Twenty Thousand Saints

Twenty Thousand Saints

Fflur
Dafydd

ALCEMI

First impression: 2008

© Fflur Dafydd 2008

Published with the financial support of the Welsh Books Council

Editor: Gwen Davies

ISBN: 9780955527227

Printed on acid-free and partly-recycled paper.
Published by Alcemi and printed and bound in Wales by
Y Lolfa Cyf., Talybont, Ceredigion SY24 5AP
e-mail ylolfa@ylolfa.com
website www.alcemi.eu
tel 01970 832 304
fax 832 782

for Siân Menai and Tom Dawson

"There are no more deserts, there are no more islands. Yet the need for them makes itself felt."

Albert Camus

"Life on this, as on every small island, is controlled by the moods of the sea; its tides, its gifts, its deprivations."

Brenda Chamberlain

1

en were scarce that summer. The women of Bardsey Island had begun giving each other languorous looks; had begun talking to each other in quivering, feverish tones. Most of them didn't even realise they were doing it. For months, all eyes had been turned outwards, towards the sea and its glittering possibilities, the arrival of each boat a benediction, a sudden breeze across the fusty, August heat. But when those weekly boats failed to deliver a single man, it wasn't long before the women started to peek, cautiously and curiously, at one another. It seemed that, by now, any flash of flesh was enough to cause certain stirrings: the subterranean shadows beneath a stranger's shirt, the surrendering of a best friend's ankle or an inner thigh, the seductive gaze of a neighbour's belly button. And unless today's boat had a man on board – as they'd been promised – it was only a matter of time before their glances and gestures sprouted hands and lips, before their wandering, unreal thoughts became the subject of island murmurs.

Or at least this is how, Leri thought, she would start her documentary, executed by a subtle, velvety voice-over, zooming in on the faces of the women lined up on the jetty, staring out to sea. She adjusted the lens, slowly pulling away from the white dot emerging on the horizon.

"Stop sticking that thing in my face," her assistant Greta said, closing a curtain of hair about her face. "I've told you I'm not going to be in it."

The camera skimmed further down the jetty. Leri focused on Elin, one of the island's volunteers, knowing full well she wouldn't resist being filmed. The camera loved her, her porcelain poise, the flutter of fabric in her faux-modest flinches. She was the perfect siren. If only she were a little more articulate.

"You can *feel* it, can't you?" she said, looking right into the eye of the camera, something Leri had repeatedly asked her not to do. "That we might be starting to fancy each other a bit. It's surprising how quickly your body adjusts to these things – your mind might take a little more time to catch up but… I mean, I could, if I *had* to, I may even *want* to in the end… but maybe it's a good thing after all that they're sending a man at last, I mean, it might help restore the…."

The sentence found its own way home, as Elin's sentences were prone to do. Leri framed her face while she waited. This was the problem with Elin. You could get her to start but you couldn't get her to finish. It frustrated Leri, seeing her hoist those phrases up into the air like kites, but lose interest as they took to the wind, loosening her grip; not even aware of the kite's dismal descent. Sometimes Leri would have to hoist it back up again, if only to rid herself of that vacant feel of the fragmentary, the incomplete.

"*Balance*," she added briskly, tying the kite to a post. "Just say the word balance, and I can edit it later."

"I'm not sure balance is what I meant," Elin said, "I think I meant… oh I'm not sure what I meant… I think it's difficult to know what I…."

For once, Leri was prepared to let the sentence dwindle. She shut down the camera and looked at Greta. Greta looked back at her for a second before looking off again. Leri wondered if either one could bring themselves to discuss what was happening between them. Balance wasn't the right word, Elin was right. If there had ever been any, it had long sloped into some asymmetrical, slanting mess. Leri's entire world had tilted towards Greta; the green bottles rolling away from the bed, the bed springs bending, and her words, like her clothes, in disarray at the bottom of the mattress, jumbled, ruffled. It was the kind of thing you didn't mention, until the tilt solidified, until the whole world seemed a little off centre. It was never meant to be part of the documentary, she was very sure of that. *Stay focused Leri,* she kept telling herself. She turned to face the sea; being surprised once again how its swelling mass closed in on them, binding them to their tiny tuft of land. Everywhere you looked, there it was, encroaching ever closer. It was nothing like the distant mirage of sea she was used to; this was real, pulsating.

"Then again, since when has a man had anything to do with *balance?*" continued Elin, as two herring gulls perched themselves on the jetty behind her, chests puffing proudly as they circled her words with their pink splay of feet. "What we need is a good *body*." She kicked the squawking duo away, "everything in the right place, all the necessary bits. I'm fed up of these sweet, pretty men... when you get them into bed, it's all bones and skin and soft kisses. There's no weight there, no force, no rhythm. It's like making love to a... feather, like being invaded by a..." Another kite fell from the sky. Leri was annoyed. Making love to a feather, that was fine. It was a nice comparison, simple and compact, it said everything that needed to be said. She could instantly imagine what it would feel like; the feather softly grazing her neck as it attempted its seduction. Why Elin had to go and spoil it all by adding another simile, she didn't know. She was about to tackle her on it when the final word landed at her feet, a gunk of feather and saliva: "Quill. Like being invaded by a quill."

There was something mesmerising about Elin's movements across the jetty, which made Leri turn the camera back on. The early morning sun was bursting out of the still waters around them, dazzling them. The jetty fell from view, and it seemed that Elin was walking on water. She might be able to do something with that for the opening credits, thought Leri excitedly. Not your average documentary, her viewers would say, noting her name as it flashed in bold white type across the bottom of the screen.

"Just keep walking Elin, OK, and keep your head poised like that. Let your arms go so we can see a little more flesh. That's it. Beautiful, just beautiful..."

Elin needed no coaxing. She was continuously emphasising her angular dimensions by wearing short skirts, crop-tops, and those subtly-sexual swimming costumes that came undone in the back if you jolted about a little too eagerly, as she was prone to do. Today she was wearing a short, yellow skirt, picking incessantly at its hem. She was always touching herself in some way, Leri had noticed – rubbing that tight, concrete back of hers, caressing her long arms, or reshuffling her breasts. Leri had given up complaining about it, finding that even speaking to Elin forced a sentence to retreat, to curl in on itself ("Do you have to keep fiddling with yourself like that, it's so…" she had said, her voice losing its verve.) Elin had argued she needed reassurance that she was still whole. "I mean, in a place like this you can easily forget that you're a *complete*, real person. Your mind plays tricks," she said, cupping her left breast in her hand. Leri zoomed in on this last gesture.

She wasn't sure she could use it, but it had something; a kind of absurdity that would be otherwise difficult to capture.

"He could be the most 'balanced' man in the world and still not have anything to talk about," Greta complained. "We don't know anything about him, do we? At least give the poor boy…"

"Man," Elin corrected, stepping out of her golden silhouette. "We want him to be a man. He's twenty six, apparently. If he's not a man at thirty two then… well…."

Leri saw the boat advancing in the distance. Suddenly, Elin seemed plain and the jetty no more than a strip of pale wood. Raising her camera once more, she could make out the boatman's face, as well as a host of faceless life jackets.

"You have to ask yourself serious questions about a man who wants to come and live on a bloody island, especially *this* one, on his own, at twenty six years old," Greta threw this last comment over the jetty, into the sea.

"Well you won't have to bother with him, will you? He's staying with me at the lighthouse," said Elin, as she bent down to dismantle a stray, desiccated crab claw on the jetty, "so it makes sense that I should have first refusal, doesn't it? I mean he's *one* man and… well I'm not sharing him with….

"Well you might have to!" Leri shouted, as the kite morphed into a balloon and glided silently away.

A writer-in-residence had been suggested by Gwyn, the island's manager. Leri had been present at the meeting. Despite seeming so joyous on the phone, layering his small talk with biscuit-crunches and coffee-slurps, saying what a wonderful idea a documentary was, he was brusque when he met her in person. "Don't make a nuisance of yourself," he'd said, twisting a greying eyebrow, "they won't like that I've brought you." She soon realised that she'd been set-up, that Gwyn had planned to propose the writer in residence at a choice moment, knowing that the board members were unlikely to show their objection with a camera present. Which was exactly what Gwyn wanted; quiet approval, no-nonsense acquiescence. It hadn't particularly mattered to Leri, either, considering the material was irrelevant. "The first meeting is just the first step in the game-plan," the executive producer had told her. "Get them to trust you. If you can appear a little bit stupid, then great. If they see you filming the really mundane stuff like a board meeting, they're less likely to think you've got an agenda."

But as it turns out, Gwyn was the only one with the agenda; and she was at the bottom of it, while the writer's residency sat smugly at the top. The board members, eyeing the camera as though it were a wild animal waiting to be roused from its lair, were polite enough in their objection. The thought of squandering the island's minuscule funds on a writer, when there was a jetty waiting to be extended, a tractor waiting to be painted, and a field waiting to be excavated was almost beyond hilarity, said a ginger-haired woman in a purple cardigan. Never mind about that, said a balding man with a thin voice; it was perfectly obvious that the scheme was a whitewash. "After that Venus woman," he added, coughing into his lukewarm latte.

Leri learnt that the proposal came soon after the sudden, premature departure of Chiara Venus, the island's first ever artist-in-residence. The islanders, despite their initial scepticism, had begun to accept Chiara as one of their own, and there had been talk of making her position permanent. That is, until Chiara's first exhibition in the school-house had revealed that they themselves featured in several of her oil-paintings. Howard, the island's farmer, had seen himself portrayed as an archangel, who seemed to be, from a great height, zapping a cat's genitals with his lazer-beam eyes.

"We don't even have cats on this island!" Howard snapped, slapping his palm down on the mahogany table. "We don't want another fantasist like that on the island! A camera crew is bad enough!"

The writer-in-residence, Gwyn argued, would be a different

experiment altogether. Someone to survey and observe, to live quietly in their midst; a watchful, probing eye.

"A perv, you mean," said a young woman whom she now recognised as Elin. "Plenty of those here already, thank you." Howard shifted uneasily in his seat.

"You're not seeing the whole picture here," Gwyn gestured with his hands, "a writer could really do wonders for the place. Write something dynamic, exciting about the island. Something racy – something to really sell the place."

"We don't want to sell the place, Gwyn," Elin noted, disapprovingly, "we need to make the island... well... sort of..."

"Sexy," shouted Gwyn. "Yes you're right, Elin. We need to make the island sexy."

"That's not what I..."

"A writer should do it. He'll really be the making of us..."

"He?" Elin raised an eyebrow. "It would be a..."

"Yes," Gwyn thundered, his eyes flaming. "A man, yes. It would, of course, be a man."

When she'd got back to the editing suite in Cardiff, Leri had deleted the entire sequence.

He'd been clever, thought Leri, as she saw the boat approaching that afternoon. He knew the clincher would be to offer them a man.

The boat was now gliding into place by the jetty, the ropes slithering from the boatman's hands.

Leri flung the camera over her shoulder and started filming. She focused on the boatman's brown face and scanned the inside of the boat, trying to locate the writer in question. As usual, it was impossible to distinguish one particular man from the dark mass of bobbing heads, all penned into their puffs of orange. She turned around again to focus on the beads of sweat gathering on Elin's brow – these were much more interesting, travelling their way southwards over the smooth stream of her face, stilling suddenly in that pert, pointed chin.

"Not now, alright, it's just not a good time to... I'm not really in the... just don't."

Leri turned the camera lens towards Greta, who was picking the skin from her lips, throwing Leri a bloodied smile. Leri filmed her pacing back and forth on the jetty, her raisin-coloured hair rising now and again in the wind, her cheeks shading a sudden pink, her glasses hiding her eyes. Leri thought warmly of those evenings they'd spent together, each glass of wine a little sweeter, a little denser. She still found it hard to believe that she had reached out towards her and she had not been rejected. Her drunken memory kept on replaying the one solitary image, that of Greta's shirt sliding from her shoulder, the cool moon skin rising to her touch.

The camera had been idle during those few days, tucked away in the canvas bag underneath the table in their cottage, Carreg Bach. The documentary hadn't seemed important then, and she'd let the islanders be, knowing how much they disliked its dark gaze. She'd done what Greta had suggested they do all along, what she viewed as the best way to start the documentary: see people beyond the cold contours of the camera, peel away the layers gently, so that when they did some *real* filming they wouldn't always be trying to find things. *Like found poetry*, she'd said, *it is what it is*. All very well and good, thought Leri, if there was nothing more to it. But she knew better.

Greta was someone who refused to be a subject; that's why she liked her so much. But it was a hindrance when you were trying to get a job done, especially one as covert and complex as hers. Greta was now distracting the linear narrative she had planned for the documentary. She was always enthusing about histories and reconstructions, about different emotional journeys that needed prompting, flashbacks that had to be cut in. Greta had been getting to know the islanders, by way of taking part in the archaeological dig at the north end, and seemed to think that along with the bones and artefacts and worthless pieces of jewellery, she was unearthing something else entirely. "I just don't know why you're so dismissive of the documentary, Leri, you've got a real wealth of material here, and all you want to film is lichen and choughs. You've got a chance here to really make a difference."

Leri knew this, of course. She knew it, and she had her own plan, and she hated staring into that pleading face night after night, not being able to voice it, unable to unfurl the exquisite map of her story at Greta's feet. But she was too close, now, to start sharing things. If you shared something, someone soon forgot whose idea it had been, and she'd learnt that the hard way.

As was customary, the islanders formed a chain in order to sweep the cargo swiftly from boat to trailer. Greta stood right at the front, so that she could get the first peep at the new arrival, while Elin stood right at the back, hands on her hips. Leri recognised this as a quiet, skilled manoeuvre. Better still if the stranger saw her last of all. He would be glad he had waited for such a glorious scene. Leri climbed up towards the boathouse, perched for the right angle. As the chain dismembered itself, the real cargo came. An elderly couple in matching hats, taking what looked like a first retirement holiday; three nuns, carrying their Bibles and baskets, and two birdwatchers, binoculars hung like macho medallions on their grey-feathered chests.

And that was all. The white boat swayed emptily in front of them, laughing. Foam rose and dissolved, in and out of shot. Leri lowered the camera.

Eventually, Brian, the boatman gazed back at them, bemused.

"What the hell are you lot gawping at?" she heard Brian say. "I know you're desperate for a man, but you must be joking. I'm flattered, of course."

She saw Elin charge up to the edge of the jetty, young enough not to be afraid of Brian's rope-burn temperament. He was waiting to raze your skin with that rope at any moment, holding it out in friendly gesture.

"Where is he?"

"Who?"

In one gracious leap, Elin was off the jetty, and into the boat.

"The writer, the one who was supposed to arrive today!" she said, steadying herself as Brian loosened the ropes and sucked on his cigarette.

"Don't know what you're talking about, darling," puffed Brian, tilting his eyes.

"Stop looking at my tits, Brian," she snapped, "and answer the question."

That really wasn't the protocol for talking to Brian, Leri thought. Her register was two octaves off the scale. Greta looked at her, urging her to get filming. She lifted her camera once more. Brian *was* kind of fascinating. He was the kind of man she'd only seen in a good mood when his wife had been taken seriously ill, a man who had recently refused to come back and collect twenty day-visitors, because one of them had vomited on his dog during the crossing.

"If you don't mind, darling, I've got things to do," he said, turning his back on Elin.

This was good, this was very good, Leri thought, the camera whirring its approval. Greta flashed a conciliatory smile.

The roar of the engine drowned out the rest of the scene. The residual crowd watched as Elin flailed her arms around in protest, and Brian sneakily started steering the boat away, the rope closing in on Elin. But Elin wouldn't have it. Once she realised what was happening, they saw her, at a fifty metre distance, jumping off the boat, into the water.

They hauled her back onto the jetty, where she made the most of her audience, draping herself over the pale wood, imprinting her dampness onto it, barely moving, whispering the occasional breath. Her small, brown eyes bolted open.

"A woman!" she spluttered.

Leri forced her way forward.

"Are you alright?"

Elin looked up into the black eye of the camera.

"Oh for God's sake Leri, this is not going in your programme, I'm not... I mean I don't, but that's not why..." Elin choked, sitting up. "It's a woman." Her voice was slick and salty. "Brian told me just now. The writer. She phoned him to say she'd missed the boat... she's coming on the next one, not that that's...."

"Another woman," groaned Greta. "That's *all* we need."

"A woman who missed the boat," Leri mused, as the camera's eye shut tight.

2

She misses the boat, as she somehow always knew she would. The result of which is this long, uneasy day; Mererid sitting in a pale blue car next to a man she's never been sure about, not really. He buys her a bacon roll while they're waiting for a boat that has already sailed. She delves into it; tasting only her own disappointment in its rubbery rind. Everything now is about texture, sensation. Like Pwllheli harbour; its sneering white barriers, the fondant waves. *It'll be alright*, Mark says; one of the many platitudes he reserves only for her. She puts her hand to his stony face, and is surprised by this unfamiliar feel, like the rugged surface of a planet. Unable to enjoy his own bacon roll until his car has been reverse-parked at a more orderly angle, he re-starts the engine. His bacon roll falls from his lap, onto the floor. Yolk pulsates out. He picks it up, dusting away flecks of dirt, his lips feeling for the join of egg and bacon.

"There wasn't egg in mine," she says, sulkily.

"They only had one left," he replies, unashamedly, his words forming a yellow crust.

Mererid is informed, by a gruff-beard at Pwllheli harbour's reception, that there won't be another boat today, and that the best thing for her to do now is to phone the boatman – some Brian or other – on his mobile. She dials the number. Imagining the tremor in his loose, perhaps navy, trousers.

"You'll have to go over to Aberdaron," he says, the tide gurgling in his throat, "there'll be another boat from there at three."

Three seems all wrong, somehow. She had wanted to go at half past eight. She was ready for this at half past eight.

She sees from the look on his face that Mark is pleased. It means the whole day together in Aberdaron, it means that the ending will not be abrupt, half-awake, as she had wanted it to be. She hates the idea of the whole day becoming one elongated goodbye, a trickling of farewells along the north-west coast.

She had wanted to jump out of the pale blue car, and onto the boat, and she had wanted it to be half past eight in the morning, before his face had even begun to form that bewildered look, before she would have had to look him properly in the eye.

★ ★ ★

Last night sways gently between them. She had been lying in the dark on the sofa bed, waiting for him, unable to sleep, listening to the stifled murmurings of the late summer night against the windowsill. He had been away at a conference in Germany, and was arriving back at Manchester at eleven-fifteen. She calculated the amount of time it would take him to drive to Bangor, roughly one and three quarter hours, allowing for the eventuality of a misplaced bag or a sudden stomach lurch on landing. She waited, she must wait, she thought. He is flying back to her, leaning forward, arms outstretched, falling through the air. And tomorrow, she will be sailing away from him. She will stand up straight, clamber on a boat, turn her back on him. She will be rising and falling to the rhythm of the waves and rock of a boat, but it will be impossible to quantify how far she is really travelling away from him. The distance between them will be as indefinable as ever.

She remembers seeing the headlights come flooding through the room, signalling his arrival. The gravel path grinding its teeth, a sturdy case rollicking over the doorstep. She remembers the creak of a door, and him falling into her darkness, kissing her, laughing. She was naked, he was in combats and a T-shirt; his classic flying outfit. She had bathed before bed; he had carried the stale air of the flight with him. He kissed her again and again and again, and she let her lips do what they do best, reciprocate rhythmically, an accomplished performance. *I am good at this,* she told herself, this act she has been playing out almost every night for the past two years.

It is Mark, she thinks, peeking at him now in a sliver of side mirror. It is Mark who she does not *quite* love, but it isn't as if she *doesn't* love him, either. She's just not sure where she stands on this. She is nowhere.

She shouldn't have been naked, she thinks, recalling the feel of the long, predictable swell against her inner thigh. She wouldn't, she couldn't; not then, not now. Her stomach was bulging, her head fuzzy with it, and she was plagued by thoughts of those laxative adverts, the one where the woman carries around with her in her bag, all the food she'd eaten that day. If she owned a handbag, hers would now be bulging with one penne arrabiata, two Greek salads, seven jaffa cakes, and two smoked salmon and spring onion *paninis*. They are all conspiring together inside her, huddling close, holding fast. And now they have a bacon roll for company.

She has been constipated most of the time since meeting Mark. It's always there somehow. She secretly blames him for it. That small, echoey, pale green bathroom with the weak handle and no lock. She's always perching on the edge of that rather faded seat, ready to lunge forward to stop the intruder if need be. But there are other factors, those she tries to stop herself thinking about. There's more than a mere physical, internal blockage. She's somehow blocked from herself. Something isn't quite moving through in the way it should; everything is in some way clogged.

She drifted off in the end, or at least, pretended to. Within seconds he was snoring on top of her, only the top two buttons of his shirt undone.

She hasn't written a poem in weeks.

★ ★ ★

And so there it stands between them, now, as they reach Aberdaron, the fact that they have not had sex in the three weeks Mark had been away. And she is going away for eight weeks. She knows Mark, he has not yet given up. It's the first thing that sprung to his mind when she'd been told she'd missed the boat. They have an entire day. A day full of hills, caves, Caverns, woodlands, rocky enclosures – a day full of her eyes reflecting the calm blue sky as he writhes on top of her.

She opens her red notebook and scribbles: *I am the poem waiting to be written.* She hides it from him, knowing how trite he would find it. She slams the notebook shut, angry with him for having done nothing but be himself, and leans forward as they descend into Aberdaron. It

18

is a dead-end of a village, a seaside town framed only by a vast ocean and pasty, smiling buildings. Nicknamed by locals as *pen draw'r byd* – the far end of the earth. *In my end is my beginning,* she adds, the last letter smudging as Mark swerves to avoid a limping seagull.

In the Aberdaron ticket office, she is told to go to Porthmeudwy. It seems an endless endeavour – the boat getting further and further away from her. How could she have misunderstood? She, who always listens to every detail, had somehow not listened that particular day to the man on the phone. She had heard what she wanted to hear, and it created this day she wasn't prepared for.

Lunch in Aberdaron. Still the blockage is there and the limp cheese sandwich does little to dispel it. The toilets are dark and smell of lavender. Entering them after being out in the brash sunlight is like stepping into a cool cave. She pulls the metal chain and listens to the water gurgling through the pipes. She thinks about living without these familiar sounds, of filling the compost toilet with grass, of emptying the decay daily into the large sewage pit on the island, like she's been told to do in the letter that is now missing.

Her eyes meet the mirror. *I am part-whole,* she thinks, something she cannot bring herself to write down.

★ ★ ★

Mark insists on climbing Uwch Mynydd, the mountain side from which the whole island can be seen. It's the last thing she wants. To see it from that great height, from that colossal distance, will cement the impossibility of ever getting there. But she follows him. She lets him guide her; even though she's far more familiar with the mountain, she lets him pull her up, she lets her hand be squeezed and caressed by him. The sun gets stronger and stronger, and every time Mark turns around to smile at her, she finds herself squinting at him, unable to see his face. Mererid loves being in love with a shadow, it seems more real to her somehow, and she has one of these sudden urges to tackle him from behind and wrestle him down to the ground. She hears his soft, fleshy thud against the turf. The shadows cower, leaving only his face. She loves it, suddenly. Those covert dimples on the left side of his cheek, the commanding, sturdy nose, those brown speckles in his green-grey eyes.

"I *do* love you," she says. "I do."

They roll around in the sheep droppings, laughing, kissing.

"I love it when you say it," he says, quietly, holding on to the sentence with both hands.

They both sit up, and look across. There it is. Bardsey Island, lazy in the water. It looks like an outstretched cat, its long green paws leading up to its gorse-carpeted, rising hind.

"It's so small," she gasps, "and so beautiful." She looks across to what will be her home. Though she cannot see the cottage, the tip of the lighthouse is visible, winking at her. She imagines walking out at night, looking up at it and feeling its greatness, its towering mystery.

"You'll be bored out of your brain," says Mark. His face becomes a shadow once more.

They arrive at Porthmeudwy, with half an hour to spare. He drives the car down the small, rickety lane. He opens the boot, and she starts leaving him, bag by bag. He helps her choose her life jacket from the glistening orange pile on the shore. She wants simply to go, to be gone. But there is so much scuffling, rustling, interchanging. The boat arrives, and fragments into a flurry of smaller boats, returning passengers to shore. First come the rubbish bags, the bulging bin-liners, all alone in a separate boat, a dark, bowing congregation. Mererid greets each and every islander and holidaymaker as they walk past, knowing they are somehow ahead of her, that they possess knowledge that is, as yet, beyond her. She tries to hide the urgency in her eyes. She feels Mark's hand on the small of her back and she cannot help but take small steps away from him. His fingers, one by one, fold away.

She is thankful, therefore, for the one elderly lady who changes everything, the one struggling with her bags as she starts her arduous walk to the top of the path. They both see her, dwarfed by her suitcase, the wheels of which are unsteady, turning the bag over, twisting her frail, shrivelled wrist. Suddenly Mark is no longer by her side. She sees him opening his hands in a kind gesture, the woman smiling, nodding, turning around and wheeling her case towards the car.

"I'll be five minutes," he says, with a gaze that is supposed to fix her, keep her standing there, waiting for him. "Don't leave until I get back."

The dwindling sun irritates her; the empty boat becomes a glare. The boatman gestures for her to come forward. She decides to obey silently, seeing her own hands hurling her luggage on the boat without a word of resistance. She will later recognise this, in a poem, as the moment she truly leaves Mark behind. She simply can't stay there, suspended, for five minutes. She tells Mark later, in a text, that it was because she was afraid of the boatman, and that he is renowned for being volatile and rude to visitors. It is true that she feels her own inadequacy in missing the boat has already roused this stranger to something in her he intensely dislikes. But part of her will always realise that wanting to be liked by an unpleasant boatman should never have come before a proper farewell with this man she says she loves. She tries to let her mind be flooded as she sees the boat cutting silver across the water, urging her on, taking her away.

She sees the blue nose of Mark's car arriving once more at the waterfront. He gets out, stands at the edge of the water, and potters around. She is relieved she can't see the look on his face. She can't really see him at all.

3

She had the best view of the whole island. At least, that's what Viv would tell Sister Mary Catherine in her letters. She omitted to mention that it was the best view if you were primarily interested in people. On a clear day, like today, she could see all the way down to the Cavern through her window. And she saw much more than mere arrivals and departures. She saw expectations. The surrendering flag of Elin's yellow skirt communicated everything she needed to know.

She longed to be among them; to leave her peppermint tea cooling in the shade, to feel the back door slamming its full stop. It only took a few minutes for her to get to the Cavern. It was the perfect day for a jaunty stroll, dog at heel, the whole island a glinting, exultant green. But Sister Mary Catherine had told her categorically not to. "It wouldn't be appropriate," she'd said, in her squat, black handwriting. "Hermits like us must not congregate among others of a disparate inclination. You must remain at the hermitage and God will lead us to you."

Howard, the farmer, would lead them to her, and he certainly was no God, she wanted to write back. But despite the fact that it was *her* island they were on this time, she still didn't have the nerve to challenge Sister Mary Catherine's authority. When she saw the boat come in, she got as far as the front door, with Elfyn, her black Labrador, urging her on with his wet nose. But she couldn't do it.

"They've zapped the anarchy out of me," she told Elfyn's bruised eyes, as she settled down to watch the pantomime from her kitchen window. The second she heard the roar of Howard's tractor, she peeled off her cheese-cloth shirt and sank glumly into her habit, regretting instantly what she'd begun.

She had no idea why she'd offered to host this year's conference on Bardsey. As far as she could tell, she was the only one who saw the notion of an annual conference of hermits as quite absurd. From the moment she saw Sister Mary Catherine, Sister Lucy Violet and Sister Anna Melangell ascending into view, gazing in wonder at the surroundings as they rattled against one another on the trailer's mobile-pulpit, she was already feeling crowded. She'd attended the first, at Sister Mary Catherine's island, Caldey, ten years ago, a few months into her postulancy, as an attempt to prove herself. It had been a rather stagnant affair, the days as labyrinthine as Caldey's paths, which she'd walked in silent exile among numerous silent, faceless others, never seemingly getting anywhere. The only bonus had been the chocolate, or at least, the promise of it. It was made by the island's monks, and had a dense, soap-like quality and a taste that scalded the ridge of your teeth. It wasn't until she found out that the monks *also* made soap that she realized she'd been munching on a bar of herbal fusion.

When she got back, she chided herself for having ventured there in the first place; it was surely against all she believed in, having to traipse through Wales in the back of that hot car. Then again, she'd kept her head on her knees the whole time, allowing herself nothing but a quick glimpse of a neutral sky, so that her journey was through the landscape of clouds, down into the valleys of fog and rain. She could have been anywhere, she reasoned to herself later. By the time she opened her eyes again, she was on that red boat to Caldey; balance was restored. She would do the same when she returned – blanking out the bit in the middle as she went into her trance, sinking deeper into the back seat, this time strapping herself down with both seat belts.

That should have been her last trip. She wasn't to know that once you'd attended one of these events, there was no turning back, that the islo-manic hermits hounded you with newsletters and gift-packs, loyalty cards and special offers. She'd since been on a day-trip to the Blaskets – two for the price of one that year, so she took Elfyn – and had rather enjoyed herself, primarily because the wind was strong enough to drown out the offending silence. Then on to Lundy, Sister Lucy Violet's territory, and then on to the calm shores of Ynys Llanddwyn, near where Anna Melangell lived – not technically an island, Sister Mary Catherine had argued – but all had been forgiven once she'd laid eyes on the grey-blue skeleton of St. Dwynwen's Chapel, the windmill-shaped lighthouse of Twr Mawr, the sloping, golden dunes of Llanddwyn beach. "Her chastity brought us this beauty," she'd said, crinkled bottom lip quivering. "She renounced love to live in purity. It's important that we remain close to the saints, at all times, so that we can continue to be inspired by their frugal lives." She fixed Viv with a potent stare. But Viv refused to budge. She'd done nothing but downplay Bardsey from the very beginning, keeping tight-lipped on the subject of the twenty thousand saints, and of the hermitage next to her cottage. She certainly wasn't going to volunteer the information that three pilgrimages to Bardsey equalled one to Rome. *They can go to Rome on a special offer,* she'd thought, *it's not that expensive.* But soon enough, another special offer had leaked its way from Sister Mary Catherine's fountain pen to the boathouse mailbox: *an opportunity to host the 2007 conference on your own island!* The fine print, which she'd never bothered to read, had firmly stated that *not replying* to the attached slip confirmed acceptance of the offer.

Most nuns would have loved the opportunity, she supposed. Her problem was that she wasn't really *like* most nuns. She'd been a lax holy woman at the best of times, popping on the habit mainly when it suited her, namely when she'd been caught doing something she shouldn't have. When Mwynwen, the farmer's wife, had come knocking the other week, she'd hoisted the habit about herself like armour, had stooped at the door, and had argued that God had insisted that she dig up all that rhubarb in Mwynwen's garden, that it had been a call she couldn't ignore. Mwynwen's face reminded her of the bold flashes of red in rhubarb as it boiled. She'd had the most terrific crumble.

It had been a few years now since she'd taken her temporary vows, and no one, not even the sharp-eyed Mwynwen, had noticed her rather slipshod attitude towards her calling. But it was simply the way of things on Bardsey. She lacked comparison; a context. On a two mile long piece of land, you rarely had two of anything, unless you were a chough. And while she didn't question the mechanics of Mwynwen's home baking or Howard's lobster-baiting, they were perfectly content to see her vocation as equally legitimate to theirs, fulfilling their need for spiritual service just by being there, even if she didn't always wear a habit, read her Bible or wish to listen to their crises of faith during those long, mean winters.

In short, there was no one to check up on her. No point of reference which singled her out as a fake. Not that she was a fraud. But she wanted to do it in her own way. She always had done things in her own way. As far as she could see it was the only way, when you'd had a life as troublesome as hers. Many had viewed her decision of becoming a nun as another anarchical moment in her history; that perhaps moving to the island in the first place had not been extreme enough for her, and that becoming a nun was a means of finding a new level of extremity. But she knew it was nothing to do with being extreme. It was more to do with safeguarding herself; keeping people out. And although the emotion that had spurred her decision, all those years ago, had indeed been extreme, she was nothing now if not moderate, the quiet life of prayer having grown on her, like she'd grown into the habit. People left her alone now; they didn't ask her things, they didn't probe into what had happened to her, like they used to. People had believed they had a right, until she'd signed that right over to God. He now had the exclusive. Even tough-tongued Mwynwen knew that there were certain things she couldn't ask anymore.

There was nothing she wanted more than to take those permanent, lifelong vows, and to dedicate her life to something that would bring her peace, unlike her previous endeavours. She'd grown closer to the island these past few years. It was speaking to her in a different voice. It wasn't merely the island's beauty that kept her going now, year after stubborn year, but something deeper, something so indelibly woven into the island's landscape it didn't even have a name. She was used to decorating the island in her letters to Sister Mary Catherine, wondering how best to conjure up what it felt like, what it really felt like to be roaming around here in a summer dusk; the heat roasting the sky a deep auburn, the lavender sea lathering at her feet, carrying with it air that was clean like spring water. But now she found it necessary to try to go beyond that, to explain that one sudden moment when the fresh breeze came gushing in, just before the door slammed, the sense she had in her own house, of someone being *with* her. Or what she felt when she roamed around the south end of the island, around those purple rocks, looking down into that thrashing whiteness. Living on Bardsey was somehow to live on the brink of things, but with a sense that there was something, or some*one* there, tenderly pushing back her toes from the precipice. There was always something bursting out of the place these days for her, flowers spilling over one another to be noticed, lichen sprouting its soft regalia along the stone walls, Manx Shearwaters racing out of their round-homes, and her among them, breathing quietly. And it wasn't just what was around her that made it such a sanctuary, but the sea, a mainland unto itself. She still gazed at it with wonder every morning. Each night, she let it soothe her, praying in gratitude for its boundless mass which somehow spelled at once freedom and incarceration. The tide-race around her pulsed with life, but she knew that true power was here on this earth, blessed, beneath her feet.

And it had been blessed, of course. Those Celtic saints, all those years ago, had made sure of that, all twenty thousand of them. She'd been dismissive enough at first, when living her secular life on the island. Had guffawed at the legend, saying it was nothing more than a marketing strategy. But she knew how wrong she'd been. They were here, she could feel them. They'd offered up a connection, a sign of some sorts, that day at the Abbey, when she was erecting the plaque. They'd let her in. She'd become quite protective, viewing the likes of Saint Deiniol, Saint Beuno and Saint Cadfan as her silent comrades, while Elgar, the renegade executioner-turned-saint, this darker horse among the brooding pack, got her pulses racing, and her prayers muddled. There was no way she was sharing them. They all spoke Welsh, anyhow, a language neither Sister Mary Catherine nor Sister Lucy Violet had any grasp of, and the saints couldn't be forced, at this late stage, to learn English, now could they? Everyone knew it was much more difficult to acquire a language when you got older.

Most of all, she felt the island was hers now, more so than it had ever been. She was one of the longest-standing residents of the Seventies influx, and certainly the most stubborn-standing, as she'd heard Mwynwen whitter once over the hedge, the way she never left the island unless she absolutely had to. Not like the others, who were forever boat-bouncing to Aberdaron to the beck and call of some errand or other, or flocking to their cottages in Uwch Mynydd when the winter wound its way around them. Not her. She was staying put. She'd already decided that these annual jollies had to end, that this would be the last one. She simply couldn't face that unsettling feeling she always got when she left, the feeling that she was betraying the place somehow, the sea in front of her foaming its disgust. The second you left everything was different, the island changed shape behind your back. It made faces at you. She never again wanted to see the feral delight in Elfyn's eyes that she'd seen on her return one day, bounding out from beneath Mwynwen's skirt as though it were his home.

There really was no need to leave, after all. She ordered her groceries on the island's pay-phone, she healed her own tiny ailments with grass and lichen, and she cured her own neuroses through meditation and prayer. Admittedly God wasn't a dentist, but she'd only had minor toothache so far. She had everything she needed right here. She'd had everyone she needed here once, too, she mused, before tucking the thought under her headdress with her last stray strand of hair.

She opened the door and bowed her head.

"Sister Mary Catherine, Sister Lucy Violet, Sister Anna Melangell, I welcome you to Bardsey Island. *Croeso i fy nghartref, fy hafan, fy myd.*"

She smiled conspiratorially at Anna Melangell, who mouthed an appreciative *diolch* while Sister Mary Catherine ploughed straight across the sentence.

"Sister Vivian, what an honour it is to be here, in your divine company." They formed three black shadows at her feet. "What a bounty has been bestowed upon you by God's grace."

Viv bowed down once more to greet their faces, silently praying that Sister Mary Catherine would close her mouth so that she wouldn't have to see the brown remnants of the cheese sandwich embedded between her ageing teeth. She ushered them in, one by one, while Elfyn sniffed his way around them. She momentarily lost him in the dark mass. On cue, Sister Teresa started to sneeze, and Sister Anna gave her a pleading nod which instructed her to take the dog outside.

Before long, they were sat around her table in silent communion with God, with Viv leading them in a prayer which, at Sister Mary

Catherine's request, also contained an itinerary of the week's activities. Mid-prayer, Viv cautiously turned her head ever so slightly to the left, to exchange a sly, complicit look with Elfyn. The dog was rubbing his grumpy wet nose against the window, wondering why on earth he'd been ousted to make way for a pack of brooding Dalmatians.

4

When the purr of Howard's tractor was heard for a second time that day, a crescendo above Cae Uchaf's hedges, Deian saw his own reflection landing threefold, as three small silver trowels were hurled into the soil.

"Oi!" shouted Deian. "We're not done yet!"

"Well I've had enough," Leri retorted. "There's only so much soil-gazing I can take today. I've got some filming to do."

"Yes, being the first on the scene is very important," said Greta. "Knowing when to stick your nose in, it's quite an art."

"If anyone should be sticking their nose in, it's *me*," said Elin, "I'm the one who has to live with her... I mean, at the end of the day she is supposed to be a writer-*in-residence*... and as her fellow resident, I need to know what I'm dealing with here..."

"What *we*'re dealing with," added Greta. "It doesn't just affect you, Elin. I mean one person can change everything on an island. It's the dramatic entry, isn't it? We need it. And for the documentary's sake, let's hope it does change something. It's been a little stagnant here recently, we need someone to perk things up."

"Oh, and since when are you a seasoned islander, Greta? I've been here five months and you've been here five minutes, I hardly think that makes you a...."

The sentence dissipated in the dust.

"It's important, for our documentary," Greta said. "Isn't it Leri?"

Leri was halfway through the gate.

"Of course. But Howard won't talk if there's too many of us. I think you'd best stay where you are, Greta. I just want to get a nice, uncomplicated piece to camera. First impression of the writer, that sort of thing."

Greta's face started crumpling in on itself. She assembled a quick, squinting smile from the ruins.

"I'm supposed to be the assistant producer," she told Leri. "Don't start taking over."

"Well you can be *my* assistant producer," Deian said, kicking the soil in annoyance, splattering both Elin and Greta's faces with brown flecks. He stared out across the orange expanse of the field known as Cae Uchaf, where his team had spent the best part of a month working on the excavation. It wasn't actually an excavation, it was a survey, but he'd long discovered that the word survey didn't seduce anyone. The word excavation, on the other hand, made his novices believe they were digging deep, that they were unearthing mysteries, and that they might actually find something. It made them turn up in the morning. The problem was that it didn't make them stay. He watched on, helpless, as Elin, too, ignored his pleas and left the site, dusting off the last bits of soil over his fresh, white worksheet. At the far end, Greta continued to pummel away with interest.

"Unbelievable!" he shouted, reshuffling the trowels. "How on earth do they think we're going to get anything done if they keep running off like that! It was bad enough this morning. There I am, raring to go at nine o' clock, and you lot go running off to the Cavern, just because of some man or other…"

"And now there is no man," Greta sighed, rubbing her red, worn knees. "I feel sorry for her already. She doesn't know what she's in for."

"Well if she's got a pair of hands, I'll tell you exactly what she's in for." Deian dusted the soil from his clip-board. "Need all the help I can get, at this rate."

Once she'd finished her patch, Greta lay back, her eyes reflecting the breadth of clear sky above. He stood over her, blocking the blue.

"Greta! Don't you start slacking on me now as well! And if you are going to collapse in sheer nervous and emotional exhaustion, please do it on an unmarked area!"

"I think I'll go and see what's going on," she said. "You can cope without me for half and hour, can't you darling?"

Her final comment landed clumsily, along with her trowel. Deian spent the next five minutes rearranging the newly-strewn row, while Greta's tiny frame slipped from view through the gate, blowing him a kiss as she went. These women didn't half make a mess.

As he combed on, scraping the surface of the soil, fragments of the story were hurled deliberately, loudly towards him from the enclave of the goat yard, where the women had gathered around Howard for their tea. It seems the word being bandied around by Howard was *poetess*, and he heard it echoed and savoured, a crude coo of syllables rustling in the air like a bird. With Howard it was always a curiously devised synonym, never quite the actual thing itself. The artist had been the *artiste*, the puppet maker the *puppetrice*. Soon enough he would become the *archaeologiste*, pronounced in a French accent, if he was lucky.

Deian stood at the centre of the deserted field. He remembered the satisfaction he once felt, looking out over the soft furrows, recording his finds in his sheet. Usually, he'd need that time alone, just to savour the soil's offerings. But now, he felt nothing but emptiness. *Getting nowhere fast*, he'd said to Greta. And it was even worse than that. It was exactly what he wanted, what he'd been ordered to do – to find nothing. The board had instructed him to choose a site of little archaeological interest, and to keep churning up the emptiness until it was deemed a suitable site for their new pet-cemetery. It was difficult enough gearing up enthusiasm for archaeology among a gang of sex-starved women as it was, without revealing his true, pathetic quest. The fact that they were digging as a pure formality, an exercise in nothingness – so that another hoard of furry nothingness could go in there instead, was enough to dishearten the most stoic of archaeologists.

It was easy enough to execute his plan, to keep them going, to keep the enthusiasm alive. As long as he gave them *something*, it was easy enough to keep the nothingness at bay. He rummaged around in his coat pocket for a few interesting objects. A few animal bones he'd kicked from the dust in Porthmeudwy, a copper bracelet that contained a hint of something medieval (yet he'd bought it in the market in Bangor for 30p) and a few interesting looking (but worthless) stones from his own private collection. He found suitable holes to place them in, and worked quickly while the women were on their breaks, with one eye on the gate. He thought of Elin suddenly discovering the bracelet, the yelps of disbelief that would sound across the field after her rare and precious find. It was sure to ignite the rest of them; make them determined to sweat it out through the rest of the afternoon, hoping that they too, would find something. He might even throw in one of his rare flints, as a treat. It would all be coming back to him anyway. Once the discovery was made and relished and shrieked-over, they all handed over their finds, acknowledging that he was the only qualified one among them, legitimate hoarder of all discoveries. He would keep them for a few days, until they'd had time to forget their feel and shape, before the whole process started again, before they mysteriously reappeared in the soil.

He'd claim to be putting it all down in his report, of course; noting all discoveries. He was getting quite good at pretending to write. He sometimes felt a pang of guilt for deceiving them. But then he remembered his deadline, his promises. They had to finish surveying that field by the end of summer, and that was that. He was not dishonest, he was merely being pragmatic.

Despite his desperation, there was no way he was willing to share his truly precious finds, those he found when he went digging on the south end of the island, without the rest of them tugging at his coat tails. He'd found countless bones, several mysterious and unaccountable ones, but kept them to himself. Over on the south side, he felt his old archaeological flame ignite once again, and it reminded him of the thrill of being with his old team in France all those years ago, when he had first met Fran. In those days, he didn't have to listen to people complaining about the heat, and he recalled those intense afternoons when they unearthed bone after bone, the sweat mingling with the cold beer they drank, the nights gently cooling as they huddled around outside their tents. Those days people really did discover things. At least he had. That summer, in Burgundy, with Fran. That summer was the very cusp of their relationship. He remembered how he'd stared at her all day on the site, only to spend each night staring at her at the far end of the tent, bodies stacked in between, an impossible barricade.

Fran was gone. He kept having to tell himself that. He still couldn't quite believe what had happened; how last minute her decision had been. But his ultimate treasure would become somebody else's find soon enough. He presumed it was why she left him in the way she did, so that she could get on with finding someone else, before it was too late. She would have loved Bardsey, he thought, playing a ray of sun against one of his rare flints. She should be here now, by his side, as they'd planned. Instead, he had only his flint collection as company; and he'd become the joke of the site, the only man, yet one nobody wanted.

The random team he'd accumulated over the past few weeks was an arbitrary collection, that was certain, but in his experience, serendipitous gatherings seemed to work perfectly well. Leri and Greta had found the dig intriguing, so much so that they had restructured their documentary to include some of the most significant finds (he was confident that, being a Welsh language documentary, no other archaeologists he knew would watch it, and would never know what lies he'd told that summer, what truths he'd buried), while Elin, the island's chief ecologist, seemed to be using the dig as her excuse for not completing any of her island tasks. For once, he found himself the head of a tribe, not merely a minion as he had been in Burgundy, but a true dictator. He found it bizarre that they all listened to him.

He'd been put out by their sudden thirst for a man. The more he thought of it, it was completely rational for them to want something. Anything. Elin had been there for five months already. It was a hot, sticky summer. It did things to people, or so Howard informed him, winking. But he hadn't even thought of it. On some sleepless nights in his loft he'd let his hand wander, rather undecidedly, to his wilting penis, but when it had arrived there, he found that his own touch did nothing for him. He wanted Fran's hand around it. Her determined, warm white hand, and if he couldn't have that, he didn't want anything else.

He didn't even particularly mind when they kept complaining that there were no single men. "Deian's single," Leri chirruped. And they had all laughed. They wouldn't have laughed if they'd known how strenuous these last few years with Fran had been, he thought, how being single at the end of it all felt like the worse kind of desertion. But considering they saw him as single, he wasn't sure why they didn't even count him as a possibility. Perhaps the problem was that he couldn't really bring himself to *be counted*. It was the soil that was important to him, and had been for twenty years. Every morning he couldn't help but wonder whether he'd find what (or rather who) he'd always been looking for, even though he knew it was improbable, impossible even. Returning once more to this inexorable, dark thought, he raised his head to gaze over towards the old Abbey tower that signalled the cemetery. Apparently there was a plaque there now – *in loving memory*. He'd resisted looking at it so far.

Before leaving the site, he turned his head once more to face a sea of oblivion, shaking his head at the thought of having spent the whole day motivating his team for the discovery of a great, looming absence, only to lose out to a presence, a mere someone.

Yet at least it had given him a chance to fill in the site, plant some finds for the morning, something to get the women's pulses racing and their elbows bending with a new-found-fervour. A bone here, a bracelet there, and he'd stamped the nothingness back down.

5

When she awoke the next morning, Leri was pleasantly surprised to see Greta snuggled up in her shoulder like a child. Despite the dryness of her mouth, she was reluctant to reach out for her glass of water, for fear of destroying the perfect stillness of the moment. She clung on to it for dear life, while also hoping for some sign from Greta, a gentle squeeze, maybe just to confirm that it was where she intended to be, and that she hadn't just been washed ashore there on the tide of her dreams.

She stared at the ceiling of their cottage. It was called Carreg Bach, the small rock; a red and white cottage perched just on the lower limbs of the Bardsey mountain, a pop-up house, springing out of the grass. She'd known, somehow, that it was the perfect cottage for them when she'd first seen it. Right at the heart of the island, yet somehow resolutely apart; looking across at the other houses, yet without being looked into. It had a curious smell, a strange infusion of damp and cinnamon, that was now starting to get saturated with sweat, stale coffee, discarded shirts. But it was perfect, nevertheless. The one sofa, the wide, wax-dribbling candle. The dark corners, the low ceilings. The tiny windows that offered small puffs of blue and white. She'd had a recurrent vision of how it would happen between them; she imagined bumping into the low-beams, Greta's sympathetic hand raising to the back of the head, and her own travelling to meet it. The sofa catching them as they tumbled. She'd envisaged it in short, neat scenes, heightened by the odd close up of their entangled toes. And it had gone more or less as she'd scripted it, apart from the smash of the gas lamp that she'd knocked over as she'd wrestled with Greta's shirt.

But she'd never really envisaged what would happen after those gasping, tangled-up nights that eventually had to give way into days, and longer nights. Or what dangers they might bring, that Greta might blur her focus, make her lose sight of what she was there to achieve. Worst of all, she could end up telling Greta too much.

Last night had been a close call. They'd been at a dinner party at the lighthouse, a warm evening of faces lit by candles and gas-lamps, the heat going to her head; she'd forgotten herself again. Had let down her guard, along with the camera, and had found herself having fun, becoming truly interested in those around her. It wasn't how it was supposed to be. Greta had been on at her all night about her *ideas* for the documentary, telling her which direction it should take. It wouldn't be taking any direction yet, she'd told her, slamming down her glass of wine by the sink. It hadn't even started. Greta's eyes sprung out beneath her glasses. "What do you mean by that?"

She'd had to leave, then, before she'd told Greta exactly what she meant, before she'd revealed that all these *ideas* of hers would amount to nothing. She remembered slipping out of the noisy kitchen unnoticed, being hit by the pure air, steadying herself against the dark wall. Looking up at the colossus of a lighthouse in front of her through the eerie orange sidelights, wondering, if at some point, someone would let her in to the lighthouse so she could get some shots from the top. It could be useful, especially when things got interesting, it was the perfect vantage point to get shots without being seen. Perhaps Howard had a key. She couldn't resist one last look through the steamed window of the cottage, seeing Greta squashed in between Elin and the writer, laughing at something one of them had said. It was so easy for her, she thought, because she had nothing to lose by getting close to these people. She saw Elin put her hand on Greta's shoulder and something shot through her, urgent like poison.

Soon enough, Greta was running after her, a small glimmer of a gas lamp visible in the distance, still shouting "what do you mean?" in dark echoes. Leri was so drunk she kept thinking, *the camera, god, where is the camera?* It was so black she couldn't see anything, not forward, not back, the night thick like wool. The moment she'd found the cottage, Greta was gone it seemed, swallowed up by the fug. She remembered slamming the red door and clunking across the

36

floor, barefoot. Smashing the bottle of wine she was trying to open, showering glass all over the slate flooring. It took a few attempts on the ladder to reach her bed, and even then, she couldn't sleep. She remembered lying on her back in the loft, wondering, hoping, that she'd hear the creak of the ladder. The thought *where's the camera?* being chased breathlessly by a second, more pressing thought, *where's Greta? Where's my Greta?* Finally, the door opened, and after she'd heard some non-descript shuffling and brushing, Greta's face appeared above the mahogany. In her drunkenness and desperation, there had never been a sight like it, and Leri began to cry.

"You're so silly," Greta had said, smiling.

"The camera," she remembers slurring, "where's the camera?"

"Don't worry. Packed it. Tried to get some shots in after you'd left. Elin was willing to talk, it was only that writer who was being difficult. But I didn't get anything. You'd forgotten to put a tape in. Call yourself a film-maker?"

"I didn't want to..."

"Didn't want to what? You weren't making sense tonight Ler, what were you trying to tell me earlier? What are we waiting for?" Greta slid in beside her.

"Nothing," Leri said, the word pressing down on her, easing her gently into a deep sleep.

She knew she'd made a mistake bringing Greta. She should never have listened to Clive. "One woman there on her own with a camera, they won't like it, but two of you, now there's a chance to really get involved in the island, make them trust you. Take Greta Williams with you. She's good with people, got a gentle way about her, people will talk to her, open up to her. And you wouldn't even have to tell her what was going on. Just get her to help out. Researcher, or give her a title, assistant producer or something, that sort of thing. Let her think you're doing a lifestyle documentary. No, better still, make it something about the saints, give it a historical focus. That's right. Say you're going to call it *Twenty Thousand Saints*. She's a bit of an archaeology geek that one, she's got a degree in it or something."

She'd resented the way Clive thought she needed Greta for

communicative purposes, as though her own manner were as abrasive as his own. But she put that quibble to one side for the time being, considering that what he was offering her was something she'd dreamt of for years.

"Great. It sounds great, Leri," Greta had said, not even looking up from her computer. "I'll make sure the dates are up on the board. Let me know when you want a meeting so we can work out our itinerary. We'll have a laugh." At that point she'd swivelled around to meet her, pulling her hair free from her ponytail, her face on the verge of one of her curious, endearing face-scrunches. "I went there on a school trip when I was nine. Don't remember a thing, mind. It was in the papers a lot a few years back wasn't it?"

"Was it?" Leri had said, dampening her voice with nonchalant notes. "I'll look it up."

When Greta had first arrived at the company, four years ago, she'd knocked the breath right out of Leri. She wasn't what most people would call beautiful, but she'd had something about her, something Leri liked to think only she could magnify. Long hair that was somehow always changing shade in the light, so much so you could never pinpoint exactly what colour it was. Sometimes it was coal, at other times a grape, on some days it was like sunlit tar, the deepest blood. Her glasses worked with her beauty, somehow, hiding her eyes when it suited her, yet giving them a strange clarity in a dark room. She was young looking for her twenty nine years, and she always had something discerning at the brim of her lips, something that was waiting to bubble over.

She'd been seeing some bloke, some Dafydd or other, when she'd first got there, and the next she'd heard, she was seeing a woman. She'd come with her to the Christmas party, a girl with these peculiar pale green eyes, and they'd spent the night, heads-huddled, giggling, their index fingers linked. Next thing, she'd heard that they'd moved in together. And that was the end of that.

. Until, she'd come in early one morning and found Greta snivelling by her computer, her hair streaked out in long, straggly strings across her desk; this time taking on a bluish tinge, lit up by the monitor in front of her.

"My God, Greta, did you sleep here last night?"

"Don't tell Clive please, I couldn't cope with him this morning, after everything."

"It's alright," she'd said. "I won't. Do you need a tissue?"

Greta blew her nose noisily.

"Nia and me, we're finished. It's over. I never want to sleep with a woman again."

"I know how you feel," she'd said, smiling.

And somehow, that had been it; the start of a slow, cautious friendship. Meeting up whenever one of them had been mistreated by a woman or a man (as it turns out, Greta was forever changing her mind) and laughing at the ridiculous intensity of same sex relationships. Their favourite topic was the sorority of the Welsh-language-lesbians, whom they avoided at all costs. When Leri's arch-nemesis, Angharad Eden, was awarded a BAFTA Cymru for her documentary on the subject of the Welsh-language gay scene (beating Leri's own entry on the subject of autism) it was Greta Leri had phoned, leaning against the wall outside the St David's Hotel, her mouth a mess of champagne and mascara. "Don't worry about it," Greta had said, silvering her sentences with a low, compassionate tone. "At least it's done now. She's won it. It won't happen again. It's your time next time."

And she believed her, because it was Greta telling her. And though she'd wanted to ring her again the following morning, after she'd snuck out of the flat of Lisa-someone-or-other in Cardiff Bay, she'd had to stop herself, knowing the conditions of the friendship. They didn't soothe one another's neuroses or help one another 'work through things'. It wasn't one of those friendships (of which she'd had many) where they slept over at one another's houses, talking long into the night, huddling around wine bottles and eventually trying to kiss each other. One of those friendships which eventually gave way to a labyrinth of slammed doors. In this friendship, the door was always half-open, but you should never pop your head around it without announcing your presence first.

There had been four years of this, and naturally, Leri had had to busy herself. She needed the stories, after all, to keep the friendship going. There had been a curious cast of lovers during those years. Kirsi, the

Finnish exchange student, with cropped beachy hair and fantastically clear blue eyes, an ice hockey fanatic, who had loved her diligently for a year, and yet who shed no tears at the airport, and had never contacted her since. The shy Megan, from Llandudno, uncomfortable in her own skin and oversized clothes, a shriveling, weak-voiced social worker. There had been the addictive, butch Nina, a Great Wales and Western trolley-dolly who had stolen from her to fund her love of amphetamines, and the detestable Melita, a truly bad playwright who frequently cried in bed because she thought herself a substandard lover. Then there had been the tender, near-Greta experience of Alison, a guide-dog trainer, who had allowed herself, for a year and seven months, to be blamed secretly on every occasion for not being quite-Greta, for not being Greta *enough*.

But at the time of sailing out to Bardsey, they were both single. Greta had recently given Nia the boot for the eleventh time, and Leri had finally had the guts to leave Alison, who'd kicked her bicycle wheel as she'd sped down Beda Road. There was nothing stopping them. It felt good, seeing Greta descend into the boat that first day, turning round and looking at her, her tiny face boxed in by her life jacket, the itinerary of *Twenty Thousand Saints* already dampening under her raincoat. Crossing that sea, seeing the island rising out of the depths in front of her, feeling Greta squeeze her hand, she knew it could happen. Not straightaway, perhaps, but eventually.

And now, here they were. A week into their new-found relationship, if that's what it was. Or maybe it was merely a bit of island madness, the intensity of the enclosed space fooling them both. Didn't she know all this from her own notes, from what had happened here all those years ago? Yet being here, it kind of made you forget the theory that it was cabin-fever, stir-crazy seduction. What was happening now, between her and Greta, it just *was,* and she didn't want to spoil things by thinking about what it meant. Everything she had ever wanted had suddenly happened, and yet she was restless and impatient to know how it would be played out.

But you can't be thinking about this now, she scolded herself. *You've got things to do. You've come too far to let it slip for this, for what this may or may not be.*

40

People undoubtedly did seem more attractive, day by day, when you were in such an environment. Imperfections became lustrous features, sharp angles were softened. But Greta hadn't changed for her, she was simply what she had always been. But what was Greta seeing? Perhaps Leri's rather long, equine face had suddenly become round to Greta, sweet, beautiful. Maybe Greta was going mad, or having some kind of breakdown.

She was suddenly hauled out of her thoughts by an unexpected sneeze on her bare left shoulder. Greta was awake. She drew her in closer and closer again into the crook of her shoulder, until the smell of her lavender body lotion wafted warmly towards her. Leri reached out and kissed her. Greta kissed her back, softly, curtly, a full stop of a kiss. It wasn't enough. She wanted a sentence, a paragraph, something more. Leri gently rolled on top of her, running her hands back through her hair, wishing, as she had done so often recently, that Greta wouldn't look so complacent. She didn't want to be one of these women Greta said she somehow 'found' herself in bed with, too polite to say no. How was Leri to know she was any different? She'd never considered the fact that knowing the ins and outs of Greta's sex life could make the sex annoyingly impossible. She nervously started her journey down Greta's naked body, kissing her oval breasts before then gently kneading them, waiting for them to arise warmly as they had done last night. Greta's voice rang out, again and again.

When it was over, they lay side by side, not touching, both staring out of the skylight of Carreg Bach, watching the fog erasing itself. They listened to the mismatched rhythms of one another's breath. Somewhere, far away, they heard Howard's tractor grinding past, and the voices of children laughing. The sound of the island awakening to yet another day jolted Leri. Suddenly things were real again. She sat up. What time was it? She never knew what time it was on this island, ever since she'd lost her watch in the first midnight swim with Greta. It had its own time, that's what the islanders kept on telling her, but she knew that wouldn't go down too well in Cardiff. She'd need to go up the mountain today and ring Clive. See how things were getting on, if things were going to plan at his end. It should only be a few days now.

And then you'll have to forget this silly little fling and get to work, she told herself. *They don't give out BAFTAs for holiday romances.*

"We should get up, I suppose," Greta said. "Deian will be wondering where we are. I'll go and get dressed."

"I'm not coming with you today," Leri answered. "I've got some shots to do at the south end. Seals and sheep and stuff."

"Let me come with you then," Greta said.

"No, it's OK. I know you enjoy the dig."

"I do, but, well I'm here to help you…"

"I know, but Deian might have a tantrum, you know what he was like yesterday."

They both laughed.

"I suppose, if you're sure… Deian seems to think we're going to find something amazing today… that we're close to the remains of Cadfan or someone…"

"Fascinating."

"Oh alright! Well *I* find it interesting. If you ask me, we haven't done half enough filming of that site. Maybe we can do it tomorrow."

"Yeah, OK," said Leri, trying not to think about the offending tomorrow, creeping ever closer.

"You're sure you don't need me today?"

"No, I'll be OK."

"Well remember to get some good shots of the lighthouse this time, seeing as how you were too drunk last night."

She tried not to look Greta in the eye. She had every intention of forgetting to insert the tape again today.

6

Mererid wakes in a dark room with orange curtains. She is aware of a force that shakes the room, that makes the bed shudder. The fog horn rings on and on, and by the seventh time she hears it, it's become familiar, like the ticking of a clock. She peels back one small layer of curtain and is dwarfed by the sight of the lighthouse that stands above her, its ruthless red and white stripes, its unusual rectangular shape. *I'm here*, she thinks, *really here*. On Bardsey Island. She gets up to hoist the curtains open, to throw back the wooden shutters, letting light flood the room. She lies back down and waits for the fog to lift, the way Elin has told her it will. "You can wake, thinking it's going to be the most miserable day," she'd said, fiddling with her bra strap, "and then the fog lifts and it's just beautiful. It's like the island's playing games."

She paces around her memory of last night. Elin, Leri, Greta and herself sitting around the table until the night had pervaded the room, their faces caked in blue shadow, until there was nothing to do but light the gas lamp and open up their faces once more, grappling all the while with something, anything that could be constituted as a middle ground between a poet, an ecologist and two film-makers. She remembers hating the camera that seemed always to be on, always in her face, but being too cautious to say anything. She's come to the island to get away from this sort of thing, she thinks, these incessant interviews she's always doing about nothing. "S4C must be desperate," Mark keeps telling her, "I mean there are supposed to be nearly a million of you Welsh-speakers now, can't they find someone else?" She told Leri she didn't really want to be in the documentary, and she recalls Leri's unease, her rubbing of Greta's back, her narrowing eyes in the window as she left without saying goodbye.

Most of all, she got through to Elin, cemented something important. After the second round of beer got into her veins, Mererid remembers informing them that she didn't consider herself a very good poet – had won only the one prize, and a trifling one, in fact – for a rather shabby collection of poems, that she considered herself as more of an academic at heart (though her lecturer boyfriend was constantly telling her that academia certainly wasn't her forte, if her latest conference paper on Derek Walcott was anything to go by – she has a tendency to homogenize shamelessly, he says). She also told them that she was rather reserved about coming to such an island and following in the footsteps of the many *real* poets who had been inspired by the place. The whole thing was a bit of a joke, really, a young poet like her claiming to have anything at all to say in the first place – something one of her reviewers had rigidly installed in her consciousness.

"I don't like poetry anyway," Elin had said.

Elin was softer after a while. She let her hair be. Put on an oversized jumper and forgot about what was underneath it. Knowing her beauty was safe. But she might be different today. Mererid knows you can never accept anything at face value. At least, this is what things are like in her world. Everything stands for something else. Everyone is someone else. Perhaps islanders are different, she thinks; when the world shrinks to the size of a pebble – perhaps there's no need for games, there's no such thing as disguise. The island itself just *is*.

The conversation had turned to men. She told them about Mark, jokes that she should have sent him instead, and then regretted mentioning him, for she was asked by Elin what kind of man he is. She found herself reeling off what she knows are the facts, that they've been living together for two years, that they will get married a month after she leaves the island (feeling a sudden pang with the memory of that dress hung in her mother's wardrobe back in Swansea), that they fell in love while working in the same English department, that working together somehow works for them, that he's handsome; not to everybody, but to her (while thinking that she's wrong, that he is to everybody *but* her), and that she might even enjoy being married to him, that settling down is something she doesn't particularly mind doing. Elin had laughed when she threw this last comment at them, having no idea that most of Mererid's life with Mark *is* carried out in this haze of *not minding*, of giving in.

She's been allowed some small space into which to crawl – a space where they understand her and she understands them. Even though these women have been together for weeks, sharing the same air, getting used to one another's company, they don't mind having someone else here. It's a small island, but it doesn't mean that there's no room for her. Though she was armed to the hilt, ready to assert that she can't – won't – force her presence on them, and that she'll quietly skim around until they're used to her being there – she'd over-prepared as usual. They don't mind. She's different. *Makes a nice change*, Elin had said, *from pottering around this cottage on my own.*

"*Nos da*," they'd said to one another, bidding one another goodnight, the slow release of syllables echoing down the corridor.

Mererid remembers dragging her gas lamp to her bedside, staring into its white orb, believing that there's something truly special about being so close to such light, of growing used to it, of forgetting about switches, about the brash, blaring light Mark always insists on putting on in the bedroom rather than the subtler side-lamp. There's something comforting about living life in a slightly dimmer reality, of watching the blunt contours of a room fading away and each angle becoming soft like fur.

It is the very same lamp, cold and dull to the touch, that she's now staring at, longing for an opportunity to use it again. The fog is rising, as Elin said it would, revealing a dense blue. Mererid slides closer to the window. To the south she can see the last desperate fingers of the island reaching out into the sea, to the north, sees the distant top end of the island where there are buildings, the silhouettes of people moving around. She rummages around in her case for the binoculars Mark has given her. She deliberately disregards everything he told her, in his tarmac-thick voice, about how best to use the contraption, and uses it recklessly through the closed window; seeing nothing but a blur of green and yellow in the distance.

Still in her pyjamas, she goes out into the corridor, the tiles cold against her bare feet, and flaps her way down towards the unfamiliar kitchen, frayed pyjama bottoms shuffling. She hears nothing now, no movement, no tinkling of pots – she doesn't know if Elin is still here, even. She is yet to know the pattern of a day on this island. She walks to the front door, notices that there is no lock, that the door may have been slightly ajar all night. She walks out into a dewy, bright promise of a morning, and is hit by the reality of it – the sea all around her. Everywhere she looks, there it is. Blue silver under that dense sky, pounding, positively pounding.

She wanders around the corner of the cottage, expecting to see the mainland. But she can't. She walks to the other side of the lighthouse courtyard, it can't be seen from there, either. The mainland can't be seen at all, as she expected it would. It's gone. Bardsey mountain stands as a bulk between, and allows the whole island to turn its back to it. So they were right, she thinks. Bardsey allows her to lose sight of things; those things she had been trying to find an excuse to lose sight of. She thinks about Mark saying a few weeks ago how he would climb to Uwch Mynydd at the end of the month and look across to see if she were visible. She shudders at the thought of it – but now she sees she's safe. The island guards her, as it guards all the islanders. She would have to climb the harsh, craggy mountain to wave back at him, although she knows he's already climbed half that amount to get close to her.

To the left she sees an old flagstaff on a risen hill, dotted with dawdling sheep. Walking closer, she startles them, they rush off in different directions. All around this island something or other is glistening, awakening, stirring. She listens again and hears the strange, unearthly moaning of seals. She is hit by the fact that even as this is happening to her – as eight weeks stretch out gloriously ahead of her, this space, this life, those dimly lit nights, the untouched bright white pad, the poems waiting to be written – even now this moment is leaving her too soon.

"Looking for inspiration?" Elin's voice echoes somewhere behind her. She turns to see Elin in a pale purple bra, stripy pyjama bottoms loose on her hips.

"No, I wasn't," Mererid replies, following the voice back to the cottage door.

"A phone signal then…" She hoists a white T-shirt on. The purple

46

bra remains prominent, the two cups poking through, now a muted pink. "If you're desperate, walk with your phone further on to the south end. The flagstaff's usually a good spot for it. I mean we have it easier than most, you need to be near the sea to catch any of the signal, poor buggers up top need to climb halfway up the mountain to have any chance of a decent conversation." Elin's sentence is swallowed by a yawn, and she walks back in, heading for the kitchen. Mererid realises that she doesn't even know where her phone is. The kitchen smells of rainwater mist, of lingering leftovers, of compost. Elin pulls out two plates on which she piles last night's left over tikka massala. "Want some?"

"Why not?" Mererid answers, remembering suddenly about the bulge, the blockage. She's surprised she's been able to forget about it for so long.

They eat the leftovers in silence, rhythmically munching away. Elin offers to take Mererid around today, to let her get to know people. Take her up the mountain. Show her most of the island – and there isn't much, she says – so that she knows what to do, where to go. Not that she has to do anything, or go anywhere – Gwyn, the island's manager, has reminded them all that they should let her choose her own path over the coming weeks. Then Elin says, "But choosing your own path doesn't mean straying from the designated paths. I won't have anyone spoiling my paths. And don't go grabbing the lichen for support either. Lichen is like *gold* to me." Mererid thinks that she will scribble this down later, this thing about lichen being like *gold*, it sounds like a poem half-forming. Although she isn't quite sure what lichen is. Mark would know. Mark always knows.

The remainder of breakfast is spent explaining to Mererid her toilet duties – that she isn't to place any paper in the bowl itself, but fold it away neatly in a nearby box. And how she's not to flush, only to pour water from the water-tank down the toilet, from a red bucket, in whooshing, non-specific quantities. She's only to flush if there's waste involved. "*Real waste*, you know…" Elin says, blushing, and Mererid is surprised to find the more demure part of this striking girl smiling back at her. "And consider it a luxury that you have the option," she says, reminding Mererid that it's the only flush toilet on this island, that the rest of them have to make do with compost toilets, which need emptying every day.

All this talk of toilets makes Mererid realize that she's ready to go after all. And she has no difficulty. Despite there being no lock, no key, no closing of the door. The blockage is part-removed; her body is starting to find its own rhythm again. Elin's waiting for her outside the door, bag on her back. The water is still rushing through the pipes. Mererid is embarrassed, thinking all the while about this loud signalling of waste, until Elin laughs at her.

"We all do it," Elin says, "We all have to, I mean it's…"

They link arms.

She tries not to think of Mark. She promised to ring him the minute she got there. She's already twelve hours away from that minute. She looks out to the sea on either side, feeling totally safe, utterly unreachable.

7

It was the first hour of their three-day-meditation, and Viv had not been prepared to have to justify her own specific brand of silence. Last night, on departing from the cottage, the sisters had agreed that they would travel down to Henllwyn Bay in the morning to offer their silence up to God, and that morning, Viv had made the mistake of trying to greet them verbally to start, thinking that their vow of silence only started once God had given it the OK. Sister Mary Catherine had clamped her hand over her mouth, while Sister Lucy repaired the air with a sudden wave. Sister Anna merely whispered a *bore da* and chewed another smile from view.

She'd then been urged, through a series of hand gestures, to lead the way. Elfyn, who'd been out roaming all morning, now came wagging about her heels, tripping her up, asking for breakfast. Sister Mary Catherine had been offended by the barking, pointing at the dog, glaring at Viv as though she'd somehow commanded him to do so. Viv had stopped the procession, and taken him back to the house. "*Sori cariad*," she'd mouthed as she shut the door, thrusting a handful of dog biscuits at him. When she turned round she was face to purple-face with Sister Lucy, who had been waiting for the slip-up. Even when she rejoined the procession it was indicated, through a myriad of confusing hand signals, that she was still somehow breaking the silence with the flapping of her habit in the breeze. It seemed that Sister Lucy's sneezing and less-than-silent wind-breaking were allowed by means of some devout loophole in the fine-print of Godly silence.

Yr arglwydd yw fy mugail, she started, *ni bydd eisiau arnaf*. The ultimate crime, she thought, conversing with God in Welsh behind Sister Mary Catherine's back. The second the thought passed through her mind Sister Mary Catherine's eyes slid towards her, like a pendulum. "Your thoughts are breaking the silence, Sister Vivian," she mouthed.

They started the journey to Henllwyn Beach, with Viv travelling a little in front of the others. She found that she could let her thoughts roam as freely, and as noisily as she wanted, as long as she could keep up her stoic, head-stiff poise that made her look as though her mind were full of arid whiteness. She'd been wanting to get Sister Anna alone since they'd arrived, to ask her how things were going with that awful daughter of hers, who kept turning up at Llanddwyn wanting to put her in a home. "It's obvious that this is some kind of breakdown you're having, Mam," the witch-daughter had apparently said to her. "The sooner we get proper care for you, the better." Whenever she heard this story – in its annual installments – it enlivened her to think that others, too, like her, had had something resembling a normal life before taking their vows. That Sister Anna knew what it was like to have a child, too, however awful the consequence of such a thing sometimes was, kept something alive between them, an understanding that was brimming even now, as they traversed noiselessly down past the Cavern, their eyes meeting every now and then in covert communion.

It was ten o' clock, the sun already scalding hot through her habit. The smell of summer was intoxicating, the freshly-cut grass woven with the odour of a wild sea, which transported her back to a day when she would have been able to wear anything she wanted to greet the summer season. She had one defining memory of walking down the lane of their cottage, wearing a patterned blue and white short sleeved dress, with Iestyn, her son, asleep in the crook of her shoulder. He clung to her too tightly even then, she thought, before chastising herself for betraying her silence with another memory of her unholy life. Sister Lucy was close enough behind her to detect it, she was sure of that.

By the Cavern, they came across Leri hovering around by the boathouse, camera dangling from her hand. She prayed that Leri didn't notice them. She didn't want her turning her camera on them, as she so often did, primarily because Viv wasn't sure what Sister Mary Catherine would make of such an intrusion. Mainly though, she was worried Leri might let slip she'd already filmed her. She didn't want

Sister Mary Catherine finding out about that. That she'd been in her house, setting up her camera in the corner while Viv made the tea, asking her all sorts of questions that, in the end, she hadn't minded answering. Even worse, for Sister Mary to find out that she'd enjoyed it: that she'd thought it was nice for someone to care about her, someone who wanted to know her particular story. She didn't tell Leri everything, of course, although she'd got the strange feeling that Leri had known some things anyway. She *was* in the media, after all. She might have seen her picture on the news. Either way, she'd felt as though she'd represented herself adequately. Most people didn't get the chance, did they? It wasn't as if Sister Anna would even get the chance to tell the nation her particular side of the story, while the witch-daughter looked on, seething.

She would probably be quite safe, she thought. Sister Mary Catherine was hardly going to be watching S4C. ITV was the channel of choice at Caldey, apparently. They were sticklers for those *Midsomer Murders*.

At the last minute, she decided to take them to Solfach Beach instead, as it was more private there. Henllwyn opened up on the sea, the Cavern, the jetty; the islanders would all be able to see them, make fun of them. The seals would belch in mockery. Leri would get all the footage she wanted. Solfach was easier. It was that kind of bay into which the sea drifted in and stayed silently put, the seals didn't frolic as much in this water, they kept their dark eyes just above the surface. She suddenly ushered them to the left, confusing Sister Lucy who yelped as she tripped over a piece of driftwood. Viv had great pleasure in giving her a sudden glare for trespassing on the silence.

On they went, down past the bleating, curious sheep, across one more field, until they reached what would be the perfect alcove for a day's silence. Porth Solfach, on a day like today, was the purest, crescent moon of a beach, curling around the shore. She heard them gasping at the sight of it and suddenly felt proud of what she had. Yes, this was hers. This mute beach where she often sat alone, shoving her wrinkled hands deep in the sand, disturbing the sand-flies.

This exposed the beauty of Bardsey better than any of her letters ever could. This is where Viv imagined the pirates would have arrived all those years ago, or the smugglers, reeling up under the light of the moon to the bright silver sand, their coarse whispers echoing all around. Once again, she caught Sister Mary Catherine looking at her, as if she somehow knew she was thinking about something ungodly, that her mind had dwindled from the reality of the twenty thousand saints to the material reality of ten gruffly bearded men throwing their loot onto the sand. She focused her gaze once again on the morning's golden waves. *Clear your mind*, she said, again and again, as the waves sashayed up to greet her.

They took off their clunky black boots, and walked on towards the sea. Viv was the first to hoist up the habit and go in, with the other three standing back, curiously watching her do it. Yet by now Viv had started to get a little tetchy – they were on *her* island, they would do as she gestured for them to do. She'd had to perform a Celtic dance in her awkward feet at the Lundy conference (Sister Lucy had a theory that God was mad on dancing), and had been forced into a workshop on chocolate-making on Caldey. All she was asking for was a little cooperation.

And so she went into the water, habit hoisted just below the hips, the thickness of the sea absolving her veined legs as she went. She felt the water dressing her ankles, hoisting its wetness about her, until the prickles of cold fell away and the warmth seeped through her. This was it, she thought, this was the closest she got to feeling that she was part of something again. But it was something that moved independently without her, something that didn't need her persistence to survive. These waves would never stop coming. Feeling the usual exultation fill her, she let go of the habit and felt it descending into the water, lolling heavily around her as she waded further and further in, until the water was pushing against the top of her thighs, her habit draped behind like a black mane.

She opened her eyes. To her surprise, she saw that they had followed her in. They probably thought it was protocol for connecting with the saints, that it was some ancient Celtic ritual that called the likes of Beuno and Cadfan to the surface, entwined in seaweed. They needn't know it was a ritual of her making; that it was absurd, possibly meaningless. Sister Lucy, who was considerably shorter than her, winced as the waters reached her waist. Sister Mary Catherine ordered them with her eyes to stop, to allow the silence to congeal about them once more.

The sloshing gradually gave way to stillness. They stood in a line, perfectly still, eyes closed (Viv's eyes half-open, still scouring for Leri and her camera) as Sister Mary Catherine gave them the nod to link hands, and offer their silence to God. Viv saw a seal pop its curious head above the water, moving towards them with a flash of recognition in its eyes.

Sister Anna's hand drifted to meet Viv's, Viv's reached out for Sister Lucy's.

Sister Mary Catherine's hand was never on offer.

8

In the end, Deian allowed Greta to come with him to see the plaque. Although he'd only known her for three weeks, it was enough on Bardsey, where a few weeks somehow amounted to a few years of friendship. He'd told her about his mother on the third night of meeting her, because her face seemed open to it somehow. Some people had that kind of face; he knew they did because Fran had once told him that his was the furthest point from that face imaginable. "You have the kind of face that stops people from saying what they really think," she'd spat at him, "all closed off. No through road." He could only imagine that Greta's face, strangely shaped as it was, made somehow comical and unserious by those unsteady glasses, and uniquely set by her almost unfathomable eyes, was furthest from his own jutting brow, his rough beard, his clear blue nothingness, another term Fran had invented for one of his stares. He knew somehow, just in the way Greta fell into him ever so slightly when she laughed at his poor jokes, that she was not repulsed by him as a person, that she could accommodate closeness, and that she would listen to him. And she did. She understood that it was possible to feel one poignant loss for ten years and more, and that he didn't particularly want to move on – as people always told him to do – because he was afraid of forgetting his mother. "If you miss out on a mother, certain bits of your life don't fit," she'd said, her eyes grimy with sea-salt.

And so they'd stood there together, amidst the ruins of the Abbey tower, like man and wife almost, hands almost touching, reading a plaque that read: "*Er Cof am Delyth Davies, un o'r seintiau anwylaf a gollwyd*" and then in smaller, writing beneath, *In loving memory of Delyth Davies, one of Bardsey's most treasured saints.*

"I don't know why they decided to make her a saint. She wasn't a saint," he said, without looking up. He found the gold glint of the plaque a little offensive.

"Sainthood comes in many forms," Greta had said. "I mean, if some people want to remember her as a saint, then…"

"Some people might want to. Viv might want to. But she wasn't one. That's all I'm saying. Not in a bad way. But a saint, I mean, what does it mean? Honestly. She might not even be here. I mean, no one knows, do they?"

"No," Greta drawled, "I mean no one can know where a soul goes after…"

"I'm not talking about souls, Greta, I'm talking about *her*. I mean never mind about her soul, it might be a start knowing what happened to the body."

"Right," said Greta, grappling with his arm. He shrugged her off.

"It looks crap, doesn't it?"

"No, it doesn't. It's nice that it's there."

"Well it wasn't my decision, anyway. You don't get much say when you're only here once a year. I don't like it. Makes it seem conclusive. And it isn't. To be conclusive you need evidence. I just don't think Viv had the right."

He turned to look at Greta. He didn't know why he'd brought her here. It seemed odd, standing by a plaque that had never been there before, with a woman he hardly knew. And yet it was Bardsey-sense, the kind of thing you did here. He stared again at the plaque, and at his mother's name. It looked fresh, the soil around it still a dark brown. They must have done it recently. Someone could have told him. Why hadn't Gwyn mentioned it, when they'd spoken about the survey? He hadn't wanted to hear it tumbling out of Viv's mouth when he'd first arrived, squashed in between apologies and offers of ginger cake.

"She spoke Welsh, then, your mother?" Greta asked.

"Of course. So did I. *Unwaith.*"

"*You* spoke it?" Greta smiled. "*W't ti'n siarad Cymraeg 'lly?*"

"Yeah, I did once. It's, it was, my first language. Why's that so funny?"

"It's just that you sound so *English.*"

"That'll be Preston for you – I had to go and live with my father after my mother went missing. I mean, I was eighteen, but, my Dad still saw me as this little kid who needed looking after, and, to be fair to him, he wanted a chance to get to know me. He hadn't seen me since I was a baby. He's a decent bloke, unlike what my mother told me. I felt like I owed it to him. I still live in Preston now, you know, only a few miles away from where he is. I suppose it's no wonder that my Welsh just... faded."

"Why do people let that happen?" Greta let out. "For someone just to lose a language like that... happens all the time with Welsh, it's like they think it isn't really important."

"It wasn't, after a few years in Preston. I just sort of forgot about it. It's amazing what you can get used to, you know, when you have such little choice."

"*Ond ma'n rhaid bo chdi'n cofio chydig?*" Greta said, trying to prompt him. He recognised all of those words on their own, but strewn together they seemed a little overwhelming. Cofio was to remember. He'd forgotten what to forget was. "*Ti 'di anghofio?*"

That was it.

"*Do, wedi anghofio.*"

"Forgetting isn't the same as losing, now, is it?" Greta said, taking his hand. For once he didn't flinch. It felt good, this woman's whisper of a touch.

"It must still be there, somewhere," Greta argued. "Things like that don't just go away. It just needs unearthing. Excavating."

She was smiling when he looked up, head cocked to one side, laugher lines opening up like cracks across her face. She knew how to get to him.

"Maybe after the excavation of the saints," he retorted. "I suppose you're going to tell me now that that's good material."

"What do you mean?"

"For the documentary... you know, the mother tongue and the missing mother. Suppose you want me to play out some reconstruction or something, film me crying, holding on to the plaque like some crazed loon...." He heard a grasshopper chirrupping around the plaque, dancing in and out of the grass in a ghostly green shadow.

"Why would you think that?" Greta said, taking off her glasses, giving him her eyes. "Is that what you think we're like?"

"Aren't you all the same?" Even as he said it, he knew they were not. He recalled Leri's straight-back poise, the semblance of indifference in that baseball cap (that was completely cancelled out by her clipboard), and the pointed questions that she threw over her shoulder at him when she thought no one was listening. Leri brought a breeze with her onto the site, cold air that lodged itself under his shirt.

Greta, on the other hand, was like the gate to Cae Uchaf, always open, always drawing people in. She had a smile that rose higher on one end of her mouth, her beautiful face pretending to be plain, that chameleon hair of hers always flying about, speaking to you. She came at you in swathes of light-coloured linen; disarming, opaque.

"I'm sorry – I didn't mean it like that," he said, placing a hand on her shoulder. "You end up getting defensive about these things."

"It's alright," Greta said. "It's just, I don't want you to think I don't understand. I lost my mother, too. To cancer. Few years back."

"I'm sorry," he said, hoping that she wouldn't be able to see the envy that crept up his neck in crimson blotches. Cancer. A death certificate. It all seemed so much more decorous somehow; finite.

"I'm sorry Grets," he said, abbreviating her name in a slip of sincerity. "It can't have been easy…"

"No it wasn't," she said. "I mean, being this age, everybody expects you to get on with things. But it's not easy to get on with things, it's more a matter of things getting on with you. Still, it's nice that you've got this, isn't it?" She said, her voice brightening, the gate swinging wide open once again. She traced the outline of his mother's name on the plaque. "It must be an honour to have your mother made a saint."

"She wasn't a saint, Greta, I've already told you that, this is Viv's idea of cementing my mother in this island's history. She always did get stupid ideas."

"She must have cared for her…"

"She did, but she forgets sometimes that she wasn't the only one."

"Wouldn't the language be," Greta hesitated. He knew what she was going to say, "wouldn't it be some kind of... you know, path, back to her? You must still remember it."

"It's kind of... locked," he said, thinking about all those phrases that were somehow bound as one, inseparable, inside him. "It would take a lot of practice, and I'm a very busy man," he said, in mock earnestness.

"You've got your harem, haven't you, all here waiting for you. Me, Leri, Elin. All the practice you need. Even the poet's a Welshie."

"Ah yes, the poet," he'd said. "Sent to unearth us all, no doubt."

"Looking for a muse," Greta said.

"Aren't we all?" Deian replied, finally placing his bouquet of wild flowers at the foot of the glinting plaque.

Walking back from the chapel, Deian thought once more about the plaque. What it was saying, confirming. That his mother was dead. Of course, he'd known that there was a chance that she must be dead; ever since her disappearance, he'd had to face the fact that in all probability she was indeed dead and would not be coming back. But seeing her name there had seemed a little too finite. It was the gravestone they'd never had, that they'd resisted getting. For him, she had always been missing, never dead. And though most people hated the liminality of the notion of the 'missing' person, lost forever in time and mystery and circumstance, he had found it strangely comforting.

For as long as she was missing, it allowed certain parts of himself to remain missing too. Not gone, but missing. Forgetting isn't the same as losing, Greta had said, and she'd been right. All around him he heard the whispers and brogues of the island, the island that had spoken to him when he was a child, in Welsh, telling him where the best finds were. He'd run over to the south end and always find something, some little rectangular dark shape in the soil that would seem worthless until he'd cleaned it all up. The island's voice, hoarse and haunting, guided him there, he was sure of it. Now, ten years on, the voices were absent, but they weren't gone. He'd pass *Tŷ'r Ysgol* and think of how his mother would call him a *hogyn da* and *y 'nghariad bach i* and *yr hen ddiawl bach drwg* and he'd know what they meant. He remembered how he and Iestyn, Viv's son, would spy on the farmer's wife getting undressed from the mountain side and when they'd been caught he'd screamed his blamelessness as he was dragged up the lane, *nid fi nath Mam, nid fi nath!*

But he couldn't quite keep ahead of the language, the way it was now. All trendy, modern, slacked-out in Greta's linen combats and shiny across Leri's expensive sunglasses, bursting with flesh and energy and Cardiff-isms, there was always something he couldn't-quite-catch. It was the angular, hard-hitting language of the camera, bouncing and bounding at the touch of a button, the whirr of the tape. Leri and Greta used words like *strwythur* and *cyfarwyddo*, *esblygiad* and *goblygiadau*, officious lingo that made his head turn once more towards the simpler vernacular of the soil.

So he'd rather pretend that he couldn't speak it. It was less embarrassing than trying. And it was easy to blame Preston. The truth was that his father had never discouraged it. There had been the obligatory bout of holidays at Anti Mair's in Llithfaen, the drawn out weekends at the odd Eisteddfod. But he'd come home in a bad mood, saying he never wanted to go back. Because for him it was the language of the island and his childhood, of kind faces, caves and bird-hides, rock-pools and lime-kilns, of the chattering choughs and the Manx shearwaters, Viv, Iestyn, his mum, their own little enclosed world. The language was Bardsey, Bardsey was the language. And even when he started coming back, a few summers ago, his Anti Mair always discouraged his decision. "It isn't good for you," she'd said. "After everything that happened, to go brooding about the place. You won't find her, Deian. She's gone."

But he still came here, each summer, to brood. Too look for things. And to regret the fact that the language had been lost – in his stubbornness, somewhere on the A55 back to Preston, such a dismal way for a language to die. No, not *die*. Go missing. Just like his mother.

When he arrived back on site, Elin was there, with the resident poet in tow. He hadn't seen her at first, for Mererid was actually small enough to be entirely engulfed if someone happened to be standing in front of her. Being unaware of her presence, he'd come hurdling into the scene in his usual way, yelling at Elin to stop wasting time, informing Greta she was on the wrong side of the field, kicking a path for himself toward his trowel, before finally falling to his knees in his designated spot. It wasn't until he'd heard Elin say, "Sorry about this," in Welsh, and, "He isn't usually this rude," that he turned his eyes skyward to see them both standing above him, Elin, in her usual strange quarter-of-a-dress and the poet, black hair framing her tiny, translucent-white face.

"Deian, this is Mererid, the poet. Mererid this is Deian. The archaeologist, or so he says. The one who is…"

"The one sane person on the island," he said, shaking her marble-cool hand.

"I hardly think so Dei," Elin said, fiddling with a strap that wasn't there, "that would be something, wouldn't it. I mean it's not as if you… you…"

"Do you know that Deian speaks…?" Greta started. He turned around and fixed her with a look that said, *don't you dare,* "speaks complete and utter bollocks most of the time?" Elin said.

Mererid laughed. The kind of laugh that folded itself away, neatly, when it was done.

"Done much digging before?" he asked.

"Only in theory," she'd said.

Liking her answer, he handed her a trowel.

9

L ast night Leri had been shaken awake by Greta, opening her eyes to a frantic swinging of hair and blankets.

"It's an attraction," she said.

"Of course it's an attraction," Leri replied, her words gloopy. "Come here."

"A lighthouse attraction," she said.

The phrase made no sense to Leri. She imagined the lighthouse walking towards her, gathering her up in its arms.

"Leri don't go back to sleep…"

"Greta please will you…"

"If you don't get up and film this, you'll regret it, I promise you."

Greta was already half way down the ladder. She heard the squeeze of toes-in-boots, the zipping of jackets. She peered her head over the side of the loft. Every few seconds or so, the dark rose in shocks of light, giving her powdery glimpses of Greta, moving towards the small window.

"It amazing, unbelievable… Leri get up, you've got to see this."

"What time is it?"

"Who cares what bloody time it is, get dressed. We need to go over to the lighthouse."

"What's your obsession with this bloody lighthouse?"

"It's not an obsession, it's the birds… look, the birds, the attraction. Elin said this might happen."

"Elin this, Elin that," Leri couldn't help herself but whine this last sentence. She expected some reprisal, but was offered nothing. Nothing but the quiet clicking of the door as it shut behind Greta.

"Greta? Greta!"

The camera, she thought, *she's taken the bloody camera.*

When she woke a second time, just before sunrise, the bed was still empty. There was no warmth, no imprint of a body. The sheet was a smooth, derisive white. Greta had obviously been gone all night. Leri had a sudden flashback of her dream; Greta and Elin, entangled, ponytails meshing together. Dreams stayed with her these days, floating around her consciousness, blending a little too easily with the reality all around her. She knew she wouldn't be able to look Greta in the eye when she returned.

She was getting too attached, she thought, too close. That night, they'd tumbled into sleep like a couple who'd been together for years, hands crossing over one another's chests, looking at the egg-moon being swallowed up by the dark. The blackness soon enveloped them, too, so that they could see nothing at all, not even one another's faces. Leri recalled how she'd traced the tip of Greta's nose in the dark. It had character, even on her fingertips. A sharp descent finished by a sudden ascent; a ski-ramp of a nose. She dived off it and plummeted into a deep sleep, feeling Greta's hand slip in and out of her grasp as she went. Suddenly, she was being fished out of the dark with a huge net.

"It's an attraction," Greta said, and then she was gone.

Leri flipped up the blinds. Another beautiful day on Bardsey. And it was a little ridiculous, the weather swimming around them in caramelized, sunny clichés, everything coated with a syrupy film – the greenness looking almost edible. The buildings set off by the indigo blue they lived under, even the path's yellow dust drifting like star dust. You couldn't even escape it as you looked up, where a pair of choughs launched red legs above the cliff tops.

It wasn't what she wanted for the documentary. Beauty is difficult to work with, Clive always told her, beauty of any kind is a distraction. And beauty wouldn't work for her story. She knew it wouldn't.

She deliberated every movement she made from bed to front door that morning, hoping that if she moved slowly, time would somehow bring Greta back, that she wouldn't have to open the door to an island which knew more than she did. She was nervous about the camera. About whatever had taken Greta away from that warm bed. She pottered around the kitchen, choosing a random array of Bardsey foods for her breakfast; rice cakes, with some of the farm's homemade goat's cheese. She'd bought the goat's cheese from Howard, after being charmed by its taste at one of the beach barbecues. But she'd found the taste to be nothing like any of those she'd tasted previously. She'd taken it back, and Howard had laughed at her.

"It's them you want to be talking to," he said, gesturing towards the goats, who looked at her as though they'd taken offence. "Damn things don't know what they're doing. If they're having a bad week, you can taste it in the cheese. It's that one there, it is. Bullying the other one."

Before she'd been able to trail the direction of his finger, he'd shut the door on her, leaving her staring into the eyes of two seemingly docile goats, trying to pick out the abuser from the abused. They both bleated at her, hair raised in cotton wool tufts, their tilted heads like two question marks.

But thinking about it now, shoving the cheese down in clumpy, bitter pieces, she saw that he was right. What the cheese was lacking was not the culinary skill of its producer, but the warmth of its creator. It was sharp and stinging, not like the creamy slice she'd had at the barbecue. You could actually taste the fear, she thought, thinking again of those doppelganger goats, their cold, identical stare.

She wrapped it up again in the white paper Howard had given her, writing Greta's name in nervy angles across the top. Greta had tasted something different from her, and saw the cheese as a delicacy to be devoured in small, sanctimonious slices. "Kept this for you," she wrote, hoping it would serve like an apology of sorts, a white flag in cheese form.

Just as she shut the fridge door, Greta came in, her ever-changing hair like seaweed, her eyes electrified by the thrill of the sleepless night.

"What an attraction," she gasped, before collapsing in a heap on the small sofa.

"What do you mean, attraction? Tell me what happened." Leri

heard herself trying to sound nonchalant.

"You want to know now, do you?"

"Don't be like that, Greta. Let me make up a bed for you, you look exhausted."

She reached for a blanket and spread it over Greta.

"You must be tired," she said, one eye on the camera's canvas bag at her feet. "I was worried."

"Worried about the camera, more like."

Leri unzipped the case and peered inside. The tapes were still where she'd left them. Flicking the tape deck open she saw it was empty.

"Did you…"

"No, I didn't…"

"But, I thought that's why…"

"There wasn't time. It was all a mad rush. I had to help out."

"Help out with?"

"With the attraction!" Greta shouted, pulling the blankets over her head.

The word, at once both alien and familiar, like Greta's scowl, acquired significance during the day.

"Hear about the attraction? I hate bloody birds. Especially that many of them," Howard said, disappearing in a cloud of dust on his tractor.

"I don't sleep well, at the best of times," Mwynwen said, "but it had to happen on the one night when I was drifting off, really drifting off, you know, when you fall really *deep*. Next thing I'm sat upright, eyes wide open. They made such a racket, going past, all squawking their heads off."

"The birds came past the house?"

"Not the birds, those birdwatchers from the Obs. Chattering away like they'd never seen anything so exciting in their lives. They were practically sprinting to that lighthouse."

She recalled the bird observatory that morning. The place was usually teeming with groups of people, holding onto their lukewarm teas, their binoculars glued to their eyes. That morning the blinds were down.

"Not many dead this time," Mwynwen added, flapping a rug in the breeze.

"Birdwatchers?"

"No; birds, love," said Mwynwen. "The birdwatchers aren't exactly high-flyers."

She had no choice but to make her way to the lighthouse gradually, camera pressing into her back, the sun hot on her exposed toes. Not that she intended filming anything in particular, but she still needed some establishing shots of the lighthouse, and she knew she'd get away with doing this nicely if it were in the guise of asking some basic questions about the attraction. It annoyed her that whatever had happened had caused such a stir, because it took the edge off her own little drama. Her drama would begin when the last boat came in, which was, according to Mwynwen, when the blouses on her washing line began puffing with air.

She didn't *need* to know, of course. But she wanted to. Primarily because what she'd seen hidden in Greta's eyes was something she wanted some share of. She'd already discovered the main body of what had happened, only that it was a mesh of bird feathers and bones in her hand. It had something to do with birds, thousands of them, all up at the lighthouse. She imagined a huge flock of them surging past, a moving cloud across the sky, with the crowd mirroring them below, mouths agape.

Squealing in through the rusty gate, she first passed the side window and saw Mererid sitting at her desk, writing. She waved cautiously and Mererid waved back. They were yet to talk to each other properly. That first night at the lighthouse they had been cautious of one another. Mererid had resisted being filmed; she remembered it well, that pretence of demureness, those hiding eyes and that flickering half-smile. Leri found herself wondering what on earth a person like that could find to write about. She tried to avoid poets as much as she could, ever since that documentary film she'd made about them back in the late nineties, where one overbearing bard with a tweed coat and hat had snuck into her hotel room, oozing sweat and tobacco breath, clasping her in his puny arms. When she'd thrown him out, she'd found a poem under her door the next day, stale reassurance in strict metre. She still avoided him at every Eisteddfod.

Walking across the courtyard, she saw that patches of gravel were carpeted with grey and black feathers, with one or two dead birds lying on the ground. She remembered something in her notes about dead birds; something that had been used in evidence in the court case. Maybe this could fit in, somehow. She started rolling, focusing intently on the bird's dead face. It didn't look peaceful as she was half expecting it to look, but crazed, manic, still holding in its crystal gaze the horror of its last hour. She then filmed the lighthouse courtyard, noticing how different it was to the other end of the island. It wasn't silent for one thing. There was the constant hum of some generator or other, with the messages from other parts of the island blaring out of the kitchen's radio system. Even as she peered through the lens, she was aware of Howard telling Deian that there was an injured sheep on the cliffs at Bae'r Nant. "The bloody thing's bleeding to buggery," Howard's saying, "get over here to help, will you?"

She was startled by a sudden knock on the kitchen window. Elin pushed it open, and splayed herself out of it like a cuckoo-clock figurine, hand on scantily clad hip.

"What you doing? Shouldn't you...?"

"You don't need permission from a dead bird, do you?"

"Have you asked Mererid? She's a bit..."

"What on earth happened here?" Leri asked. "It looks like you had a bird massacre or something."

"You television people know nothing!" Elin complained. "Get in here, and I might tell you."

Ten minutes later, Leri was trying her best to digest the last of Elin's too-sweet toffee, washing it to the pit of her protesting stomach with a cup of rainwater-tea. Mererid joined them, complaining that she was getting nowhere with the sonnet about the bird attraction, that she'd got stuck on: "Another night pours forth a feathered sky", a line that, to Leri, sounded completely overdone. Then again, all literature sounded a little laboured to her, as though writers had a complete refusal to see things as they actually were.

"So what happened last night?" Leri asked.

"An attraction," Elin said.

"If I hear that word one more time… I *know* it was an attraction, Greta told me."

"Greta was great wasn't she?" Mererid said. "I mean, she had no more idea what she was doing than I did, but she coped with it better, I think, a real trooper!"

"Don't run yourself down, Mererid," Elin said, "you were great, too, considering you'd never seen anything like that before, it was so…"

"It was amazing," Mererid said. "I'll never see anything like that again. Pity you weren't here to film it."

"I thought you didn't like cameras," Leri said, trying to mute her menace in a tea-sip.

"But this wasn't about me," Mererid replied.

"Would you mind then," Leri said, treading softly, "if I filmed you two talking about it? About what happened."

Elin and Mererid exchanged glances.

"Ok, then," Mererid said, swallowing the last bit of toffee with a wince, "if I have to."

Leri started filming. Mererid gave her the preamble: how they'd come home from a late night drinking session with Deian to see the birds circling the lighthouse. She'd gasped, and hadn't known what it was. Elin's hands reconstructed the journey of the migratory bird through the foggy, starless night, using a small torch as a substitute lighthouse. She then placed the torch at the centre of the table, pretending to circle it like a bird, her arms punching the air as she went.

"And that's if they're lucky," Elin added, her voice hoarse from her pseudo-squawks. "Because some of them just fly straight into it and die – *bam!*" She slammed her fist on the table a little too hard, leaving a cereal bowl trembling.

"It was so beautiful to look at," Mererid added, "all those birds with their wings glowing with light, until you realised that what you're looking at is something that's gone horribly wrong, something unnatural."

"And unnatural things happen for a reason," Elin continued, getting ahead of her own story, relishing the details in the way a nature presenter would, draping herself around chairs and tables in the room, her eyes dense with drama. She was fabulous, it seemed to Leri, more of an attraction than the attraction itself. She made a mental note to show her producer the tape. Perhaps Elin was quite a find; they were seriously lacking in good-looking presenters for Welsh-language nature programmes. "And where were you?" Elin asked her. Leri clicked off the camera. She knew what Elin and Mererid wanted, as they looked up at her with their sleepless eyes. They wanted Leri to tell them that she was sorry she had missed seeing the birds circling the lighthouse, seeing their strange, bewildered gaze for herself: that she'd rather have been there than here this morning, without a story, without a narrative, a dead bird in her pocket. But she wasn't.

"I was asleep," she'd said, sticking her head out of the window to watch the make-shift washing line. Elin's T-shirts were starting to swell. It was nearly time for the boat.

10

Mererid is back at her desk, trying to write a poem. She hurls out lines, watching them soar across the whiteness. Some of them, like the birds last night, are blinded by the light, and are extinguished before they've even begun their journey. The language flaps about the page. She bins her sonnet, and starts again without rules, without limitations. *A ring of feathers / like unfinished poems / streak the sky's page.* Yes, that's it, Mererid thinks: the birds circling the lighthouse are like her ongoing poems, entranced, which cannot take their eyes off themselves long enough to finish what they've begun. She feels a pulsation deep within her; this is what she feels when she is able to write, really write, and the second line gushes forth from her fountain pen: *their eyes grey / with moonlight.* She sits back, stares at it. She thinks of greying whites in decaying eggs, and is sure she's heard the line somewhere before. She remembers another line from a recent review: *here is a poet with technical skill in abundance, as though she were flying a jet-plane or manoeuvring a forty-tonne truck – but one wishes at times that she'd let the controls be, let these machines plummet to the ground or teeter off the edge, so that one would find in the wreckage, something far more interesting.* She pushes the pen deeper into the page. The page that is like Solfach beach, a new canvas that she will approach without technicality, she tells herself. Slowly, silently, she treads it, her word-prints ruffling the white sand.

Then she starts to think what Mark would say about this poem – ah yes, a uniquely female predicament, her affinity with nature, he would say. She remembers the comments he made on the paper she wrote about ornithology and Welsh poetry for last year's research seminar. It's a little tepid, he'd said, not rigorously argued, reaching for one of his own papers in comparison. She wanted to tell him then that there's nothing more tepid than those words he hides behind – nexus, acerbic, paradigmatic. But she realises that the only power she can have over him is silence.

Had he been there, he would have argued and theorized his way out of the attraction. He wouldn't have let the awe touch him. He wouldn't have been able to stand the people who took so kindly to her last night. Nothing but the light shadow of a gas lamp to give colour to the sparse meal, while two goats gazed on from their dark corners. The shadows pacing and jumping, the strange names evolving into hair and gestures, into questions and friendly accusations.

Deian, one of the few men on the island, is everything that Mark is not. Something in his eyes, his laugh, something warm, enticing, secretive. He is one of those men Mererid gets on with without trying – a man possessing a certain whimsicality and femininity (it belongs to Mark too, only he won't allow it), something that disarms her; allows her not to think too much before she speaks.

All too soon she was being dragged away by Elin back to their home, her arm linked with hers. "It isn't bad having you around," Elin had laughed, a little drunk, Mererid feeling the thrill of her arm against hers – the closeness, the flickering friendship between them. She wonders if when she gets married, that door to friendship will be closed off altogether. She thinks again about Mark, about how she must ring him. She is now two days away from the second she arrived.

She watched the piercingly bright flashes of the lighthouse ahead of her. Five flashes every fifteen seconds, Elin told her. It wasn't until they were at the Cavern that they saw something patterned against the light, throwing shadows across the beams. Then, they heard it, the screeching of hundreds of birds, mesmerized by light, being unable to do anything but follow the path of whiteness, towards death.

"It's really happening," Elin had said, letting go of her arm, running towards the lighthouse, leaving her behind.

Passing her own bedroom window, she saw a man inside, dressed in thick clothing, throwing his torch light about the place, illuminating her books, her notes, her unmade bed. "Don't worry," Elin said, "he's looking for more lamps to guide the birds back down." She followed

Elin's eyes to the scene above them, a furnace of feathers, all twisting and turning above the light, mistaking the circular path for a forward journey. The horizon had fallen away, the world was upside down, and now for these birds there was only the one star, a false lunar light made of prisms and lenses, urging them on.

It's only some birds that were able to make it that high (waders, she will later learn) whereas the darting crakes and rails come plummeting towards the light, a smatter of blood on the tower, disrupting the regularity of white and red. She heard the final screech as one sudden redwing scraped past her left ear. Shining her torch into its eyes, she saw the silver light still trapped within. This is what gave her the line: *grey with moonlight.* But now she knows it won't do. She is still flying her jet plane and accelerating along in her forty-tonne truck.

"You can help, if you want," Elin said, handing her a box. "You could collect them."

She wanted desperately to help, to be seen to be doing something. The courtyard was a congregation of birdwatchers holding up bright strips of light, trying to attract the birds back down to safety. It looked like a ritual of some kind, their brows furrowed with the intensity of religious fervour, their straight backs poised with purpose. And slowly, silently, the birds came to them, flitting down, their feathers weakening, to be taken in tender palms and stored away in the bird shack.

But Mererid didn't have the technique to do this. Her job was to clear away the dead birds. To rescue the flailing and injured. She started her journey across the courtyard, which was a mesh of trembling feathers. Most of them were dead, with only the breeze bringing them to life. Picking up their still warm bodies, she wondered if this was what undertakers felt when they were first called upon to collect the dead, the shifting of a warm body that was ever so gradually stiffening, stilling, at each passing moment.

Feathery shadows filled the box. She felt a hand on her shoulder and started – looking up she saw Greta's face, her eyes questioning and clear. It didn't take long for her to explain what must be done – she felt proud in that one moment that she knew what she was doing, that she now had this new knowledge that she could impart to others, as she and Greta filled the boxes together.

71

The small coffins piled up by the cottage doorstep. Mererid resisted looking at the birds as she collected them, letting her hands do the decoding. The next bird slumped in and she shut the top of the box. But then she felt something exploding to life within, protesting against its own death. She opened the box and the bird was there looking at her, wide-eyed and accusatory. It tried to fly away, scratching the side of her face, but fell at her feet, where it remained, gently wobbling. She picked it up. It pecked at her hands, drawing blood, the sharp beak all too easily shedding her white skin. Kicking the bird-shack door open, she hurled it to safety among the others, and closed the dark about them once more, muting their angry chorus.

They did this for hours, silently moving around one another, around the myriad lamps and birdwatchers, weaving their way in and out of their own patches of death. Their hands a maze of scars. All around them, the deathly down was being swept away, the birds drifting from the sky towards the iridescent glow of the lamps, nature being restored, repaired, pieced-back-together. The chatter of birds was replaced by the chatter of eager birdwatchers, huddled in the blue kitchen, drinking black coffee and spouting names she had never heard before: White Wagtail, Thrush Nightingale, River Warbler, a whoosh of words rustling past.

At five o' clock, the three of them were delirious and laughing, the dawn breaking across the corridor. The three of them fit together somehow, she thought; her, Greta, Elin, leaning against one another before they went their separate ways, Greta taking the spare room. It had been so long since she'd been in a unisex household like this; she had always convinced herself she could never stand it. She thought again of Mark. She didn't know how much longer she could keep him away.

And now she is here. This warm, blank mid-afternoon, trying to squeeze a poem out of her bird-bitten fingers; trying to turn the blood into ink on the page.

But she can't.

11

Sister Mary's Catherine's silence was driving Viv mad. She had never noticed before how essential voices were, how much they were needed to alleviate the aggravations of human behaviour. A distraction here, a distraction there, and it was easy not to be annoyed by the way a particular silver spoon was thrust intrusively into egg yolk, spilling its gluey contents all over the pale ochre shell, gearing its way into the all-too-confined space between shell and cup. It annoyed her even more when Sister Mary Catherine lifted the egg up to go chasing after the remnants, poking her fingers in around the rim, licking each finger while allowing a little more yellow gloop to spill out of the shell. Even the butter seemed to have sunk in a little too densely to the sister's bread. When hoisted from the porcelain plate on the table, it began a sparkling golden journey down her wrist, and had to be chased by her purple tongue. The other two, in comparison, carved the egg out noiselessly, graciously, scooping out the egg bit by bit, but then when it came to placing the egg in their mouths, there were all manner of obstacles to be overcome before the grey matter could be lodged firmly in their stomachs. Sister Lucy couldn't swallow anything without coughing, the spittle speckled bright yellow as it hit her water glass. Sister Anna had decorum, however, her only indiscretion being the way she ground the rough mass of Anglesey sea salt with her false teeth.

All this noise led to Viv having little appetite for her own egg, and she made her excuses, through a series of gesticulations that were now becoming tedious, to leave the darkness of the cottage and attend to her small patch of garden. Over the past few days, this had become a haven for her, a place where she could relish certain sounds after two days of stale nun silence, the flitting of pale yellow butterflies above her

73

cabbage patch, the incessant buzzing of the wasps that flapped about her hands, the spongy thump of Elfyn's black coat in the greenery, her own hands warm about his sun-swept stomach. The distant, consoling whisper of the tide-race all about the island, its soft slow tugging, which gave only the slightest hint of the dark rhythms that lay beneath. Her only wish was that it should remain peaceful until the day of the sisters' departure, so that they could be carried effortlessly away from her. Every day she held her hand out to the wind, looking for reassurance that nothing would stop their departure. If her sleeve merely ruffled, she was safe, the wind was on her side.

Then again, there was nothing stopping them from wilfully staying on the island for another week. She had been to visit Mwynwen that morning, checking the bookings.

"If they ask you, tell them the hermitage is fully booked," she'd said, pilfering a piece of bara brith from Mwynwen's plate.

"How are they going to ask me if they're not allowed to speak?"

"We're allowed to speak on the sixth day. Then it's feast day," she said, grinning, the sugary crumbs cascading from her mouth.

"You've got a funny way of fasting, Viv."

"I'm not eating, I'm meditating," Viv protested, shoving in another thick slice. "This is just like some sort of meditative preparation," she said, choking.

"Look Viv," Mwynwen had said, her laughing face grinding to a halt. "I'm glad you came. I wanted to talk to you. About something I heard. On the radio just now…"

"I haven't been allowed to listen to the radio this week," she'd said hurriedly, knowing what was coming. She shook the brown crumbs from her habit's safety net. "Best be off."

"Viv, wait." She was halfway down the path by now, the goats blocking her way. "It was about Iestyn. Apparently he's…"

"Oh, it's always about Iestyn. They're always finding something new to say about him."

Mwynwen stared at her. A stare that could penetrate silence, she thought, wishing Mwynwen were putting it to better use.

"You know, don't you?" Mwynwen had said. "You knew he was…"

"As I said, I haven't been allowed to listen to the radio. It interferes with the silence, doesn't it? You know I don't bother much with it anyway. I'm finished with politics…"

"But Viv this is…"

Turning her head slightly to the left, Viv caught sight of Sister Mary Catherine, Sister Lucy and Sister Anna descending from the mountain, winding down slowly to the farmhouse path.

"Promise me you'll tell them it's booked," she whispered, before paving her way between the goats.

"Viv!" Mwynwen grabbed hold of her sleeve. "Get back in here and talk to me, will you?"

Sister Mary Catherine landed in a bulk of black, just in the nick of time. She gave Mwynwen a glare, took Viv by the shoulders, and urged her on, away from Mwynwen's questioning eyes, and back into the depth of her own silence.

The afternoon was spent reflecting upon the solitary predicament of Elgar the Hermit, Viv's main inspiration, as she had told Sister Mary Catherine in several of her letters. *A man who was thrust from the sea, his heart ship-wrecked*, she wrote, *his eyes full to the brim with the flotsam and jetsam of life*. And the island forgave him his deeds, granted him solitude and peace, offering him a gloriously chaste, frugal life, where he was able to live on little more than air, grace and stolen potatoes. She had never mentioned, however, that he had once been an executioner, or that there was evidence to suggest that he was an Englishman by birth, for she had already forgiven him both these shortcomings in her prayers.

It was Elgar's life that she wanted, right now, Viv realised, staring up at his embroidered scripture in the yellowing light of Bardsey Chapel. She wanted to be like this sturdy ascetic, roaming the island, living on grass and vegetables, with no one for company but the waves. According to the book of Llandaf, he had even dug his own grave, rolling silently into it as his heart went down with the sun. Things had been so much easier in the twelfth century. No one around to meddle with things, Viv thought. Things would be different for her. Even if she did manage to dig herself a hole by the cabbage patch, and trained

Elfyn to push her in, there would always be some bugger (Howard, probably) who'd come and fish her out in the name of health and safety, dead or otherwise.

Sister Mary Catherine's left eye shot open, confirming that she'd caught another of Viv's noisy, roaming thoughts. Viv lowered her head. Moving her gaze away from Elgar made her confront Mwynwen's words.

"You know, don't you?"

Yes, she knew, she thought bitterly. What mother wouldn't? It didn't matter, she kept telling herself. Iestyn had made his own life, and she wasn't accountable for it. God had said so. He was gone, just like Delyth was gone, just like all the reasons she had ever come here in the first place were gone, carried out to sea by the wind. And like Elgar, those thoughts might find dry land one of these days; become somebody else's problem.

She wondered if it had ever crossed Elgar's mind, the moment he'd hollered that first greeting into the concave silence of the island, realising that there was no one there but him, that perhaps it was better to be dead than alone.

But even if he had, he had given it a chance. And aloneness grew on you. And soon enough, you'd rather be dead than be among people, she thought, staring at the bowed heads of her companions.

Walking out from the dark chapel and into the bright August sunlight was painful. Viv saw the gelatinous dots circling her vision, while Sister Lucy walked head on into the stone wall. Having established that there was nothing but a minor scratch on her ageing forehead, she guided them around the remains of the old Abbey. For them it was thrilling; they reached out their wrinkled fingers to the lukewarm stone, and looked at one another as if they were on the verge of discovery. She smiled weakly back at them, and wished, for the first time that summer, that it would rain. It was one of the most glorious summers they'd had for years, each day a kaleidoscope of morphing colours, glazing even this tepid grey stone with a sepia gleam, the sea awash with deep, moving blues. *Stuck between the devil and the deep blue sea,* she thought, smirking while Sister Mary's back was turned.

Sister Mary was pressing her face into the stone, deeply inhaling and exhaling its sanctity, no doubt. Viv couldn't help wondering if there was such a thing as limestone-on-the-lungs.

Let them try and survive the winters, she thought suddenly, recalling those wild months when she'd been alone here with Iestyn. When the fresh food ran out, when there was nothing to eat but tinned tomatoes and those horrible, bitter apples that grew at the side of Plas. Apple and tomato broth, day in, day out. She remembered too well his tantrums, the way he'd streak the pale blue walls with the blood-red-concoction. That was the first time she forced her way into his room, and had found the dead birds under the bed. He'd refused to let them be prised away from him by the bird observation team, so she'd taken to stealing them, one by one, from underneath his bed by the light of the candle, wincing at seeing how he'd gouged out their eyes. She remembered seeing him toss and turn in the pale light, terrified that he'd suddenly awaken, and seize her. And then do what? she always thought afterwards, gently mocking the thought as she closed the door softly on her beautiful boy alone with his dreams. Plenty of other children who'd grown up on this island developed a morbid fascination with dead animals, it was a positive thing, Mwynwen had once told her, it meant they were closer to nature, and more realistic about life. It didn't mean they were going to grow up to become murderers, did it? Even now, Viv remembers not answering this question, staring off out of her small window to the garden, where Iestyn was crucifying a fish with a crab claw. Though the fish was long gone, its stare cold in its silvery body, it was the way Iestyn stuck the claw in again and again that bothered her. It was as if he were looking for some reaction; proof, maybe, that there was more than one way to hang a fish from a washing line.

When they'd finished kneeling by the side of the Abbey, Viv steered them out through the gravestones, veering away from Delyth's plaque the best she could. But the sun had picked it out, throwing traces of gold against the blank wall, guiding Sister Lucy, and then Sister Anna to stare at the inscription. Viv regretted getting gold; it did seem a bit much, Deian was right. She stood aside a little, not wanting to look at it again. Sister Mary was the last to see it, and her back cricked as she bent down.

Not important, she tried to gesture, *not a real saint. Honorary.*

She saw from Sister Anna's nod that she understood. The eyes of the other two kept bulging.

Like Santes Dwynwen? Sister Lucy asked with her eyes, pulling out a worn postcard of Llanddwyn Island from her bum-bag.

Yes, she concurred, smiling, wanting the interrogation to be over. *Like Dwynwen. Saint of Hearts.*

Nothing like Dwynwen, is what she actually thought, thinking of Delyth's prickly laughter, her arctic eyes.

Sister Mary Catherine traced the plaque with her fingers, smudging it with sweat. She'd go back and clean it later, Viv thought, hurrying them on through the cemetery gates.

12

Word was out that the last boat of the day had brought with it a man. Deian had first heard Howard and Mwynwen mumbling about it in the goat yard that afternoon, their voices hushed, their pacing shadows amid the day's final flickers of light. "You don't think I'm going to be threatened by the competition, do you?" Deian had joked, slicking back his hair and raising his dirty T-shirt to greet them. Mwynwen had looked at him the way she sometimes did when he mentioned his mother, like she was searching for a sentence to restore the balance of his life; as though it were that simple.

"Leri got him out here," Mwynwen had said. "Or at least that's what I think. Howard thinks he might have come off his own bat. But anyway he's, he's, well, you'll see soon enough who it is."

Great, he thought, *more television people. More disruption.* He'd shuffled uneasily on past Howard and Mwynwen, quickening his pace, hoping to keep the news out of Cae Uchaf. He didn't want them rushing off again. Greta and Elin had only just arrived, still slow-moving after last night's attraction. He shut the gate and decided he would tell them later, when the work was done.

But it was too late. When he came back to the field Elin had risen from the soil to perch on one bare foot on Cae Uchaf's gate, binoculars in hand. "Where is he, then? Can't see anything, now," she complained, "apart from those bloody nuns. They're everywhere these days. Caught them walking on the stone walls the other day on their way down the mountain, can you believe it? Dancing on the lichen like there was no tomorrow. No consideration for nature, and Viv should know better, I mean she's supposed to be…"

"Give it here," Deian had said, pushing her gently off the post.

She made a huge show of falling, clinging on to invisible threads in the air, imprinting a soil-angel on the site.

"Can't see anything, either," Deian said. "It might be a mirage. You're so desperate for a man, you're seeing things…"

"I definitely thought I saw…."

"Well you didn't, so get back to work. You'll see him sooner or later, won't you? It's only some television guy, anyway."

"What do you mean, television guy?" Greta said, elbows arching.

"Something to do with Leri," Deian said.

"It can't be," Greta said, scratching her hair, "I'd know about it. It's not down on the itinerary."

"Well, standing around and talking rubbish isn't on my itinerary either," he snapped. "Now please, could we just have one last concentrated push to get this finished…"

"But Deian," Elin moaned, her eyes sloping from view. "I'm just so tired, and after last night it's just too…"

"It's not too much to ask," said Deian, clamping the discussion shut.

When he looked up he saw, to his surprise, that they were back at work, Elin and Greta having wriggled their weary bodies into position, shovelling with a new found gusto. A frustrated woman makes an excellent digger, Fran had once told him.

An hour later, her palms imprinting orange stains on her face, Elin climbed back onto the post.

"I don't understand it, I mean usually by now we'd know something, there would be…"

"I thought we were getting down to work," Deian said, his voice clogged with dirt.

"It's obviously not what you think," Greta said, sulkily.

"But it is," Elin said. "They said it was a…"

"Who said?" Deian asked, scraping some empty soil from the naked ground. He wished he'd planted more finds overnight. The copper bracelet he'd intended them to find couldn't compete with a man.

"Mwynwen said. Oh my God," Elin went on, "I can see… yes

it's definitely a man!"

"Let me see," Greta said, knocking Elin from her perch. "That's definitely Leri with him."

"Do you know him?"

"I don't know, I can't really see him properly. Are you sure it's a man?"

"I suppose it has been a long time," Elin said, slumping down.

At that point Mererid came swinging in through the gate, a flash of black waves over a green and white print dress. Deian smiled. So she had come, as she had promised him last night. She wasn't one of those who merely said she would.

"Save me," he said, handing her a trowel.

He tried not to notice how she had to lift her dress to bend down onto the site, or how ill at ease those pale knees looked in the beige soil. He didn't tell her what to do either, and watched bemused as she emulated Greta's gentle strokes, sifting the soil towards her in gentle waves. She'd never get anywhere like that, of course, but something made him keep the thought to himself.

It was Mererid who found the bracelet, in the end, scraping its glinting bronze to view in the far end of Cae Uchaf.

"What's this?" she said, quizzically, holding it up to the sun. "Don't tell me the saints wore bracelets."

"They might have done," he said, making a show of getting up and hurrying over, hoping to engage the interest of Greta and Elin. He only needed one more hour to finish today's section. "Hmm," he said, scratching his head and fiddling with the bracelet, "I think there may even be some medieval amethyst in there."

"And that's the definition of the frugal life, is it? Amethyst-studded bracelets?" ·

He looked down at her green eyes. She looked a bit like Fran, her mouth flinching at the side, as if she were hoping to suck in words from the air.

"They were pretty eccentric," he said, his mouth trembling with the promise of laughter. "I mean Cadfan especially was a bit of a goer apparently…"

"Oh really? And I suppose Beuno was a transvestite."

"No, that was Deiniol."

"This doesn't feel like Deiniol's," she'd said, swinging the red circle in the air.

"Whose does it feel like, then?"

"Dyfrig's – he always had an eye for a bargain."

The laughter broke forth from them both in rippling giggles, mingling with one another in the air. He hurled the bracelet in Elin's direction. It rolled across the soil and tinkled against Elin's trowel. He hadn't realised until that moment that both Elin and Greta were gone.

Later on, when they'd finished, they'd sat there for a while in silence. She proceeded to roll a cigarette on the far end of the field, while he wrote down his imaginary finds on his blank sheet. She eventually came towards him in cautious strides, and he pretended not to notice. Her shadow fell across his page; and he found himself accepting an invitation to show her the mountain. He didn't quite know how it had happened, there was an ease to it, the sun hiding her face, his eyes small, the world he saw through them feeling manageable for the moment, the survey fading to the nothing that it was. He made his way towards the wilderness of Bardsey Mountain, trying not to look at that small, smiling bottom in its flowery, swaying patterns.

"Let me go in front," he insisted.

They wound their way up through the rugged path from Cae Uchaf, up through the dark greenery, curving around the shadows and out into the light. It was quite easy to get lost if you didn't know where you were going, to keep coming back on yourself, as he'd done here as a child. She followed him dutifully, her feet sliding over the gravel in her trainers, yet always resisting the hand he tried to throw back in her direction as support. He talked about the dig, about how well it was going. She asked him a few questions about the twenty thousand saints, about if he really did think they'd find anything, and began to feel a slight pang of guilt. For the first time since beginning the dig, he thought maybe he'd underestimated his volunteers. Who was to say they wouldn't love the craft of digging, the sheer exercise of unearthing, without having to be enticed by some *find* every now and then? Wasn't the sheer mystery of nothingness enough? Maybe it would be to Mererid. Then he remembered Elin's irritated exhalations and knew he would have to keep on lying.

When they reached the far corner of the mountain top, they looked across to the mainland, a mass of rising slopes above the blue. There came an intake of breath – a sprained-ankle of a breath, he'd thought at the time – turning around to catch her. But she was standing perfectly upright, perfectly still.

"It's just that you almost forget it's there, don't you," she said, with a hint of deep sadness in her voice. "It's as if the island protects you from it, and makes it your choice to climb up here and face it." She took out a small, silver, mobile from her rucksack. He heard one, two, four, six messages come hurtling out of the air and into her inbox. She read them in silence.

They ascended higher up again, this time reaching a small plain in the middle of the heather. He almost always felt the exultation when he got here, feeling as though he were really at the top of the world, king of the castle. She, too, stopped for a while, taking out a small camera to take photos. The island was shimmering with a stillness that only a perfect summer's day could give it, littered with chaffinch and wild flowers, radiant, rolling Bardsey. Then suddenly, their sense of being the only people in the world was diminished by the presence of four dark figures.

They both stood transfixed as the nuns approached, each one with a pair of binoculars hung awkwardly on their chests. Mererid attempted to say a few words in Welsh, words he remembered, and understood, but she was greeted only with fading smiles. The four walked on, starting their descent in the purple haze of heather.

"Charming!" Mererid laughed. "They don't speak Welsh, I take it."

"They don't speak, full stop. Not this week. They've taken a vow of silence. It's the annual conference for hermits this week. Viv's idea."

"Viv? You're on intimate terms with Sister Vivian, are you?"

"She hasn't always been a nun."

"Hasn't she?"

"No, she only became one around ten years ago. She was a warden here in the old days, quite vocal then of course. She could put the fear of God into you then, mind, so nothing much has changed."

"But why become a nun? What happened?"

"People change, I suppose."

He looked back to see the dark shadows descending from view. He had a vision of Viv coming at him on the mountain, stick in hand, shouting at him and Iestyn to get off the walls. He'd never told Iestyn that he'd found something quite attractive about her then, the wild dark curly hair, the side-angle of an angry mouth. It had been different then, of course, when his mum was still alive. It was a different kind of anger, passing, mutable, falling away into breathless chuckles as she herded them back down to the cottage, urging them on as though they were cattle. He didn't want to think about that other anger of hers, the one he'd seen the day his mother disappeared. The one that had led to her telling him to leave the island, go back to Preston where he belonged. The anger that had been responsible for hoisting that habit over her.

"I sometimes think I wouldn't mind being a nun," Mererid told him, skipping over a patch of heather. "Living here in silent communion with God, with the great big sea and sky, it really wouldn't be that bad, would it? I think I'd quite enjoy separating myself from mainland life for a while. The time seems to be going too quickly. 'Sister Mererid': it has a certain something, don't you think?"

"Why don't you then?" Deian asked her.

"I think my fiancé would have something to say about it," she remarked.

Deian sneezed suddenly. It was that word – fiancé – it always got up his nose.

As they were edging closer to the east side of the mountain, he risked asking about him. He'd heard the others mentioning him on the site, of course, in that kind of absent-minded way they did on those long afternoons, clinging to anything they could find that wasn't quite right, that warranted some speculation. He remembered Elin's words: "It's just that when she mentions him, she's got a sort of vacant look, and it's as if she's on auto-pilot."

And it was there again, right now. She told him how he was an academic, that they worked together at the same university, that he'd written a lot of books on medieval poetry, that he was an avid film watcher, and lover of cities. Suddenly, it wasn't the same voice that had joked with him at the site about Cadfan. It was as if she was telling him a story that she knew off by heart, but one she'd recited so often she couldn't separate the story from her voice. He didn't speak Welsh, she continued, but he was from Wales, well Shotton to be exact, and didn't consider it as important as she did; it annoyed him that people always had to be defined by their nationalities. He couldn't fathom her wanting to come to the island, either, but he was willing to condone it as her last shot at freedom before they got married.

"When's the wedding?" he'd asked, surprised at his boldness.

"A month after I get back," she said, her smile fading as the sun slipped from view behind the lighthouse. "I want something small. Quiet."

"And does he?"

"He's never been small or quiet in anything," she laughed. "He's a real giant of a man. Bulky, tall, larger than life, you know the type. I'm sure we'll work it out. He's coming over tomorrow. That's why he was texting me."

"It will be nice to meet him," Deian said, hoping he sounded genuine.

"What about you, Deian?"

"What about me?"

"Is there someone? I mean, I know they all go on about you being the only available man on the island..."

"They think I'm desperate," he laughed.

"And you're not," she'd said. A confirmation, not a question.

"No. They don't do much for me, really. The others. I mean, they're holiday makers, really, aren't they? Frivolous tarts, the lot of them!"

She laughed. He wondered if she laughed like that at *his* jokes. He wondered what the fiancé would make of this now, what Fran, who had always refused to be his fiancée, would think of him and Mererid on top of this mountain together, laughing, throwing the word tarts out over the wind, startling the birds.

"But you're not looking..."

"You don't come to Bardsey Island to look for things," he said, thinking of Fran at Porthmeudwy, where he'd left her on the mainland, shaking her head, her hair wet, while he stayed on the boat, unable to speak. She should have been here now, as his lover. They should have been on this mountain together. "It's never been about romance."

"Maybe not," she said. "But Elin's got all these romantic notions about meeting someone, hasn't she? She thinks that it's going to happen. Every day she thinks that the boat will bring her what she wants."

His boat had nearly contained everything he needed, he thought bitterly. It wasn't until Brian had reached for Fran's hand to guide her from the dinghy into the boat that Fran had left him. Swam away from him, in fact. "I can't do this with you," she'd said, choking on sobs and salt water. "It isn't fair. If we can't have a future, these memories will be too painful."

He'd consoled himself often with the thought that what Fran had done had been a spur of the moment decision, that something in the shallow sea of Porthmeudwy had frightened her as they'd started their journey. But he saw now that this line was too rehearsed. Too perfect. She'd known all along she'd leave at the last possible moment; so that he wouldn't have been able to stop her. She knew he wouldn't swim after her, in front of all those people. It would have looked absurd, grappling with her in the water, their life jackets getting in the way of their faces.

What happened with Fran was still biting at his conscience, still there in every single dream. Still making him writhe around in those cold sheets in his damp, loft wishing she was there with him like they'd planned.

"The boat never brings you what you want," he told Mererid, bitterly. "It only brings you what you need."

A little further down, they stopped to admire the lighthouse. She took out her camera and started taking pictures of it. He told her a story about him and Iestyn, how they'd taken a picture of the lighthouse when they were children, with Iestyn holding his fingers over the lens, to make it look like he was holding the lighthouse between his fingers.

"You've been coming here for years, then," she'd said, clicking the camera with her fingers shaking. He knew she'd done it wrong. That she'd develop the picture weeks later and that two women behind the photo counter would be laughing at it when she arrived to pick it up.

"I grew up here. I didn't leave until I was eighteen."

"Didn't you? I didn't know that."

"You didn't think I sounded it, you mean."

"You don't speak Welsh, do you?"

"I did, until I left. Then I kind of, forgot it. Nobody really spoke much Welsh in Preston."

"Mark reckons he forgot his, too. It's so annoying. He speaks it when it suits him. He can't bear the thought of me having a better grasp of it, so he just pretends it isn't there."

"I've never pretended it wasn't there," he protested. His voice seemed small all of a sudden, and the girl in front of him no longer small and bird-like but larger, looming.

"I'm sorry, Deian. It's not the same for you, probably. Everybody's different. Sometimes there's nothing you can do about it. It just goes. But it's only ten years. So much of it must still be there, somewhere."

"It's more or less gone," he said, thinking once again about Fran sinking into the water, his future trailing behind her. What did he have left? His past was shrunk to the size of a small, golden plaque. His future had swum away from him in a life jacket. His present was that dark patch of nothingness in Cae Uchaf. And the only thing he could have clung on to, that thing that people kept telling him was still inside him, was too far down to even begin dredging up.

They said their farewells by the lime kiln. She'd looked right at him when saying goodbye, right into him, somehow. None of the others

87

ever looked at him that way, he was always at the margins of their eye-line. They shifted about, looked off in other directions when they were telling him something – Elin rubbed her eyes, Greta twisted her hair into tangled knots, Leri only looked at him through a lens. Mererid's glance, he'd noticed, never veered very far from what was in front of her, and being caught in that gaze was something he was grateful for.

He sat in the lime kiln watching her fade from his view, round the corner towards the Cavern, and a little later, a small fleck ascending towards the lighthouse. He kicked the stones in front of him, gazing up the path towards the top of the island, then gazing back down to the Cavern. It was unusually quiet on this side of the island. Where were they all? Mwynwen's sentence about the recent arrival was rolling around in his mind: *Leri got him out here.*

He decided to go and investigate at the south end. If nothing else, he could do some digging over there, he needed to find something interesting to plant in the site for the next day. The Cavern was a mess, a land cluttered with discarded bits of boat, ropes, leftover mail fluttering in the evening breeze. They really needed to sort this out, he thought, it was such a dismal site for visitors, this clutter, this archaic wasteland. "Exactly, Deian *bach*," Howard told him, "as long as we keep this place a little bit messy they won't want to live here, will they? A week will be enough."

An echo of voices sounded from Solfach Beach. He recognised Elin's squealing. He approached the beach slowly, cautiously, like he was planning an attack. He didn't want them to see him, not yet. He crouched down lower and stuck his head above the tufts of grass. Leri was there, the camera darkening her shoulder, while Greta was lost in a flutter of flapping pages. Elin was poised much in the same way as she had been in Cae Uchaf, her back slightly arched, her long arms dwindling behind her like discarded sentences. Her hair was slightly different, he'd noticed, a little more ruffled than before, sticking out in clumpy feathers, the way Fran's hair sometimes was when she returned from the bathroom in a restaurant. And she'd changed out of her shorts into that little yellow skirt. Which could only mean one thing.

It wasn't until he was right there at the edge of Solfach Beach that he really allowed himself to see what was there. He must have seen him earlier, of course, he would tell himself later, or rather heard it, in Mwynwen's voice. Even in the waning sunlight, that bulk of a torso could easily be separated from the women all around him, that ripped-throat laugh couldn't be anybody else's.

Walking away from the scene, he thought he heard his name being uttered softly across the beach, but he didn't turn back. He kept on going at a steady pace until he was back in the safety of his loft, behind the closed, bolted door, watching the last strips of light illuminating his flint collection. He didn't light a gas lamp that night, he just lay down on the low bed, and let the night come seeping into this room until it was all around him. Even when he was woken hours later by a soft knocking at his door, he didn't flinch, just lay there until he heard the swift scurry of footsteps retreating on the wooden stairs.

Let me have tonight, Iestyn, he thought. Let me at least have tonight.

13

The Iestyn Daniels that arrived that afternoon was not the same one she'd interviewed in Cardiff prison, thought Leri, zooming in on his face as the boat made its final, confident strides through the surf. Something in him had changed. She couldn't quite ascertain what. There was none of the erratic pacing. The blue smoke that was always pouring straight towards you from the cave of his mouth was now curbed in tiny, sidewards exhalations, and his craggy face seemed to have softer edges. He'd shaved, that was it. But it was more than that. Though his eyes still darted about in his head like flies, his body was no longer a tangle of twitches. No, the man who hurled his bag onto the jetty and instantly joined the cargo-chain was someone far more placid, somehow. "Don't let him see you straightaway," Clive had told her over the phone that morning. "Because it will all seem too easy, we want a little agitation to start it all off. And besides, we can't have the islanders associating you too strongly with him, because soon enough you'll be the enemy, not him."

Leri stepped cautiously into the shadows by the boathouse, letting the camera hang by her side for a while. She saw him casting his eyes skywards, taking in the scene in front of him, and for one moment his eyes seemed to land on her. She didn't move. Soon enough, his eyes had swung in the other direction, towards the lighthouse. She started filming.

"There's bound to be some kind of scuffle, some reaction when they realise who he is," Clive had said. "It's essential not to miss any of that initial tension." And so there she stood, up by the boathouse, poised at an angle, her feet quivering with energy, ready to swoop from sight if need be. He seemed to know where he was going, and made his purposeful way towards Howard and Mwynwen. She'd seen the horrified look on Mwynwen's face when the boat came in, moving from an agitated pink flush to a furious burst of purple. She was trying to move away, but Howard was holding on to the frayed edges of her cardigan, tugging her back towards him. Leri couldn't make out what they were saying, but zoomed in on them nevertheless. Howard's eyes were at half mast. Mwynwen's hands darted about her face, landed on her hips, before hurtling back out into the air again. Howard said something with a look of earnest seriousness, and she saw Iestyn nodding his head. Mwynwen walked off, shaking her head. What she saw next disappointed Leri; the swinging of Howard's palm in Iestyn's direction, and the clamping, sturdy handshake.

"I suppose you think this is clever, do you?" said a voice. She turned to face Mwywen's quivering, cracked lips.

"I don't know what you're talking about..."

"Oh, that's right. Of course you don't. We're all supposed to think that he's just arrived here, out of the blue? Just because?"

Yes, thought Leri with irritation, that's exactly what you were supposed to think. She couldn't believe that her weeks of softening this stale-bread woman could amount to so few crumbs.

"Well you stick to that story if it helps your conscience, young lady. But I'm telling you now, I won't be having it. Howard can shake his hand all he likes, I'm not going to forget what he did."

"Look, I'm sorry, Mwynwen, but..."

"Don't you Mwynwen me," she said, her head a sharp twist. "Who do you think you are?" Mwynwen's voice peaked above the dull chatter at the boathouse, causing certain holidaymakers to peer curiously at them as they made their way to the path. Leri found herself blushing, hoping they didn't understand Welsh. As three men in their fifties approached, she saw the giveaway Three Lions on their baseball caps, indicating that she was safe. She wondered what they were saying to one another. Isn't it quaint, two women squabbling in their native tongue. Using that language to argue in, imagine! Then, just as suddenly, she saw she'd been wrong – one of them let out a booming *Sbiwch!* alerting the others to three Oystercatchers overhead, mocking the men with their sharp cries. "If you think for one second that you're doing any good here at all; you're not. It's not fair on Viv.

They may have let him out, but it doesn't mean he's innocent. And to think he was on the same boat as my grandchildren!"

Leri suddenly saw the cause of Mwynwen's anxiety. In the far distance, she saw Brian stepping up onto the jetty, with some kind of white parcel in his arms. As he got nearer, she saw that it was a baby, serene and pink faced, tiny fingers poking out of the whiteness. Two small children followed him, making their way, in a series of shrieks towards Howard, who had his arms open to greet them.

"I really don't know what you're talking about," Leri said.

"Don't you? We'll see about that!"

She sauntered off towards the jetty, taking the baby from Brian, folding it neatly into the crook of her shoulder. She ordered Howard, Iestyn, and the two children to follow her, coming back at Leri like a bullet.

"Iestyn, look who it is," she said, while the baby cooed against her. "It's your old friend, Leri. I'm sure you've got plenty to talk about."

Iestyn looked up at her. She saw the recognition in his eyes and held her breath. They'd been over this countless times, yet now they were here, she saw how easily the whole thing could drown her, how it only took a single nod of his head, a word to come splashing out of his mouth, and she and Greta would be the next ones back on the boat. Please, Iestyn, stick to the story, she thought. Please keep your head still.

"I don't believe we've met," he said, his voice a calm sea, the knowledge in his eyes being washed away, his hand floating up towards hers.

It was much later, when Greta and Elin found them on Solfach beach, the camera set on its tripod, that things had started to become difficult. Greta's eyes were searching her face for explanation. Elin's skirt was fluttering with hope in the breeze. Greta pulled Leri to one side.

"What's going on?"

"It's Iestyn Daniels," she replied, her voice flat. "He's Viv's son."

"What's that got to do with you? Mwynwen said that you brought him here."

"Well, I didn't," she said, catching the twirl of Elin's skirt at the corner of her eye. Iestyn was laughing at her. She was cart-wheeling across the beach.

"What is that girl doing?" she said, walking back towards them. She didn't like the look on Iestyn's face.

"Why are you filming him? You wouldn't have, you know, set something up, without telling me," Greta asked. "Would you?"

"Don't be so paranoid, Grets," she said. "I've just been chatting to him, that's all. I might not even use the footage in the end. But there's a story here. I can't ignore it. He's fresh out of prison, for God's sake. And he needs somewhere to stay. We can use this, Grets, I know we can."

"Why was he in prison?" Greta asked.

"Murder," said Leri, relishing the sound of the word.

Their eyes were drawn to the rather ridiculous spectacle of Elin upside-down, steadying her brown legs in a slow, mesmerising headstand. The yellow skirt flipped back over the tops of her legs, revealing her navy blue swimming costume underneath, a triangular, smiling invite. Iestyn clapped. He looked like a man applauding an exclamation mark.

"That's enough, Elin," Leri said, pushing her over in the sand.

"Did you have to? That was a good one!"

"Fair play to the girl," Iestyn had said, "she's only trying to keep me entertained."

"Haven't you got a report to write? Supper to make for your little writer friend?" Leri asked Elin, cutting across the laughter.

"I've got no plans for tonight," she said, "especially not if we've got a new playmate. Where are you staying, Iestyn? Because we've got a spare room at the…"

"He's staying with us," Greta said, arms folded. "According to Leri. Is that right?"

Iestyn threw a quick glance in Leri's direction.

"If that's alright," he said. "I suppose I should have organised it before I came, but, you know, it was a kind of a spur of the moment decision."

Don't overdo it, Leri warned him with her eyes.

"Oh well," said Elin, jumping up, the sand a sparkling pattern on her legs. "We should still have some kind of party, or something. Dinner. We should get Deian down to meet you. He's been the only eligible man on the island for long enough and I'm sure he'd be..."

"Deian?" Iestyn scrunched his face. "Deian's here? Which Deian?"

"Oh he's just an archaeologist," said Elin.

"Don't say *just an archaeologist*, Elin," Greta said, bitingly. "It's an important vocation, he's trying to find the remains of the twenty thousand saints. Doing very important work, actually."

"If you like that sort of thing," Elin said, her eyes trailing Iestyn's torso. "Up to your knees in dirt all day, I mean it can be so...."

"Deian's here," Iestyn said, a smile unfolding from the edges of his taut lips.

Don't smile, thought Leri with irritation, zooming away from him.

14

Mererid doesn't like the feel of Mark on top of her this morning, a leaden hairy body that has little to do with love. She notices now how much hair there is on his body, how she cannot land one solitary palm on a pale shore of skin, as she wishes to do. He arcs back, shaking himself into her. They lie together side by side for some time, looking at the various angles of each other's bodies through the curtains' orange glow. "You wouldn't exactly call it love, would you Mark?" is what Mererid really wants to say to him, right now, on this small single bed, and she would, if she didn't see from his eyes, when he reaches over for a cigarette, that it really *is* what he calls it, that for once he doesn't have tens of synonyms on the tip of his tongue.

"I don't know how you cope here, Mer," he says, reeling out the "r" in her name like a cluster of bells, before getting up to walk naked around the small room, opening drawers, looking under her bed, mindlessly flitting through a guide-book splayed open on the desk. "It's a bit pokey in here, don't you think? Not much room to breathe," he says, blowing his smoke into her face.

She thinks about how wrong and out of place he looks, his giant, hairy frame pacing the room, fidgeting with the crab claw she found washed up by the Cavern one morning. Seeing him touch them doesn't seem right somehow, having him here, letting him experience even the slightest bit of this island. When she saw the boat come in, she wanted to run. Because she knew that the second he had placed his two feet on her island that it would be his island, and in all subsequent conversation that they would have with friends, colleagues, strangers, he would be telling them his version of it. He would go back and read around it, write about it even, travel to conferences with his island paper in his hand. He would become the expert. It is her island. She has reeled it in for herself, cast out her net and shoaled in the island on her own. Now it's like she's found him in her net, wriggling and bright, still alive. She wishes she could throw him back into the sea.

She wonders what he would say if he knew that last night she spent hours sitting on her stone doorstep and looking up, searching desperately to find one flicker of grey in the sky's crimson underbelly, wanting for the blades of grass by the flagstaff to be moving by themselves, to be roaring away from her in a westerly direction, their sway indicating there would be no boat tomorrow. She nearly said the words, "The boat's been cancelled" when she spoke to him on the phone last night. She felt the lie racing around in her own depths, disturbing the surface.

"You sound a bit agitated, Mer," he said, "is everything OK?"

"It's just that I can't," she said, letting the sentence dwindle. Elin was having more influence on her than she thought.

"You can't what?"

"I can't write," she finally spouted. All she had so far were scribblings, fragments, blue skeleton shapes on the page. Though she had felt close to something last night, by the lime kiln, saying goodbye to Deian. There was a poem there, she was sure of it.

"So, over your writer's block now are you, my little Sappho?" he said, picking up a sheet of paper on her desk. On the top she's written – *Archaeology, the discovery of bones. My bones. His bones.*

This isn't a cottage for men. She thinks about Elin – who didn't come home last night – about the quiet understanding that's been reached between them, in just a few days. These women are not like the ones she has known, and despised, on the mainland. Elin doesn't need her, and she doesn't need Elin. But it is precisely because there is no need, dependency, involved, that they can live together side by side this way, asking nothing, giving everything. She wants to stay here. Prove herself by living through the harsh winters, and then reap the rewards of each golden summer on this island. But it won't do. Because she has to leave in four weeks, into the arms of this man who paces her room – into his arms, into her wedding dress, its white train a long goodbye on the altar steps.

The whole day she is acting, one long, superb, brilliant performance, rolling herself out on the long green pastures, her back up against the rock on the south end, throwing herself onto him, again and again. When they are finished she drags him on, from the purple stone to the mustard-coloured rocks, clambering down over them quicker than a child, before realising how far behind her he always is, his chest heaving, his cigarette smoking itself by his feet. They descend down to the enormous rock pools beneath, take off their clothes, shoot into their depths, their feet slithering over the seaweed bed. He grapples with her here, too, and she writhes in the water as he prods against her, laughing. She cups the clear water in her hands and pours it over him, watches as the river runs through his face, how some of it stills in the cleft in his chin. Eyes closed, mouth shut tight, she sees the beauty in him. She presses her lips to his, and he pulls her on to him, his hands spidery on her thighs. Mererid cannot concentrate. All the while she is thinking how open this space is, the breadth of blue air between her and the rocks, and how someone might be watching them from any number of crevices. Anyone could peer over the edge of the cliff and see her now, breasts exposed above the water, Mark arched back against a ledge, the clear water leaving little to the imagination. She doesn't want to be caught short by the nuns. She thinks about a dream she had last night about four nuns on the Waltzers at the Swansea funfair. It is this image that stays with her as she sloshes around and around on Mark's hips, then comes to a standstill.

They sit drying in the hot sun, before starting their journey back to the cottage. They stop off in the bird hide, sit in it, holding hands, looking out silently at the sliver of world they see through its small opening. He laughs that if he hadn't already asked Mererid to marry him, he would have done it now, not on some street in Manchester with the drizzle in his eyes, with that canvas hood pulled so tightly over her head he couldn't even see her eyes. She smiles back, weakly, thinking of how she'd pulled that hood over her head only seconds before, feeling the sentence bounding towards her at high speed through the tunnel of his mouth, and how she'd been so startled by the light and the commotion that she'd said yes. Just like that.

They approach the lighthouse cottage and Mererid realises how she's never really looked at it in this way before, walking towards it fresh from the sea, a picture postcard white image, standing small at the foot of the lighthouse. Her home, she thinks, so far removed from the roomy house she shares with Mark in Bangor, so far away from that terraced house in Sketty where she grew up – it's the kind of cottage she's been dreaming about all her life, and now here it is, and she isn't willing to share it with him. He wants to stay tonight; and she cannot – will not – let it happen.

"Why not?" he asks.

"Because the weather's supposed to change tomorrow and you might be stuck here."

She wishes the air wasn't this clear when she says this, so utterly uncontested by any mention of cloud.

"So?"

"You've got that conference."

"It's just a conference, Mer…"

"It's up to you."

There is a pause where she imagines the evening that lies ahead of her. Her and Mark having to walk up to the top of the island, him sitting next to her in the goat yard, drinking, as he so often does, vastly and too quickly, his voice becoming thick and salty, believing that everyone around him relishes his company. She doesn't want Elin to see this is not what she wants. Worst of all, she does not want Mark to meet Deian, for Deian to notice the difference in her when he is around.

"I suppose I really can't afford to miss the conference, you're right. You're such a thoughtful thing aren't you, my little Sappho."

He pulls her towards him and even now, Mererid can feel the desperation in him, the knowledge that he has, but which will not surface properly for hours later, that this is their last embrace, their last proper kiss. She feels her body becoming the life-raft he so desperately needs, holding on to its frayed edges even when pieces of her break off and float away. When he lets go, finally, she sees the fear in his eyes that he has not yet acknowledged, but will pound through him the second that boat starts drifting away; wondering how, after one small wave, Mererid is able to turn her back on him and start walking up towards the top of the island, up the path she'd insisted that held no appeal, to another part of her existence on that island he would never know about, until, maybe, he read it in one of her poems.

15

The vow of silence was over. Viv broke the first word around the table that morning, cracking it noisily along with her eggs, which she had decided to fry this morning, if only to hear the harmonious, noisy sizzling in the pan. Sister Mary Catherine and Sister Lucy Violet's voices were still on the same inaudible frequency, as they sat plotting the day's events, which involved a short service at the chapel, followed by a visit to Elgar's cave, and a swift game of volleyball at Solfach Beach, something a little more frivolous, they smirked, to celebrate their last day on the island. Sister Anna and Viv prepared the breakfast together, whispering quietly to each other in Welsh; Viv trying to make up for the gossiping hours that had been missed. The latest with Anna's witch-daughter was that she was having some marriage difficulties of her own, and was considering becoming a nun herself.

"She thinks it's some kind of marriage counselling service," Anna said, cutting the toast into neat triangles. "Thinks that a vow of celibacy is just something to make your husband see what he's missing. She wants to come and live with me." Viv spluttered some of her tea over the counter when she heard this. Sister Mary Catherine glared at them. "I don't think she wants us speaking in Welsh," she whispered, "She thinks we're talking about her."

"Which we now are," said Viv, coughing this last smile into her sleeve. "You haven't agreed to it, have you? To let her come and stay with you?"

"Well, no," Anna replied. "I mean it wouldn't do at all, would it? Hermits are supposed to live alone aren't they, and nuns, well most nuns don't really like to admit that they've got children, especially if those relationships are a little, what shall we say, *difficult*. We both know it's never easy. Especially you, Viv. I mean Sister Mary Catherine doesn't know about Iestyn, does she? And even if she got her head around the fact that children are a gift from God, she might feel that Iestyn was an exception of some kind. Especially considering some of the more, how can I say, *unfortunate* details of his past."

Viv refused to raise her head to meet the gaze that was fixed upon her.

"Do you mind collecting some tomatoes for me?" she asked. "I was thinking of frying them along with the eggs."

The fact that tomato translated as *tomato* should alleviate Sister Mary Catherine's anxieties, she thought, unless they thought they were comparing her to one.

As Sister Anna slipped out through the door, she heard the plotting going ahead for the last supper. Green beans were mentioned, lobster was queried, and orange was confirmed, a typically vile concoction. Viv stretched her face into a smile when she was addressed, she said it sounded *ample*. She had suffered at the hands of Sister Mary Catherine's culinary skills before, and the lamb and berry tagine was still repeating on her memory.

Still, she was prepared to suffer this final ordeal. Tomorrow, she could get back into her sack-cloth trousers, and lie in front of the fire with Elfyn on her belly, and make all the noise she wanted to. For now, she was pleased to remain the humble Sister Vivian, focused ascetic and a pillar of the hermit community. She could see from the way their worry-lines had been smoothed out, making even Sister Mary Catherine look like a woman at peace with herself, that they had enjoyed themselves, that she needn't have worried. They had been thoroughly convinced by her. The islanders had all complied, Leri had kept her distance, Mwynwen had averted her gaze, even Elfyn had assumed a more dignified air, shiny black head held high whenever the nuns passed over the threshold.

And as for providing the accompanying scenery, the associated calm that they all saw as being paramount to the hermit's wellbeing, Bardsey had done the job for her, it had beamed brightly at them throughout the week, getting itself into position just as they turned each corner, each angle more beautiful than the next. The sea had rolled in at the right time, the dense blue sky had given the mountain another dimension. Bardsey had taken their breath away, she thought proudly, time after time. Last evening, the four of them had stood in the garden watching the most incredible sunset, a burst of flame on the horizon as the sun exploded into the sea, expressing everything that was wondrous about God's creation, according to Sister Mary Catherine. And God's creation would take them away, she thought, envisaging the wondrous waters carrying them safely from view, around the corner of the mountain, never to be seen again.

In a week's time she was sure to get courteous little thank-you notes from all three, and even Sister Mary Catherine, in spite of herself, would have to admit that Bardsey was by far the superior island. "One feels the peculiarity of God's presence," she would write, "emanating from every single stone, every unearthed bone."

And Viv would reply that yes, that much was true, but it really was time to start recruiting more hermits, and throw their net further afield. She'd heard Gozo was very nice out of season, and brimful of hermits, if they could only find a Maltese link.

Sister Anna returned from the garden clutching the handful of red tomatoes. Viv thought she recognised some Bardsey-exultation about her too at this moment, but on closer inspection saw that it was something else entirely. Yielding the tomatoes into Viv's hands, she was breathless and stupefied, muttering to Viv hurriedly under her breath, fragmented sentences that Viv couldn't reconstruct.

"Would you too kindly refrain from using that ungodly language," Sister Mary Catherine whispered from the kitchen table. "A congregation of hermits only speaks two languages – English and silence – that's how *God* defines bilingualism."

God was a Welshman, Viv wanted to say. But now wasn't the time. There was something wild in Anna's eyes, something she hadn't seen before. Now she was completely silent, gesturing her head towards the door. Whatever had unnerved her had been in the garden. Elfyn, was it Elfyn? Has something happened to him? Viv suddenly had a horrified vision of Elfyn, lying in the grass, belly cut open. Had she put the lawnmower away? Still clutching the tomatoes, she left her sizzling pan and went outside.

Elfyn was as healthy as ever, but from his barking it was evident that what had upset Sister Anna had got to him too. He had leapt up out of his comforting shadow by the cabbage patch, and had run up to the gate, where he was dancing in mid air, his head reaching a different height each time he jumped. Leri and Greta stood on the path, trying to tame him with their hands. She wasn't pleased to see them, not when she was this close to acting the model nun. She would just have to tell them to go away before the other nuns noticed.

She needn't have bothered with her approaching hand gestures; instantly Leri explained she only wanted to take some quick shots of the garden. "Fine," she said, "but quickly." That was the moment Leri stepped out of the way, and Viv saw a dark haired, topless man standing right in front of her. The sun was strong and his face somewhat of a shadow. She stared at him, waiting for something to give, feeling that perhaps it already had.

"*Helo Mam,*" he'd said. "*Sut da chi?*"

Even if she were able to block out the sun and the world, there was no mistaking what was happening. The mother tongue, *her* mother's tongue, came hurtling back at her from the depths of this stranger's mouth, and she had no choice but to recognize him as her son, to recognize that he'd asked her how she was and expected some kind of answer, an answer she hadn't given him for over ten years, because the answer was obvious. What do you do after something like that happens? she'd heard Mwynwen saying to her husband as they'd passed by the house one day; *what can you possibly do?*

She couldn't have anticipated what would happen to her that moment, armed as she was with those ruby-red tomatoes, pulsating in the August heat. Seeing Iestyn's face made the world shrink to the size of his blue eyes. She landed on her tomatoes, which seeped into the white corner of her habit as she lost consciousness.

"Tomato juice," she heard him say. "My favourite."

16

It was the assumption that everything should be as it was, or that he should be as *he* was, that unnerved Deian when he was confronted with Iestyn on the site the next day. As far as he could tell, Iestyn had no idea that he already knew he was there, or that he'd purposefully ignored his knocking on his door the other night. And if he didn't know, then the homecoming swagger through the gates of Cae Uchaf was ill-chosen, distasteful even.

It hadn't taken long for the news to spread around the island that Iestyn Daniels had arrived, having succeeded in his appeal. He'd been acquitted, finally, the court having decided that most of the evidence against him was unsound. I could have told them that ten years ago, thought Deian, thinking of his head bowed low in the courtroom when the verdict came. All these years he'd felt guilty for not having performed as well as he should have, for letting his friend down.

Mwynwen was all-a-flutter, charging into people's houses without knocking, disrupting a day's calm with erratic rants about the justice system. Viv, apparently, had gone into some kind of trance and was being looked after by her nuns at Carreg, while Leri and Greta, for some peculiar reason, had taken Iestyn in at Carreg Bach. On top of it all, word had also come that there would be no more boats for the next couple of days. Mwynwen's voice had quavered as she'd given everyone the news.

He was a little heavier, a little rougher around the edges, maybe, but Deian recognised him as the same Iestyn he'd run around with all those years ago, and whose dead birds he'd given graceful burials to, whose dead birds' eyes he had hoarded, like precious flints. They'd been like brothers.

It was Iestyn, in the end, who broke the silence, tottering off in a light-hearted, bouncy sentence. Deian caught the gist of it, but couldn't – or wouldn't, perhaps – reply in the way Iestyn wanted him to. Too much had changed.

"I don't," Deian ventured, looking at the soil, "I don't speak Welsh any more."

Iestyn laughed. A distinct whirr sat underneath it which spoke of the gritty smoke in his lungs.

"*Paid â malu!*"

"I'm not joking Iest! I don't." Deian wished there was something else he could plausibly be looking at apart from Iestyn's broken face as he spoke to him. He focused on his belt. "We moved away, didn't we?"

"But your mum was…."

"I know. But after we lost her, there didn't seem much point."

There it was. The unmentionable. Deian hadn't anticipated mentioning it so soon.

"Listen, I got your letter, Deian. I've been holding on to it for the past ten years."

"Good," he said. "Then you'll know that I…"

"Yeah, I know," he said, fixing his gaze on the soil. Of course he knew. "But I didn't know you'd be here, this summer."

"I come most summers," he said, eyes cast downwards, tracing the outline of a dead moth in the soil.

"Do you?" He sounded surprised. "Don't you find it difficult, after what happened?"

"It's the opposite," he said. "Comforting, I suppose. I feel like, like she's still here."

"She might be," Iestyn replied, gazing out to sea.

Deian thought about the plaque, the blinding reflection of gold.

"Why didn't you come to see me? If you knew I didn't do it?"

"I couldn't." Deian remembered his father's insistence that he stay clear. "No one would let me. And in the end, it was easier just to forget about it."

"Do you think I could forget about it?" Iestyn said, bitterly. "Sitting in that fucking cell, with no visitors, for ten years?"

"I'm sorry," he said, looking finally into Iestyn's eyes. "But it was hard for us all. Everyone was saying that you'd done it. The courts had decided. They all told me I was stupid to think otherwise."

"Yeah, well, the courts finally decided otherwise, didn't they? Took them long enough."

"You're out now," he said, knowing how feeble the sentence sounded. "What's it like, being here again?"

"Well it's fucking weird, Deis, I'll give you that. I'm speaking to my best friend in a different language for one thing. Are you sure you've got, you know, *dim Cymraeg o gwbl*?" Iestyn stared at him with disbelief.

"*Tipyn bach.*"

"You are joking? How the fuck can you manage to lose your Welsh after a few years over the border and mine stays intact after ten years at Her Majesty's Service?"

It was the old Iestyn he could sense again. Sussing out if he was being humoured. Ready to retaliate. He looked him up and down to see if there were traces of what he'd been through. The eyes wcre as deathly as ever, and his upper body still commanded you to look at him, whether you wanted to or not.

"So, what was prison like?" Deian found himself asking.

"Not that different. Bit like here, really. Same faces. Confined space. Everybody knows everybody's business. You can't shit without someone turning it into a real drama." He started rolling himself a cigarette. "Fuck, Deis, I can't believe we're talking to each in other in English. *Tud 'laen!*" Deian could remember them both sliding on their bottoms down the back of the mountain, screaming to each other in Welsh. He could remember the words dancing in the breeze, abundant like the grass all around them. He willed those words to come back, but felt like he was shouting in a dream and no sound would come. "Suppose that's what this island's like now – all colonised by the English. That'll teach her. She thought we'd be so safe here. Boatman speaks English, shouting obscenities to a boat full of people who couldn't give a shit about the language. English holidaymakers all over the place, even the Welsh support English football teams, can you believe it? Now they've lost you as well. It's exactly what she was so afraid of on the mainland – except it hasn't happened there, has it?

They were all bloody speaking Welsh in Cardiff when I came out, I tell you. Like bloody geese they were about that castle. And I get here and I can't find one Welsh speaking fucker to talk to."

"There's a few here, actually," Deian, said nervously, trying to dissipate the anger. He recalled suddenly a day when the boat had been unable to cross and Iestyn had been crying because they'd run out of sugar to put in his tea. Deian gave him the chocolate bar that he'd been saving for months, dipping its brown head into his cup, watching the liquid darkening. Anything, just to quell that menace in his eyes. He remembered that look as fresh as he knew it then, and recognised the small triumph of seeing Iestyn's anger dissolving as his chocolate bar dribbled away to nothing.

"Lots of Welsh speakers: Mererid, the writer, Welsh speaker. Elin, ecologist, very Welsh, her, comes from Pwllheli," and on and on Deian went, dishing out his saved up chocolate bars.

"Yeah, I met most of them last night. Lovely, they are. That Elin, she's sweet. What you laughing at?"

"She's too young for you, Iest," he said.

"We'll see." He lit a cigarette.

"Few Welsh speakers passing through isn't going to change anything, is it? It's not like it was, though, is it," Iestyn said, blowing the smoke into the path of a butterfly, "not like it was when we were kids."

"You hated it here when we were kids," Deian said, suddenly resentful at this nostalgia.

"I didn't know what it was, then, did I? Didn't know how important it was…"

"And you do now?"

Iestyn stared up at the sky. Turning to look at Deian unexpectedly, Deian caught some of the softness in his eyes. Then, just as suddenly, it was gone again.

"Listen, Deis. After all those years inside, you realize that a lot of things are a hell of a lot more important than you thought they were. I wouldn't be here otherwise. I've realised what Mam was trying to do, all those years ago, by bringing me here. I mean, it didn't work, but at least she was trying to do something. And *trying* to do it is a hell of a lot better than doing nothing, I'm telling you."

"She stopped trying though, didn't she?" said Deian, thinking of Viv in her habit, the way she'd become nothing more than a face.

"Tell me about it," he said. "A nun, for fuck's sake! She used to laugh at all that stuff. It's the last thing Delyth would have wanted her to do."

His mother's name stopped them both in their tracks. Reading it off the golden plaque was one thing, hearing it, from Iestyn's mouth, was quite another. It reminded him too much of those things that had been said in that court in Cardiff. The way Iestyn said her name just now, gently, as though embracing it with his mouth, made him think at least some of what had been said may have been true. He shoved the thought back into the soil, and began trowelling away.

Iestyn paced the field. How would things work, Deian wondered. Iestyn being here, after all these years? He found himself once more making pathways for him, wondering if he could help out with the excavation, get to know the girls, maybe even spend a few evenings with them until Viv was ready to speak to him. The girls needn't know what he'd done. He could find a way to make it work, Deian thought, handing Iestyn a small trowel.

"You can shove that up your arse," Iestyn said.

Deian told him, in Welsh, to get on with it.

He resented Leri's presence later that morning, her camera close up on the two of them, like a sweltering sun. Every now and then, she took Iestyn off to the shade to film some additional pieces to camera.

"Leri," he moaned, "we've got an excavation to complete."

"Just a moment, Deian, I just want to get this last bit."

Iestyn got up from where he'd been positioned, and told Leri he'd finish the interview later. She stood there frantically pushing her hair back over her face.

"But I thought you wanted to see your Mam later," she said.

"She can wait," he said.

Iestyn knelt back in the soil and got back to work, folding his fag end into his back pocket in response to one of Deian's disapproving looks. Leri trailed him like a shadow.

"I really think we should do this now," she said, her voice strained.

"Later," he said, without looking at her.

"No, I think we should get it out of the way now so we can..."

"What does Deian think," Iestyn said suddenly, looking up at him. "What do you think's most important?"

"Nothing's more important to me than the twenty thousand saints," he replied, reeling out his rehearsed spiel with a renewed clarity. "Both Leri and I are interested in unearthing things, as far as I can see. It's just that I'm doing it in a way that's more honest."

He could see he'd given Iestyn his answer.

"Precisely," he said. "I'm all for a bit of honesty these days," said Iestyn, as Leri packed up her camera and walked off.

Iestyn had been staring at him all morning, like he was trying to equate his memory with what he now saw before him.

"Twenty thousand saints," he said, long after Leri had left, as though he'd been preparing the phrase for recital. "I thought you thought all that was bollocks?"

Deian smiled. Even as a kid his archaeological intuition had told him it was rather preposterous to think there could be twenty thousand saints buried on a single island. That it was a convenient myth to get people's pulses racing, to get the boat coming back and forth, to keep the modern day pilgrims pouring into the retreat, to keep the nuns fainting by the Cavern. The fact that Iestyn remembered this filled him with sudden affection; the fact that he knew the depths of him, the silvery surfaces of him. But just as suddenly he saw the problem – the many theories he'd expounded to the girls about how the whole thing was possible, only to find himself confronted with someone who knew him, who knew what he was doing was a farce, without and within.

"Yes well, that's what happens to people when they grow up. They sell out. I suppose you could call it the death of a career, when you end up doing the one thing you never thought you'd do."

He would never have thought he'd use his profession in this way – to make a team of archaeologists believe they were looking for something when really there was nothing.

"Career," said Iestyn contemplatively, tossing the word in the air and watching it land at his feet. "Never had one of those, did I? Right then, where do you want me to start?"

"Over there," Deian said, "and carve outwards. Don't make a mess."

The trowel was hurled through the air towards Iestyn, and in its descent, Deian thought he caught a glint of vulnerability that was with him still, beneath that hard, jutting jaw of his.

"*Ti'n newid dim, nag wyt?*" Iestyn laughed, a sentence which Deian caught between both hands perfectly. He was right. Some people never changed.

Late that afternoon, Elin and Mererid had arrived on site. It was clear, from the way Elin only threw a curt hello to Iestyn before continuing with her work, that something was already happening, the attraction polarizing them, anticipating the magnetic pull that would soon come. Deian introduced Mererid to him, briefly, and hadn't liked the look in his eyes then, lingering a little too long on Mererid's exposed shoulders as she worked. However, Mererid kept her back firmly turned towards him, and it wasn't long before the site became a playing field for the game of eyes between Iestyn and Elin, the looking on and looking away that began to make Deian feel dizzy.

He'd wanted to ask Mererid about her fiancé's visit. Word was that he'd gone back on the two o' clock boat, and he wondered how she could just come walking back up to the top of the island as though nothing had happened, volunteering no information about the visit. He found himself wondering if they'd had sex. Trying to push the thought from his mind, he had a vision of her lifting the green and white print dress, and a man – without a face – kneeling in front of her. As he watched her trowelling away he wondered how they'd said goodbye at the Cavern, whether she'd kissed him ardently in front of the other day trippers. Then, he realised he hadn't been envisaging her *fiancé* in these scenes at all, he'd been seeing himself.

It was one of the strangest nights on Bardsey since he'd arrived there four weeks ago. They sat facing one another on the small picnic table in the goat yard. Him opposite Mererid, Iestyn opposite Elin. He couldn't believe how young Mererid looked in the candlelight, her soft skin falling away in the flames. He wanted to reach out and touch her face, but was afraid he'd knock over the candle in the process, set fire to himself. The goats circled them, bleating with annoyance, edging ever so slightly into the wooden table until Deian eventually gave in and went to feed them. From the corner of the goat yard, he kept looking back at the scene, wondering how he'd adjusted so easily to what had been thrown at him that morning. Iestyn Daniels, of all people, walking back into his life through the gate of Cae Uchaf, as if no time at all had lapsed between the last, angry time he'd left that field and kicked the gate with his teenage feet, as if he hadn't gone on to be convicted of the most heinous of crimes. And while it had scared him, truly scared him when he'd seen his back turned to him last night on Solfach Beach, this morning had been entirely different. They were back where they were, they seem to have slid back into it with ease, from the moment they'd chased each other from Cae Uchaf to the goat yard like children.

Of course, things couldn't be quite as they were. The fact that they had women to entertain made this a completely different scenario. There had been no girls here when they were younger, it was an island full of women, even back then – the island being run with ruthless efficiency by baking, farming, red-cheeked active mothers, Delyth and Viv with their sleeves rolled up, their hair swept back, loaves of bread gathered under their shoulders and dead rabbits handing from their wrists. And it was hard on pubescent boys without girls around the place, so much so that they'd resorted to doing all manner of things to each other on those hot, August afternoons, behind the bushes in Cae Uchaf. Deian wondered if Iestyn remembered, and hoped he didn't, hoping that those years inside would have eroded the memory of his small, pink penis being guided ever so slowly into Deian's wary mouth, and the way the shock of this sudden, hot, wet touch had made him ejaculate almost instantly into Deian's hair. He remembered all too clearly the odd way they'd looked at one another at that moment, not quite into each other's eyes but a little off centre, and the argument that had ensued when Deian had unzipped his flies and gestured for Iestyn to do the same to him. Iestyn had point blank refused, and had run off in the direction of the mountain, screaming for Deian to leave him alone. He remembered then, how he'd sat in the bushes with his trousers around his ankles, struggling to bring himself off, and that after his weak climax (which he found out later had been witnessed by some unsuspecting holidaymakers from their barbecue at Tŷ Capel), he'd burst into tears. He could feel the emptiness even now, could remember how he'd watched the hot sun drying the semen with fascination, wondering if it was possible for him to reproduce some strange hybrid grass child with a luxurious green coat and his own brown eyes.

He thought of the grass-child often, and it had even sprung to mind when he and Fran had sat down in that clinic, listening to the hurtful, finite news. He remembered running after her in the rain, over the blue concrete outside the hospital, only to see from that look in her eyes that his future had been cut off, just like that. He felt like a child once more, the child looking at his semen drying in the sun, knowing, even then, perhaps, that it was destined to stay there, on the island, to go no further.

And this was the one thing that did unnerve him about Iestyn's arrival – the fact that he was once more that insecure child. It didn't matter what he'd achieved, the archaeological accolades he had to his name, the many countries he'd visited, the many pioneering discoveries he'd made, Iestyn had caught him out, somehow. Had found him back at the beginning, ploughing away at nothing. Still here, because of his sentimentality, his need to be close to a mother who had long gone; abandoned him, for all he knew. Pathetic, when he thought about it. Iestyn's arrival made it impossible to dress up the situation in any other way – it was his childish love of the island that drove him back here, year after year, nothing else. Iestyn knew that. The women who'd been around him all these weeks, they didn't.

Once he'd left the table, the three of them started talking to each other in Welsh, and he could hear, suddenly, the loosening of tongues. There was laughter of an entirely different rhythm resounding around the table now, and Elin was screaming piercingly in response to something Iestyn had just said, that made the other two laugh along with her, their laughter tinkling in their tin mugs. A few seconds later, they'd broken out into song. Deian stood there, his gas lamp shaking, suddenly resenting Iestyn not only for becoming the more appealing of the two, but also for bringing his language to the island. For undoing everything.

When he eventually sat back down, they continued in Welsh, their candlelit eyes addressing him constantly, until slowly, warmly, he began to nod every now and then, even to laugh in the right places. He saw Mererid looking at him curiously, with renewed vigour somehow, and he trundled along in his imperfect Welsh, until it became too exhausting for him to venture further. She laughed and touched his shoulder, just like that, and he flinched, not knowing why, not knowing if she'd noticed it even. He'd managed later to tell her, in Welsh, to leave the washing up to him, and he'd seen something affectionate shining back out of her eyes as she grabbed his shoulder this time, smiling, thanking him. "*Diolch*, Deian," she said breathlessly, perhaps a little drunk. "*Diolch i ti.*"

Her appreciation left him reeling in the side door of the small kitchen. Iestyn, somehow, was able to gracefully kiss both women on the cheeks as he bid them farewell. He stayed where he was, offering a dismissive wave. Later, they both stood at the top of the path watching the diminishing gas lamps. He was pleased that they'd left, that Elin hadn't, as he'd seen earlier in her eager eyes, asked Iestyn to accompany them home, that he hadn't been left alone in his yard thinking about the grass monster, Mererid's touch on his left shoulder, and the ghosts of himself and Iestyn that he could still feel around the place, mocking him, laughing at him in another language.

"It never goes away, you know," said Iestyn, as they climbed the wooden stairs to the loft. "You will be able to speak it again someday, if you stop being afraid of it. Don't mind if I stay, do you?"

Long after Iestyn had conked out on the floor of his loft, he tried to remember terms of endearment in Welsh. He'd heard Iestyn calling her *cariad* earlier, love in lilting, laughing tones, but he wasn't comfortable with that. It would feel like exposing himself to her, somehow. He had always preferred *bach,* like the composer, only it meant something little, small, dear. His mother had called him that when she got that

113

strange look in her eyes; smoothing down his hair, letting the word fly over the top of his head, again and again.

He fell asleep clinging on to that word, *bach*, watching it become smaller and smaller until it became so minute it fell through his hands, into darkness.

17

Leri was annoyed with Iestyn for not having returned to the cottage that evening, like he'd promised. The documentary had needed a rethink since Viv had gone squishing into her tomatoes, and she needed Iestyn to be aware of the change of plan. There would be no more courteous knocking on doors, they would simply be pressing on with the original plan, co-operation or not. She also needed his bulk around the cottage to fend off Greta's questioning eyes, which seemed to be getting a little more focused on the truth with each lie she heard. "Tell me what's going on," Greta said last night, her shadow creeping across her. "Tell me so we can work together on this." Leri looked up into her face and cupped one of Greta's breasts. She was ordered to sleep downstairs. She spent most of the night at the small window, shivering in one of Iestyn's shirts, watching the far sea swelling with silver shadows, without the faintest desire to film it.

She drank whisky, too, in petite, glittering amounts, feeling the punch in her stomach. She wondered what would become of her and Greta. They needed to get back to the rawness of those first few evenings, their moon-bleached bodies creaking in the loft, the giggles that would come with the grappling of buckles, belts and buttons. She recalled the way her hands had travelled the peripheries of Greta's body, the tops of her thighs, the crook of her shoulder, the downy length of her arms, and realised that it was those places, more than anything, that she would miss if she were never to journey there again. She found herself pining, even at this moment, for the back of Greta's head, those small, sticking-up tufts of hair, silly almost in the way they sprung to attention. She loved twirling them around her fingers, pretending they were her own. You could have sex with almost anyone, after all. But twirling someone's hair, that was different.

She tried not to hear her producer's voice driving the warmth out of her as she sat shivering by the window. But the voice forced her to see herself as she was, urgently waiting for Greta to reciprocate those needy, pleading looks she gave her every day, all the while keeping a nervous eye on Iestyn in Cae Uchaf. She knew full well she was losing her hold over them both. "Send Greta away," Clive would say if he knew, in that no-two-ways tone of his, "the first chance you get, send her away." And she'd considered it. She'd considered bumbling her way through the excuses best she could, and turning her back once the boat had sailed. But she didn't have that choice. Bardsey wasn't going to make it that easy. There wouldn't be a boat for days, now, or so they said. *Days.* The tide-race was restless, and they'd had no choice but to cancel, in fear of their visitors being swallowed up by the Bardsey Sound on their way home.

She eventually woke on the small, damp sofa, sweating underneath a thick blanket, to the accompaniment of Greta's gentle snoring, echoing off the beams. No sign of Iestyn, still. She decided to go out to look for him, being careful first to disguise her search as an early morning run, jogging pants pulled loosely about her hips. She walked out into another dazzle of a day, bright gold challenging her from every angle. She looked to the North, knowing that Cae Uchaf was the obvious choice, but she couldn't bring herself to do it. Not this early in the morning. He would sniff her desperation. To the South, the lighthouse lay before her, a long stretch of worn path, enough to work up a sweat, and it was plausible enough to call in at the lighthouse for a drink of water, for a shower even. They did have the only shower on the island, after all, not that you could tell, from looking at Mererid and Elin. But at the back of her mind was a vision of Iestyn, bare chested, laughing in that blue kitchen. She wouldn't put it past him. She'd seen the way he'd been looking at Elin.

She ran down past the early swell, past a few early morning walkers poking rocks with sticks down at Traeth Henllwyn, past the moaning seals. She didn't see what the problem was; the sea looked fine to her, perfectly crossable. But she could almost hear Mwynwen's voice chastising her, telling her that was typical of a holiday maker. "You don't see how complex it all is," she'd once heard Mwynwen telling Greta. "It may not look it, but it's real chaos down there. We're so close to the mainland, you see, the water's all squished up between the two pieces of land, it doesn't know what to do with itself, doesn't know if it's coming or going. That's why it's so dangerous. But I suppose all you telly people see is the surface prettiness, which is fine for your little programme."

Little programme. She laughed out loud, sending a nearby sheep wobbling off into a hedge. It would be anything but little. Leri loved skimming the side of this island, feeling her proximity to the sea, feeling how close she was to something so inevitable, fathomless. Sliding on a patch of gravel, a little too close to the grey, spiky rocks, she spared a thought for Delyth. Had that been it? A bend of a big toe and she was gone? Was that what Iestyn wanted to tell her? Had he been nearby, had he seen her? She was starting to wonder if Iestyn actually had anything at all to tell her. She thought about how little she'd allowed him to tell her so far about this so called theory of his. What if he knew nothing? What then? What would Clive make of it?

"What we need to focus on," Clive had said to her, "is what it was really like for him growing up on that island, and if we can find links there between what happened to Delyth, then we've got something. You and I know that he *knows* something. And we're going to be the first ones to find out what it is. *Then* we've really got a programme, and not just any programme, but a ground-breaking one, one that could guarantee prizes. And at this point in your career," he said, his beard poking outwards like an accusation, "you really should be winning prizes." Thinking of this made her charge on with renewed vigour towards the south end. It always got to her – Clive's disapproving look every year when she came into the office after the BAFTAs, having evidently drunk her disappointment into oblivion. "You don't seem to have it," he'd said, "that ability some people have to just churn out, by word of their own shameless mouth, how good they are. If you look at past winners, they win because they've convinced the world they deserve it – not because they've created great works. You're somehow not willing to do that. And if you're not, well, I'm afraid you're not going to make the distance. You have to learn that sometimes the work really doesn't speak for itself."

He was right, she saw that. She shied away from networking circles as if she was worried she would catch something, nervously sipping her first, second, third glass of champagne, and usually ending up diverting her attention to the waiters, who, to her, seemed more distinctly 'real' than any of those other white-toothed megalomaniacs. She was more comfortable with more subtle networking, becoming friends with those she wished would help her out in the long-term. She remembered spotting one of her main interviewees for the drug-ring documentary at a club in Cardiff, and literally dancing up to him, making her beeline in a series of rumba-steps, all the while inserting little snippets of information to get him interested in her, interested in the programme. And it had worked beautifully. But he wasn't the one dishing out the prizes, and when it came to talking to the Head of Communications at the Corporation, or hobnobbing with one of the BAFTA panelists, she didn't have a clue where to start. She didn't know how they danced. "Bit of a shame you're a lesbian," Clive had once said to her, "you could have made so much more of what you've got, it could have got you places much quicker, you know. It's still a male–dominated industry *cariad*, I'm afraid."

This, she'd hoped, would be her breakthrough. She'd done her research, and had seen that there had been few programmes about Bardsey in previous years. There had been plenty of nature trails and bird-watching bonanzas, but there hadn't been anything gritty, true to life, delineating a darker side to the island. And what was darker than a murder conviction; a disappearance? Let alone the potential of solving the mystery, on screen. Gripping stuff, Clive had said. It was just the kind of thing the BAFTAs would be looking to award this year, for the focus in arts was now on the small, isolated places, and if a certain work happened to fit a certain political criteria for that year then she'd got it in the bag. Iestyn had liked her instantly, she saw that in him on her first prison visit. They were from similar backgrounds, her parents having been active members of the Welsh Language Society too; they'd both known Viv, back in the seventies. And with Viv's activist past placing another tick in the panelists' box, she could almost see her face reflected in the BAFTA, elongated in its golden mirror.

But it would only happen, she thought, if what Iestyn had told her all those months ago was actually true. She thought with a shudder about the neutrality of those eyes when he'd said it. Clear his name for good, he'd said. Prove exactly what happened, once and for all. He knew what Delyth had done, he said, he'd worked it out. *He does know, you can see he knows,* Clive had agreed when he'd looked at the tape. But what had they seen, really? Cold eyes above a coffee cup, nothing more than that.

They weren't that cold, anymore, either. Anyone could see that something had happened to Iestyn the second he'd come onto the island, something that had made him lose focus, ever so slightly, on what they'd come here to do. Flicking through her itinerary she'd seen, with annoyance, that she'd missed what would have been a crucial opening to the documentary – Iestyn's thoughts on his first day, sitting at the window of her cottage, the lights of the lighthouse flashing rhythmically over his silhouette.

Instead she'd spent the night there alone, shivering in Iestyn's shirt.

Deian had been a nuisance. He hadn't been part of the plan, of course. It was one of the evident gaps in her research, something Clive would have warned her about. She knew of him, of course, from the newspaper clippings. But at no point had it been made clear that they had the kind of friendship that could be rekindled with the throw of a ball. That's all it had taken, it seemed to her. She'd filmed them from a distance, as they did nothing more than throw a tennis ball at each other in the small goat yard, the sun hot on Iestyn's bronzed back, Deian smiling placidly, as though nothing like a conviction had ever stood between them. Elin emerged every now and then from the shade to laugh at something Iestyn said, fanning the air with her skirt.

Iestyn had sat in Cae Uchaf for the remainder of the day, digging. She saw what he saw; easy, hot summer ahead of him, a little sun, a little sex perhaps, a swim, a chance to help out, to paint a few window frames, mend a few gates, chase a few cows. Chances were, even his activist mum-turned-nun would come out of her cocoon of silence and begin building bridges. That was the last thing she wanted. She and Clive had done their research when it came to Viv, they knew all about her, how to spark her, how to wrench the worst out of her. But despite her planning, all Leri could see in front of her now was shot after shot of blue skies, seas, bird watching, and mountain climbing. A complete disaster.

"Listen, Iestyn," she said, startling him one day on the site. "I know you're having a good time here, right, but let's not forget why we came here. I'm a bit worried that we haven't even started, really, and well, we haven't got that much time left to do what you want to do. Didn't you want to go around the back of the mountain? Start exploring?"

He lit a cigarette and exhaled, looking around him as if waiting for something to happen.

"I can remember you know," he said, pointing towards the stone wall that separated them from the courtyard, "running across the ridge of that stone wall with my eyes closed. Me and Deian. Nine years old, I must have been, Deian about seven. No sense of danger in the world."

"I thought you had a rotten childhood," Leri began, instantly regretting the irritated tone of her voice.

"No, I had a rotten *upbringing*. My childhood was great. It was *her* who was the problem."

"Which is why we need to get you two talking. As we agreed," Leri added, the tone of her voice becoming distinctly sterner. "Then you can start telling her what you know."

"If she'll talk," Iestyn said.

"Oh, she'll talk," Leri added. She knew that Viv liked her. It could be done.

"You know what," Iestyn added as the colour drained from Leri's cheeks, "I'm not sure I really want to force her, you know, to open up. I mean God knows; from what Deian's been telling me she's been kind of at peace, living like this. Having seen her," he stopped once more, and looked at the sky again, almost as if it were whispering an autocue into his ear, "I mean, I think it's enough. It's not really her fault, is it? What happened. So she believed everybody else, big deal. She fucking *loved* Delyth. We all did."

All the while, Iestyn was pacing the site with a kind of renewed fascination. He went rummaging around in Deian's rucksack, and came out with a bag of rice cakes. Stuffing one into his mouth, he began laughing. "Fuck knows, I'd forgotten how good these tasted. You know, some winters, there would be no fresh bread, and you'd only have these to eat – so much so that you got used to them. You started telling yourself it was bread, and then it started losing that polystyrene feel on your tongue and you really did think, some mornings, when you were nearly mad with a craving for wheat, that it was soft dough melting on your tongue." He crunched his way through another rice cake. "Where's your camera now, Leri? This is the kind of thing you ought to be filming. I mean, they've buried Delyth, haven't they? Not physically maybe, but they've erected that plaque. Made her a fucking saint, for God's sake. It's time we let her be. It's old news, practically. "

"But she didn't let you be," Leri said, "I thought that's what you said, and I quote…"

"Fuck the quotes. What I said in that cell doesn't really count, does it?"

"Look Iestyn, I appreciate we might upset a few people, but you came here to get justice, remember. To clear your name. To explain."

"My name's been cleared, hasn't it? I've been acquitted. I'm out."

"That's not the end of it, is it? She's still missing. You've got a duty to share what you know, or what you think you know. I mean, don't you think people want to know the story?"

"Ah, I see, it's a story to you isn't it? I almost forgot that. I guess this must all be getting a little boring for you now. And if what's going on in front of you doesn't suit the story then you cut the story to fit, don't you? Work it out for yourself! You've got an imagination haven't you?"

"People don't want a hypothesis, they want the truth. People need to know what happened to her. A disappearance is maddening, don't you see that? Just that bleak silence, that vacuum, the lack of answers. People need to know."

121

"Nobody needs to know *anything*."

Even though his voice was calm, his eyes hosted the threat of a storm brewing. Leri knew she couldn't push it further, at least not if she wanted to keep him level, and she let him walk away from her, her whole body trembling with the things she wanted to unleash on him, to tell him how unfair he'd been, how misleading, and how he'd ruined months of preparation, and how he'd wiped out all her prospects in one slow swagger across the goat yard towards his playmates. But she couldn't. She'd lost her cool like this before, countless times, despite Clive telling her over and over in their boardroom briefings: "the real winner is the one who refuses to bicker. Never argue with your subjects over the little things. It gets you nowhere. Keep them on side and even if they refuse to co-operate, there's always something left to play for – always. Never let them sense desperation. It's really the death of any documentary." With this in mind, she peered curiously in through the window of the lighthouse cottage. The kitchen was perfectly empty, with two empty bottles of beer on the table. She ventured around the side, peeping her head around the door. She was startled by a semi-naked Elin coming out of the shower.

"Fuck, Leri! What do you think you're doing!"

"Sorry," she apologised, "just, I was wondering if there was any chance of a shower?"

Elin acquiesced quietly, dripping her way down the corridor. Through the bathroom window, she saw Mererid out by the flagstaff, pacing in her pyjamas, talking on the phone while a solitary sheep walked an orbit of its own making around her.

Later on, clean but not fragrant (she'd rummaged around in the bathroom cabinet for something scented, and had discovered that both of the lighthouse's inhabitants were of the not-perfumed, not-coloured, just-kind variety), she jogged past the site and found it completely deserted. She stopped for a while, and listened to the noises of the morning. Usually a voice could be carried to you through the breeze in this place, and there it was, Iestyn's voice, booming out of the hollow of Deian's loft, a few yards away. She saw Deian come out and stand on the little wooden balcony at the top of the stairs.

Before he saw her, she went dashing up the side of Cae Uchaf, and up towards the mountain.

She was angry. She should have gone in there to get Iestyn, ask him what he was playing at. But she remembered Clive's words. Once they sense you're desperate for them to co-operate, the more they play with you. The higher she climbed, the louder the voices were that pounded in her head, ideas and narratives shifting back and forth. She found her mind wandering back to Greta. There was still time to remedy things. To stop the coldness come rattling in with each passing night by the window. She could forget the whole thing, concentrate on their relationship, on what was really important. But then she might blame her later on, resent her, even. By the time she'd reached a small precipice on the side of the mountain, she had a sudden rush of blood to the head, a sudden clarity. She could do this. She could have Greta and she could have her BAFTA. She wanted Greta there by her side on the big night, after all, and in her bed the morning after, two sequined dresses knotted on the floor. It would all be manageable. She flipped open her mobile phone and waited for a signal. Nothing. The phone was dead to the world – she would have to climb higher to have any chance of connecting with Clive.

Up she went, higher again, enjoying the feeling of being able to tower above the island and its inhabitants. To the left she could see the unmistakable shape of Greta's body coming up the path, dressed in khaki combats and a vest top. She resisted the urge to call out, to raise her hand. Not yet.

She looked once more at her phone and was thrilled to see three whole bars of signal flashing up to greet her. She dialled Clive's number.

"I hope you've got something good for me, Leri, I'm a very busy man," Clive boomed. "If you've kept to the schedule, you should be half way through by now."

"Not exactly," Leri whispered. She could see Greta climbing the mountain towards her.

"What? Speak up, will you, I haven't got all day."

Leri moved a little to the right and realised she was very close to the mountain side. She slid down on her bottom onto a grassy ledge.

"We've got a hiccup," Leri continued, all the while praying that Greta wouldn't find her before she was done, or that the approaching sheep wouldn't somehow force her off the cliff. "He's just starting to change his story..."

"Well he can't, you've got enough on him to..."

"I know, Clive. But he's distracted. I think he may be, I don't know, falling in love with the place again. And he's sleeping with someone, I think."

"Who?"

"Someone he's met here, an ecologist."

"Is she young?"

"Yes, I suppose so, younger than him, by about seven, eight years. Why do you ask?"

"It's obvious isn't it? What you've got to do. He's got a lot of resentment in him, that boy. What you need to do is find it. Unearth it. God knows, we know enough about him."

"I'm not with you," Leri said.

"No, you never are, are you? Listen to me. This is how we're going to play it."

In ten minutes, Clive had plotted a plan that seemed near-perfect. So perfect, Leri was slightly annoyed that she hadn't thought of it herself. He would take care of things his end, and all she had to do was work on keeping things as they were, keeping Iestyn on the even-keel, until they were ready for the big change. Filming him now would be an even better way to put the programme together, as Clive suggested. "We show the before and after, and people love seeing the after, believe me, we're geared towards it our whole lives." Leri did believe him, just like she believed that her entire world was on this island. She often found herself thinking how insignificant she was when she was in Cardiff, a mere dot on the pavement. But here, somehow, it was different, she was important, she could do anything. This was everything, it had to be. Her entire world had shrunk to the size of this island and everything that happened on it was of paramount importance; it was her last chance. She would follow Clive's plan. It would show everyone that she wasn't insignificant. By showing people this island, she would break free from the mass herself, she would float off, people would start coming to her, in flocks of white boats. Yachts, even.

She felt herself beaming as the sun filtered through her, lighting up tiny particles of hope. She stood up boldly to greet the shadow above her, that she knew, from its uneven curves, to be Greta.

18

All morning Mererid has been sitting here at her desk, warily watching the icon of her laptop battery diminishing, knowing that she doesn't have long to go, and that the re-charging of a laptop isn't considered adequate use of the lighthouse generator. She's given up on the poems. She's now writing an article about the island for a monthly magazine – the editor is a friend of Mark's and she agreed to it months before in a corner of a smoky pub in Upper Bangor. She reads the first paragraph over again and is astounded by how trite it sounds, how truly far away from the experience she is having. She fits the words together in jaunty clauses, making them link one another's arms, making them dance. "But an article isn't supposed to dance, Mer," she remembers Mark saying once, slamming one of her paler efforts down on the kitchen table. "It's supposed to walk in a straight line."

Mererid thinks about how it's always been difficult for her to walk in a straight line, following a cycling accident in her late teens. People are always asking her why she's limping. She feels that maybe this off-centred-ness of hers, this slight tilting perspective may also be infused in her work. That her prose, also, has an aversion to walking straight, that it is always tempted by the outward-splay of the foot, the slightly jerky lean forwards, not always in the right direction.

She reads back over the article, and is unimpressed, once more astounded at the transparency of it. Anyone who knows her, and thankfully there are few of them, will see that it is all there, bubbling beneath the paper-thin surface. Her relief at having left Mark behind disguised as a celebration of being without the intrusive overloading information of television, her feelings for Deian recreated as wonder at the excavation and its findings, her new sense of freedom seen in every over-detailed paragraph about the bird attraction. Every time the beam comes swishing round, there she is, Mererid, exposed, lit up in great white streaks across the page.

Once it's done, she prints it out quickly, before she can change her mind. She knows the tone is lofty, that it is both over and under-written, that it presumes to be saying something about the island, when really she's skirting the whole experience. To be honest, she doesn't really know why she's writing it at all, or why she has the column in the first place. Then suddenly she remembers, once again: because Mark's friend is the editor. And that's what they will say, her readers, in the way they so often do, "You know who she's going out with, don't you? Mark Ashford, him and Geraint are thick as thieves. That's why she has the column." Mark has a literature column in the same publication, a neat rectangular rant with his face, dark and long, like a horse – neighing knowledgeably at the top.

She faces the blank screen once more. She's heard some of the islanders talking about her, about the fact that she's been there three weeks now and they've seen little evidence of any poetry taking place. She heard Mwynwen, the farmer's wife, saying loudly over the farm wall one afternoon, "As far as I can see, she's not *done* much of anything, apart from mooch in that room of hers and hang around the excavation. Where's the product, that's what I want to know. At least you can see what you're getting with a tractor." She looks through her notebook. Four half-formed poems, stumbling along a white screen. They are all about archaeology, or at least, they assume to be about archaeology. But what does she know? She has knelt in the orange soil, she has ploughed away with her little silver trowel, she's done so believing that eventually she'll hit a bone and discover a saint.

Something has suddenly changed between her and Deian; a sudden shift. She tries to pinpoint exactly when it happened. Perhaps it was when he shouted her name over the hedge in Cae Uchaf, or when she saw his face at her window a few nights ago. Maybe it was the feel of his rough hand on her shoulder when they were climbing the mountain. Whatever it is comes to her suddenly when he's not there, too. It's in the way she sometimes sits by the kitchen table listening to the angry messages flying back and forth between Mwynwen and

Howard on the radio system, waiting for something significant to be said, without being able to imagine for one second what it is she's waiting for. Or the way she sometimes walks out of the cottage and stares at the bird hide, imagining going in and finding Deian in there, knowing that he isn't an avid birdwatcher. It's there in the strange unease she feels sitting in her cottage, so far away from the top of the island, desperately wishing for the apartness that she once craved, that she has gone there seeking, to be lost forever in the sound of the lighthouse gate opening.

And it's there now, on the screen. In between all the weak poems there is something real and solid that she somehow keeps expunging as she writes it down. And she knows from experience that it isn't ready, because whatever she's supposed to be writing about hasn't happened to her yet, *not really*.

Elin bursts into the room and the poem fragments. Mererid watches the words scurrying away, under the bed. She is pleased for the distraction, and lets Elin take her thoughts away with her own ramblings about Iestyn; the newcomer. Apparently he is coming for dinner tonight, and she thinks it's a date. She's not sure, in the way you can never be sure about anything on this island. But she thinks it is. She has plans. She wants Mererid to promise she'll stay in her room until something happens.

There is a knock at the window that frightens the life out of them both. Mererid realises she must have been laughing too loudly to hear the squeal of the gate that she is so patiently listening out for. Mererid sees Elin waving dispiritedly at the person at the window.

"What's wrong?" Mererid asks.

"He doesn't want me," she says, grumpily.

"Of course he wants you," Mererid jests. What man wouldn't, she thinks, looking at Elin's luminous, chestnut bob, that exquisite slope of neck.

"No he doesn't," Elin says, kicking the desk with mock-fury.

"Why do you say that?"

"Because he's brought Deian with him."

As she walks out of the room Mererid feels it again, the wringing of her stomach, except this time it contracts and then unfolds, sending out waves of something she hasn't felt for a long time. It's that feeling that she wants to write a poem about. But she can't just now.

She closes the laptop.

19

The last time Viv remembered craving for a boat was when she was waiting to cross over for the first time. It had been two weeks since she'd packed up and left her house in Mynytho, four weeks after the referendum and the devastating news that Wales had said no to self-government, and she was forced to leave, as she had threatened. She'd been waiting patiently in a rather shabby bed and breakfast in Aberdaron for some news of a boat, climbing every now and then to Uwch Mynydd to look over longingly at Enlli, reciting to herself a poem by T Gwynn Jones. *"Draw dros y don mae bro dirion nad ery cwyn yn ei thir,"* a poem about the promised land, free from the complaints of the ordinary world, the very poem she had chanted to herself when trying to push Iestyn out of the womb. Both times, she had wanted desperately to reach the other side, for the whole thing to be over. On both occasions, unkind voices told her otherwise.

Having put the phone down on the boatman that day, she'd put her head in her hands, wondering how much longer she could remain sane in the interim. Iestyn, who was two at the time, had been getting increasingly tetchy as the days wore on, the blank grey skies taunting him with their heaviness, the wooden door of his room all bolted up. He would not be comforted – would not sit in his mother's lap, would not come with her for walks, and would refuse to do anything but pace angrily around the house, a one-foot fury at her feet. Viv had returned from a quick shopping trip to find the landlady weeping in the small, mahogany kitchen. "My curtains," she had cried, "my wonderful Laura Ashley curtains." She found Iestyn swinging back and forth on a wave of pink-patterned polyester at the top of the stairs, the last shred of fabric ripping as she reached the landing, depositing Iestyn onto the carpet. That was the last time she remembered him crying, at least properly, nestling in the crook of her shoulder and for once, not resisting her caresses.

Thankfully, the boat had come the next morning, leaving the bed and breakfast intact. And even better, she had arrived at Porthmeudwy to find Delyth there waiting for her, with Deian in her arms; just a small face in a shawl, back then. "I haven't slept nights thinking about it," she'd said, laughing, pulling Viv towards her in one warm hug. "Jeremy thought I was positively mad even considering it. But then, in the end, I had to tell him – I can't live with what Wales has done. Viv is right. The island is the only place for us. Twenty thousand saints have got to be better than a hundred thousand disbelievers." "Oh Delyth," Viv had said, her words stumbling over her sobs, "you don't know what it means to me that you've come. We'll be fine, you know. It'll be our own little Wales out there." "I know," she'd said, her eyes glazing over. "Jeremy will understand, eventually. This is what's best for the boys, isn't it? And Deian's still young enough to forget all about this, this mainland – he won't know any different."

She'd never spared a thought for Jeremy then, of course; Viv was only pleased that Delyth had kept to her word. But she thought of him often these days, especially since they'd erected the plaque. She supposed that the whole time she'd been away he'd been thinking that Delyth would eventually come back to him. That her 'pact' with Viv was one of those silly whims of hers, and that as soon as the no vote came out, (she somehow knew that Jeremy had been one of the traitors, and knew that Delyth knew it too), she'd settle back into being a good little housewife.

But Viv knew that if she made the decision to come there would be no turning back for her. She was that kind of woman. There she had been at Porthmeudwy that day, red-cheeked and breathless, her baby pressed to her chest, her eyes full of hope. Gone was the sheer exhausting grinding-down of the past few months. They were both new again, pure. They had left, together, a family. She never could have foreseen how it would all turn out. Though she had seen that very knowledge in Jeremy's eyes the day he had come to collect Deian for good. *We knew no good would come of this,* his bulging pupils seemed to be saying.

It had now been five days with no mention of a boat. And it wasn't merely Iestyn she wanted off the island, but those annoying, conspiring so-called 'sisters' of hers. They seemed to her to have been here since the beginning of time, ordering her about, shutting doors on her, cutting off her sentences. Since the news had broken about her son, the rigorous silence had dissipated into relentless, noisy counsel, and she could not turn without one of them letting her know that the Lord would be with her during this difficult time, and that the Lord had divined for the boats to stop, for time to stand still. "So that we may have solace in stasis," Sister Mary Catherine had uttered. They had uprooted her from her home, and kept her confined to the back bedroom of Carreg like she was some long-suffering patient, and had been bringing her home-baked linseed cake to aid her recovery. It was dry and clung to her teeth, and rarely was she given anything to wash it down with; Sister Mary Catherine was apparently a little too nervous of the gas stove to attempt tea. They had been giving prayer services in her name, and told her that they were willing to rid the island of evil spirits, if she so wished. How they proposed to do this, they hadn't specified. If the gas stove was all that dangerous perhaps they could make use of that, Viv had suggested. She was met with stern faces that told her to calm herself; she wasn't in her right mind.

Every evening, they wheeled her off to the tiny white building at the side of the house, to light candles and kneel before the shrine to the saints. Viv herself knew many of the artefacts in the old pig sty was a scam, Gwyn having cobbled together a few bones that Deian had unearthed a few years back, placing them in a glass case, and calling them the bones of St Deiniol, never mind that each bone was a different colour, and that the body parts, if put together, evidently made more than one saintly body. For one, he seemed to have three hands; something the sisters must have put down to a saintly attribute. Gwyn had completed the authentic feel with a few medieval gowns and a few dusty Bibles. Shove in a guestbook, and call it a shrine, he'd said, nobody will know any different. When she saw Sister Mary Catherine putting her hands to the glass, asking for them to be blessed by the bones of Deiniol, Viv let out a small laugh, which she then disguised as a sob, Sister Lucy's arm sliding around her shoulders in compassion.

She had planned her escape with precision. She'd carefully studied their routines, and knew their patterns by now. There was no shifting them before eleven, for Sister Mary Catherine was a sound, deafeningly-noisy sleeper who kept the other two awake most of the night, and by the time she came out of her coma, the other two would be just drifting off. They would not venture out alone, and Sister Mary Catherine would be sitting in the kitchen, dribbling her tea, waiting for the other two to get ready.

That morning, she was ready for her rebellion. She had little to lose now; after all, they already knew she couldn't possibly have been a fraction of what she said she was. Not with a son like that, she'd heard Lucy Violet saying. And there was the pressing matter of Elfyn. Sister Mary Catherine wouldn't tell her what they'd done with him. For one horrific moment she'd thought that they'd panicked over the dwindling provisions, and the lack of boat, and clubbed him to death, hanging him to dry in the hermitage like a pig. She refused to eat the miscellaneous evening meal of meat stew, just in case. It was Sister Anna, passing her the salt, that had told her in Welsh, not to worry, that Elfyn was safe and had been taken in by Mwynwen, translating swiftly to Sister Mary Catherine that Mwynwen had been kind enough to provide them with this stew for their dinner. Upon hearing that the stew was a creation of Mwynwen's, Viv tucked in, her stomach rejoicing.

That morning, she tiptoed past the cave-mouthed Sister Mary Catherine in the downstairs bedroom, tweaking the heavy oak door open in seventeen discreetly slow manoeuvres. Just as she was dangling one bare foot out of the door, she heard a mucus-coated moan emanating from Sister Mary Catherine and stood perfectly still, until the moan was once more washed away in a gurgling tide of snores. Viv's second bare foot felt the warmth of the sun. The clean, fresh air seemed exhilarating, as did the dewy Carreg field beneath her bare feet as she rushed up towards the path. Just at that moment, she heard the hum of Howard's tractor and had no choice but to bow her head, so that he would mistake her for one of the others. When he was gone, she charged over the gate, and onto the path, feeling the deliciousness of deception, the elation of the convict's supreme getaway.

She stopped off at the cottage for plain clothes, relishing the feel of the canvas top and old running trousers on her, musty but homely. She pulled on her old sturdy walking boots, and enjoyed the noise they made on the path as she stamped her way down to the farm. She heard Elfyn before she saw him, a chorus of barks in the back garden, and heard Mwynwen and her grandchildren laughing and shouting out his name between enthusing shrieks. She charged on in through the house, without uttering a word to a stunned Howard, who sat at the kitchen sailing a gooey substance through the air towards the baby's mouth. She stood by the back door, watching the spectacle. They were now dancing around the dog, the smallest child being tackled to the ground by Elfyn, his face licked gently, tenderly. How normal it seemed, this grandmother, these grandchildren, her dog, she thought.

Elfyn didn't bound towards her instantly; he was too busy. Mwynwen had to lead him over, and even then, she thought she saw a slight reluctance in his eyes, as he took one last look back at the garden and its simple, green offerings.

Mwynwen reasoned with her at the kitchen counter, resuming her kneading of a deflated lump of floury matter as she spoke. The baby sat perched on its high stool, face caked in clumps, its too-blue eyes bullying her.

"It's that blasted Leri," Mwynwen said, "looking for a story. I knew there was something funny about that girl. She's obviously been planning it for months." Her words were barely audible above the pounding of fists in the soft dough. Viv thought about Leri's oval-shaped face, so unlike the baby's perfectly round, ball-shaped stare. She'd liked the earnestness of Leri's eyes in her dimly-lit kitchen, she'd liked the way she wrote down everything she'd said, and more, in looping cadences so unlike Sister Mary Catherine's. They'd both sat there one evening watching the sun sinking into the sea, stripping the light from their faces, until they could see nothing but the glimmer of eyes. For one moment, she'd allowed herself to think it was Delyth who was sat there. Nobody had listened to her like that since Delyth had gone. "If it wasn't for the blasted Sound," Mwynwen continued, white flakes flying off her wrists, "we could have got them off the island by now. You know, Howard thinks it could be days before we get another boat. Viv. Viv? Say something, Viv, will you?"

"They released him," she said suddenly, looking up at Mwynwen's face. "They released him, Mwynwen. That means something, surely?"

"We've been over this," said Mwynwen.

"It's different now," she said, sulkily, feeling the weight of her eyes.

"How is it different?" she said, sternly, carving grooves into her unbaked loaf. "Lack of evidence doesn't mean a thing. They always had a lack of evidence. You and I both know he did it."

"How do we know?" Viv said. She truly wanted to know how she knew. She'd spent so long on this place that it had become fact, hard and real. Iestyn had killed Delyth. It's what Mwynwen had told her; it's what she had told herself over and over as she had testified in court. There had been the cardigan; the blood stain. There had been the eyes of dead birds under Iestyn's bed. There had been his restlessness when the police had come. There had been his hurdle over Cae Uchaf's fence. There had been the fact that he was a difficult, violent boy.

But then again there had been very little else. She hadn't even told them about what she'd seen him do, him and Delyth, over on those rocks on the south side. Maybe she should have. It seemed to incriminate him further, at the time, but now she sees it could have been useful. Essential, even. Then again, she wasn't even sure what she'd seen now; it was all a blur of limbs and rock.

"What if she's not even dead, Mwynwen?" Viv said, trying to fine-tune the tremor in her voice. She heard Delyth's laugh in her head. Enchanting and lilting and sometimes, downright cruel.

"Oh Viv," Mwynwen had said. "Viv *fach*. Don't." The baby clapped its pudgy hands together for no apparent reason. "Stay; stay tonight. It'll give you a chance to think things through."

The baby, whose undigested dinner sat smugly on its face, stared at her, mouth forming an o-shape, emitting no sound. She reached out and touched one of its thick fingers with her own. It giggled excitedly at her. She pulled her finger back and the baby tried to grab it. The further she drew her finger back, the more animated the baby became.

When she looked up again, Mwynwen had left the room.

For some reason, this reassured her. This small, simple gesture of leaving her alone with the baby seemed to be a concession on Mwynwen's behalf that said she was willing to trust her judgement, after all. Or at least, that's what it seemed to be saying, until Viv saw the reason behind Mwynwen's sudden departure. A draft had entered the kitchen. Mwynwen returned from the front door, mouth wide open, accompanied by Sister Mary Catherine, Sister Lucy Violet and a rather rueful-looking Sister Anna Melangell. They came levitating into the kitchen space like shadows, destroying the pure aroma of the kitchen with their own peculiar gust of linseed and fusty pages.

Elfyn ran out whimpering through the back door, and the baby's face crinkled with the promise of a good cry.

20

Elin had found something. Deian knew it the second he slipped in through the gate of Cae Uchaf and saw her gaze at him quizzically. And whatever she had found, whatever caused her to cast her eyes down in that solemn, stern way, and to shuffle with unease closer to Greta, was not something he had planted there. In fact, he had been getting increasingly sloppy with his attendance at the dig recently, let alone ensuring that his workers were kept stimulated. He was spending half his time at the south end of the island with Mererid and Elin, finding excuses to arrive at the lighthouse unannounced, often to an empty cottage, the afternoons trickling away as he sat there; waiting. For what, he wasn't even sure. They were merely weeks away from the completion of the survey; hardly the time to be leaving the women to their own devices, he thought, avowing once again to confine himself to Cae Uchaf until the work was done.

Elin had her hands over Greta's shoulder. They had bound their find in a dirty cloth, and it lay on the ground before them, like an offering.

"Don't be silly, Greta," Elin was saying, "it's probably only something like a cat. They used to have cats here, before they banished them because of the birds. It's probably one of the cats they buried, isn't it Deian?"

"It's one of the saints," Greta was saying, "I can feel it. Tell her Deian – it is, isn't it?"

Without answering, Deian moved on towards the ragged pile in front of him, and peeled back the cloth. He only needed a side glance to determine what he was looking at, and he wasted no time in gathering the pile into a cardboard box. He tried his very best to remain un-fazed by it – the last thing he wanted was these women getting excited or distracted when they were so close to completing the dig.

"Well?" Greta enquired, her voice a rasp of paper.

"Nothing to worry about," he said. "Probably something left over from the building of the monastery."

"Some*one* you mean," Greta insisted, following him down the path. "Let me see it again."

"You can't be fiddling with these things at this stage," Deian said. "It needs to be inspected properly."

"It's not out of the question, though, is it," Greta said, excitedly, "for it to be a saint? It would be some find, wouldn't it? Please let me have a feel of it."

Deian gathered pace. He couldn't afford her to see that he was panicking, but he couldn't have her take the box from him, either. He stomped his way towards the gate, trying to block out the sound of the object scraping across the bottom of the box.

"It really would be a great help to me if you just continued with the dig, ladies," he ventured, trying not to look at either one of them. "I see things like this all the time, and there really is no need to hinder the dig with something that probably bears no significance to what we're doing."

"How can you say that Deian? Insignificant, honestly," Greta said. "We're looking for the bones of the twenty thousand saints, aren't we?"

No we're not, Deian thought. *We're looking for nothing.*

"It can't be a saint if it's a cat," he whispered to Elin, while Greta was out of earshot.

"I was trying to comfort her, wasn't I? She gets so emotional about things, that one. The only person alive who cries over bones. I know I'm only a student, Deis, but if that was a cat, then I'm an elephant."

"Look, just get back to work, will you, both of you, and leave this to me. There's nothing to worry about, just a few old bones, that's all."

"Leri should be here right now," Greta snapped. "Where the hell is she with that camera of hers when anything actually *happens*, God knows…"

"Why don't we go down to Carreg Bach and get her?" Elin suggested.

"No, Elin." Deian's voice was steel-solid, for once. "We are to have no cameras, no speculation, and certainly no idle gossip. This is archaeology, ladies. It isn't glamorous. And I will deal with it."

He wanted desperately to get away from them both, from this field, from the churned-up orange which now seemed nauseating. He needed to be in the coolness of his loft, the box in front of him, the wooden darkness surrounding him. His hands were quivering by now, and he managed to keep them under control just for long enough to give the girls instructions how to proceed with the next part of the dig. Having done so, he rushed out of the field and back into the goat yard. For once, he didn't even glance down the path, as he so often did at this time in the morning, in the hope of seeing Mererid coming towards him. For the first time in many mornings, Mererid was not on his mind at all. He clambered the steps to his loft, feeling sick to his stomach, his blood ricocheting through his veins. He kept telling himself that they were, in fact, looking for nothing, and that what was in the box could turn out to be nothing, too.

Opening the door of the room, he found himself spreading a sliver of light into the loft, illuminating Iestyn's dribble on the mattress.

"Jesus, Deis, I've told you before, I've no interest in archaeology until after lunchtime," he wailed, as Deian shut the door behind him.

Deian went straight over to the worktable in the far corner of the room, hurriedly clearing a space on the table, hurling things onto the floor. His flint collection went crashing down without a second thought, as did his radio and mound of maps. He could hear the faint sound of Iestyn protesting in the background, but the pounding in his ears was by now so loud that it shut out anything that lay outside the frame of this table, this box, and its contents. His immediate reality became a blur which was shaken back into focus by Iestyn's arm on his left shoulder.

"Deian, slow down. What are you doing?"

Looking up into Iestyn's face, he felt queasy. If it was what he thought it was, then where did that leave Iestyn and his so called unsound conviction? He backed away from him suddenly.

"The girls found something," he said, still unable to hear his own voice.

"Big deal," said Iestyn, nonchalantly, as he began to roll a cigarette.

"They *found* something…" he said, his eyes drifting away from him. "They found bones. I didn't put them there, either."

"Oh I see," Iestyn chirped, "you're worried that actually discovering that there *are* twenty thousand saints here could be bad for business, is that right? Or that everyone will mock you for spending so many years insisting otherwise. Get over it Deian, for fuck's sake. *Callia.*"

Iestyn's contempt made something in him slacken. Perhaps he was being daft after all. He hadn't really looked at those bones properly yet. He wanted them to be something, he always wanted each and every find to have something, some trace of something left behind. And it never did, he told himself. All these years, all these reports, all the analysing he'd done and he'd never come up with anything that suggested more than what all the history books already told him. That the monks had been here, that the pilgrims had come, that the island had been full of people and their artefacts. It was the same story he was discovering again and again, the same narrative that the ground had given him since he had been a child. Time and time again the vision returned to him of his mother walking out into the sea. Sometimes from the Cavern, sometimes leaping from Bae'r Nant, other times pulped by the rocks of the south. He suddenly realised that he was being ridiculous. If there had been something in Cae Uchaf he would have discovered it, years ago. And what would she have been doing, lying in the ground there like some earth goddess? It was the stuff of soap operas, a convenient little scene that he had played out in his head. *Hen lol*, his mum would have called it, her head tilted back, laughing.

"Well aren't you going to show me what it is?" Iestyn whispered, putting his hand on the lid.

"No," he said, slapping his hand away. "It's mine. I found it."

He pulled the box closer to him, slipping off the cardboard lid in order to peer inside. A mess of small bones came toppling out, all across one another, sliding onto the table.

"You're telling me this is it?" Iestyn said dismissively, lighting a cigarette.

Deian looked at the pile again.

"It looks like a wrist to me," he said, breathless, "a woman's wrist, smashed." He felt the last words leaving his mouth as ghosts, barely clinging to the air.

"It also looks like a tractor-squashed cat," Iestyn said. At that point, light streamed into the room, making the pile in front of them sparkle and pigment. Mererid stood in the door, dressed in her green and white print dress, her dark hair feathering her shoulders. "So does she," Iestyn laughed, putting his arms around her. "*Haia cariad*," he said. Deian looked back at his pile, and back at Mererid and Iestyn, as they left him, descending the steps into the goat yard. The bones would have to be sent off to be examined. He would have to wait. He would have to fend off the dreams that would start to tell him, once again, that his mother's body was not at sea, but that it was all smashed up somewhere, scattered across this island in a million pieces.

It could just be a cat, he told himself.

21

Still no boat

That was all Leri could send to Clive before her phone battery died.
She had no idea whether the text had even made its way out of the
black rectangle and across the sea; such technological wonders had
started to seem impossible. Then again, even if he did get the text, she
realised the words themselves communicated very little. Clive must
know, if he was going ahead with his own plan, that there was no boat,
no means of carrying out what he'd intended. And the text certainly
didn't absolve her. Whether there was a boat or not, she was supposed
to be getting on with things, making the most of it. It was a chance
to prove to Clive that she wouldn't necessarily need the salvation he
was sending over. Looking back, sending the text seemed pathetic; a
cry for help. An admission; still no boat, still no story.

She was in stasis now; every morning seeming more and more
like an impression of the morning before. The glaring sun was
getting to her, a mocking reminder that even this watercolour of a
day, these ghostly blues and greens, could still deny her a boat. She
still didn't know what the definition of a traversable sea was, but it
was constantly on her mind, her eyes fixed on the patterning of light
clouds across the sky. She sometimes saw faces pigmented in the soft
whiteness, telling her there would never be a boat, that this was her life
now; this suspension in time. The camera lay suspended on Carreg's
windowsill, appearing to be melting, dissolving from view along with
her documentary.

Iestyn's avoidance of her was also a repetitive affair. It had amounted
to an art. She had seen him jump over hedges and walls; had even

seen him dive into a white cave on the side of the mountain once, pulling Elin in with him as additional armour, though she could see, even from a distance, that she hadn't been at the forefront of his mind just then. They met head on only in situations where he knew the truth could not be tackled, like in the goat yard on a sunlit afternoon, when the throws of a green tennis ball prevented her approach, or over at the site, between puffs of his cigarette and flips of soil, guarded by Deian's shadow.

So she'd taken to following him. One day she'd jogged after him at a distance, the camera on her back, as he made his slow, swaggering journey over to the lighthouse. But she'd regretted it, walking past the open window of the lighthouse cottage to hear the unmistakable sound of Elin's dress shuffling to the floor; Iestyn's laugh becoming low and murmuring. Rounding the corner, she found herself stared at by some bearded members of a Radio Society who were staying at the lighthouse, stacked in multicoloured sleeping bags over the ground floor. She'd had to improvise a quick piece to camera about radio orienteering, before pretending to go off and film some seals.

She was getting sick of pretending to film seals. Their upturned mouths and receding eyes haunted her, following her everywhere she went. She remembered Greta, on their first day, being enthralled by their slick bodies, their unearthly moans. Now, not only were they ordinary (there really were thousands of them, it seemed, glaring at you from every slippery surface), they were positively annoying, belching and moaning at every possible opportunity, and the more she zoomed in on them, the more banal they seemed to her. Out of politeness, she'd accepted Elin's offer to film her swimming among them one day, watching on through the camera's cold body as Elin burst above the surface in a purple wetsuit, her dark crown becoming one with her blubbery companions. "It was amazing, wasn't it!" Elin had shrieked as she climbed out of the water. "They were this close to me! It was just so...." Although she hadn't really filmed it, the scene played itself over and over in her mind. Leri could still see them, a host of dark eyes surveying her above the water.

She didn't know what to make of the barbecue that was to be held later that evening, on Henllwyn Beach. It had been Mwynwen's idea, apparently, something to bring together all the marooned islanders by clubbing together their provisions, to keep them going through the latest few days of desertion. Mwynwen had asked her to kindly leave her camera at home. These were extra days, she had said, *out of time.* Technically they didn't exist, and shouldn't be filmed, to avoid them being remembered.

"She's full of shit," Leri had said, packing her camera into a food bag, regardless. "As if anything exists out of time! She's mad. Why does everyone listen to her?"

"Leri," said Greta, taking the camera back out again. "Don't mess with Mwynwen. She's been here forever. She just says what's on her mind. You used to like that in people. Some of the islanders are funny about cameras, you know that. And with all this stuff happening, it's only fair that we let it go."

Fair to whom? Leri thought, thinking about Iestyn's eyes in the prison cell when he'd told her categorically that he *knew* something; that he was willing to share it with her. This barbecue was exactly the kind of thing she should be filming. Iestyn among all those people he'd left years ago. Slinging his arm around his lover's shoulder, trying to pretend he was like everybody else; it was the real crux of the documentary. She could hear Clive saying as much. Iestyn flipping burgers, mocking the rest of them with his indifference. "Look at him," they'd be saying. "After what he did." Mwynwen glaring at him, still suspecting him, even now. Viv, cowering in the shadows (Leri was sure she could be coaxed into it), looking on, uncertain. Thinking that maybe she'd been wrong. It would be spell-binding. Prize-binding.

"Leave it," Greta's eyes warned her by the door of the cottage. "Please, Ler. It's not right. These people are our friends, now. We've already got what we came here to film. Let's just enjoy ourselves, hmm?"

Greta's lips were sucked inwards from view, her chin paling. They hadn't kissed for days now, Leri thought, although there was some covert concession in Greta's eyes that suggested that if she let the camera be, they could start getting back to where they started. But Leri had come too far. She was too close to let anything stand between her and the documentary, especially something as mutable as Greta's eyes.

"Establishing shots only," she said, slinging the bag over her shoulder and cupping Greta's chin. "I promise."

They were drawn on by the smell of burning lamb. Leri was once more annoyed by the perfection of the scene. A host of silhouettes under a lavender sky, the waves whispering in the distance. Rounding the corner by the farmhouse, they were greeted by the cold stare of the twin goats, sniffing the air.

"It'll be you next," Leri shouted at them. The goats bleated back at her.

"Don't, Leri," Greta said. "It's not nice."

"Oh don't worry," Leri laughed. "We understand each other."

"They can't kill the goats," Greta said, "or they'd have no milk. Not to mention the cheese."

"Ah yes, the cheese," Leri said, remembering the peculiar taste. "Well, they can keep one for the cheese and kill the other for its meat."

"It's not going to get that bad, is it?"

"No," she smiled. "I mean it is the twenty-first century, supposedly; they're not going to let us die, are they? There'll be a boat soon enough."

"I'm quite happy to stay," Greta said, slipping her arm in hers, her elbow a tiny truce under Leri's left breast. Again, Leri got that feeling she'd been dreading. This was all she'd ever wanted, this closeness with Greta, her smile, that warm arm in hers, this night of summer, the smell of her unwashed hair becoming fragrant as it bounced to and fro past her nose. It told you a lot about love, one of her ex-lovers had once told her, when you could bear the smell of a lover's unwashed body. It had been almost three weeks since Greta had had a proper wash, and the strong, natural smell that was emanating from her body was something intriguing, attractive. Powerful. Leri couldn't bear to think what her own smelled like, despite the occasional shower over at the lighthouse, something Greta had plainly told her was cheating.

When they arrived, they moved between clusters of islanders, soon losing one another. Leri was cornered by a member of the Radio Society; wanting to tell her about the latest communications made that afternoon, which then evolved into a discussion of futuristic microwave equipment, and where the future of amateur radio was heading. Leri watched Greta moving among the crowd, sharing a laugh with Deian, a cigarette with Mererid, eating a piece of grilled goat's cheese straight from Iestyn's palm. She saw how much Greta had become a part of things. The old holiday-maker, documentary-maker tag had long fallen off her. She was one of them now; an islander. The dig, those various chats, had made her so. In effect, she'd networked without knowing it.

She watched the evening go by as if in some kind of trance, sitting by the edge of Henllwyn beach, the night passing through fire-blurred air. They were privy to the most wonderful sunset, streaming over the small beach, over the islanders, giving everybody a golden glimmer. Iestyn and Elin seemed to be attached to one another by an invisible piece of string by now, and it only took a simple tug for one or the other to go hurtling back under a protective armpit. *Damn him*, she thought, realising how far he'd moved from her, from the documentary, from all those things that had been said in Cardiff.

"This is what happens, every time," she heard a voice behind her say, turning around to see a silhouette of Mwynwen, arms crossed. "When there's no boat, they all start to lose their heads. They seem to think it's the end for them, so they cling on to one another."

Leri and Mwynwen looked on at the spectacle of Elin wrestling Iestyn to the ground over the last piece of lamb burger. Above them, Deian and Mererid stood, laughing, avoiding one another's gaze. Standing so close, without touching. Greta stood perfectly still with her back to them all, smoking her cigarette and watching the light die out over the water. Leri wanted to go to her, put her arm around her middle, feel the stillness again.

"I suppose they can't help what they feel," Leri said. "It is like a kind of madness, I suppose."

"Yes," said Mwynwen. "It is madness. And people will tell them so over and over but they won't listen. The only way they'll ever find out what it really is, is when they leave. When they try to make it work without all this. Then they'll see it for what it is." Mwynwen's tone had softened by now. *I've won her over,* Leri thought. Maybe she'd started viewing things differently. She rose to her feet, to meet her face to face. "Look, Leri," she said, once their eyes had levelled, "I still don't think it's right that you brought him here, but as long as he's not doing anyone any harm, as long as he doesn't try to stir things up with Viv, it's fine by me. It's really good that you didn't bring the camera, tonight. I really appreciate the gesture. Greta told me you've got more or less everything you need. There should be a boat soon, and then everything can go back to normal."

Before she could reply, Mwynwen's two-year-old grandson had come hurtling into her skirts, causing much chaos and hilarity by nearby onlookers, and making his big sister bawl out, running after him in her pink dress. Hoisting the boy onto her shoulder like a shawl, she walked off to stop the girl teetering off the grass bank in a whirl of chiffon.

Leri sank back into the grass bank, clutching a canvas bag full of crisps, plastic glasses, and a camera that she may as well eat, for all it was worth.

Two hours later, the fire was dwindling in the distance, with the last few party-goers gathering in a ring around its heat. Elin's head was lodged on Iestyn's shoulder. Deian was staring into the fire. Greta and Mererid were singing a Welsh song they both knew, some pop tune Leri vaguely remembered booming off the dance-floors of Clwb Ifor Bach in Cardiff in the mid-nineties. They got to the chorus and began harmonising, swaying before the fire, arms outstretched, before collapsing into one another in a pile of out of key giggles. Seeing this spectacle now reminded her that Greta was younger than her, more adept, and could somehow ease herself into anything without making a nuisance of herself. Leri had evidently become a nuisance to them all, sat as she was a little to the left of the main party, taking small, solitary swigs of the Penderyn whisky (their emergency stash) that everyone else declined; and did not seem to need.

It would get worse, she thought suddenly, when they were off the island, when she and Greta tried to make it work without all this, as Mwynwen had said. How long would it be before she was confined, not to this tiny shore of pebbles, but back in Shorepebbles on Womanby Street, their favourite bar in Cardiff, watching Greta laughing in dark corners at something being said by a person she couldn't quite see. She imagined Greta smirking later at Leri's accusations, telling Leri to leave her alone, to get a grip. Pushing her glasses back up her beautiful nose.

She realised that this moment, tainted though it now was with the singing, the laughing, the turning of Greta and Mererid's backs to go and paddle in the water together, arms slung over one another as though they were the best of friends, was almost as good as it would get. No boat, no story; but it was all she had, she realised. And with this in mind, she rose to her feet, and made her slow, silent trudge back to the cottage, saying goodnight to no one.

22

Mererid will always remember this. This stagger up to the winding lighthouse path, drunk, swathed in the rotating light which brings her face out of the darkness, with Deian at her side. She doesn't know where everybody else has gone, all that is happening will only make sense to her tomorrow morning when she sees the littered beach, the last embers of light in the fire in the distance; for now, all she knows is that Deian is by her side and that they are headed towards the lighthouse cottage, alone. Just the two of them. He follows her into the courtyard. He's been quiet all night, not himself, somehow. She smiles at him, but knows it's too dark for him to be able to see more than the luminous glint of teeth. Once they're beyond the lighthouse, the light is no longer on their side, stretching its slivers out to sea. It abandons them as they step into the shadows of the cottage, not a gas lamp or torch between them.

She stumbles into the kitchen, grappling for a light switch first of all, for which she is mocked by him, in whispery, soft, asides. She then feels around for a drawer, finding it empty. She recalls Elin taking their matches down to the beach. She tries the pockets of her combats for a lighter, then remembers giving it to Greta. All the while she is panicking, thinking that if she finds no light, then eventually Deian will go. He won't want to sit here in the dark with her. She bangs against kitchen utensils, worktops, sends a chair flying across the floor. Deian picks it up and asks her what she's doing. She can't see anything now, she can only hear his voice, somewhere in the corner of the room. She wonders if she should follow the voice, bump into him by accident, get right up close to him to see what happens. Knowing him, she can't imagine him doing anything intimate, like kissing her. Yet he must have done this with others. There have been lovers; ones they've talked about. Fran, who he mentions every now and then, seems to have been the last; though it is never clear whether she is still in his life. She stubs her flip-flopped bare foot against the table and swallows a yelp. The whole room sways and she allows herself to be carried by the dark waves of the room, swimming in her own drunkenness.

Wherever he is in the room, he's taken a seat, and is sighing quietly to himself. He tells her he's had an odd few days, and that just being here, in this dark, is comfort enough, for now. She wonders how it looks to him, or how it doesn't look rather, to be standing in this pitch black kitchen listening to a woman searching for a light, desperate to keep him there. She stops where she is, and is glad that he cannot see this awkward pose of hers in the darkness, both hands behind her back on the rim of the sink, body pushed forward, as though it is expecting something; as though it is expecting him to react to her in some way. They stay silent for a while, listening to one another's breathing, until their eyes break ever so gently through the dark. Mererid suddenly can't remember now how this has come about, why Deian is here in this kitchen with her. The wine and vodka is still surging through her head, and she knows she cannot allow herself to sober up; it would spoil everything. She flounders her way towards the fridge, finds the two bottles of beer that she and Elin have labelled their emergency stash. Right now, this is an emergency, and nothing seems more important than handing one to Deian in the far corner of the room, and feeling his fingers brush lightly against hers.

He asks her about Mark; knowing that he was supposed to visit her again today. Mererid tries not to think about that final phone-call by the flagstaff, of Mark's frustration, of her thinly-veiled joy when she told him all boats were cancelled for the next couple of days. She doesn't want Mark's presence in this dark room, standing between them, illuminating the whole room with his brash, living-room lighting. Even in the dark you could feel Mark, somehow, he would be there with her, breathing into her, fingers pressed onto her skin on all those nights she didn't really want him. With Deian, it's not like that. It's not quite knowing where Deian is in the room that excites her, his gentle voice with its dark currents.

She wants to tell Deian of the elation she felt when Mwynwen called by to tell her there would be no boat; her round, exasperated face at her window that morning was like something she'd written into her own story. Not only was it something to keep Mark from her, but to keep her and Deian close together, to ensure that nothing changed, that he did not leave her. But she can't tell him; because she isn't, as far as she knows, supposed to know that he wants to leave the island. He isn't to know that she heard him, a few days ago, having a conversation with Howard over the radio system about using the lifeboat to get off the island. Something about work; something he needs to see to. A conversation that came crackling into her consciousness as she sat there eating her breakfast. It was what she's been waiting for, and what she's feared, all this time. The fact that he has the freedom to leave the island, to leave her, comes as a shock. She's started to lose all perception that time moves on; the fact that eventually, he will leave, they will all leave. She exhaled only when Howard's voice came booming back a few minutes later telling Deian not to be so ridiculous, he would have to be patient like everybody else. He wasn't going to risk killing them all for the sake of a few bones. Then, after a pause, a softer voice added that perhaps the bones could be sent over with the fishing boat that was soon to be passing through, as long as Deian entrusted them to the rough ride the tide-race would give them.

She hears Deian swishing the lager in the back of his throat. She does the same. They still haven't mentioned what happened at the barbecue. She knows that there's so much about Iestyn and Deian she doesn't know, that she will never understand. The way they looked at one another when Viv rose to her feet in frenzy, her hair drawn out in grey rags under the rim of her habit. Elin stopped smiling; Greta receded into the shadows, and it was then, at that moment, that Deian took Mererid's hand. She remembered the feel of it still, that palm closing around hers, yet she knows, with her head bobbing in the dark as if separate from her legs, and the vodka streaming its way through her, that it wasn't a romantic gesture. It was necessity. That's why he's sitting here now, she thinks, in the dark with her. Because of all the things she will never understand because she isn't an islander; all the things that she will never be. It's this thought that makes her loosen her grip on the side of the sink, shake her sly, seductive pose into something else more fitted to pitch black.

"Maybe I should go back and check that everything's alright," he says, suddenly, the words hurtling at her through the void.

"Maybe," she says. She wants to tell him not to go. But she can't. She can't plead with him. Not in darkness, over something she's not sure she even wants. She's scared that someone will turn on the light and she'll see that it's Mark sitting there in the corner, testing her. "I think it'll be OK," she trips over her words. She doesn't know if it will be OK. Suddenly, she cannot breathe, as her mouth releases a slow ooze of saliva, which she swallows down, again and again. "I feel sick." The darkness is coming towards her in splashes of yellow, seeping over her eyes. She fumbles her way to the toilet, trips over the red bucket. She can't remember what the protocol is for vomiting in the only flush toilet on the island, so she rushes outside. Once the air hits her, that's it. She pukes unceremoniously over the lighthouse wall. She doesn't get up, she hangs there for a bit, arms over the wall like two strips of meat, the wall cool against her forehead. When she lifts her head she sees that it isn't as dark as she thought it was, and Deian is sitting on the side of the wall with her, handing her a tissue. "Thanks," she says, gurgling.

"No worries," he says, his voice far away. "Want to go for a walk?"

They reach the bird hide, and go inside. She's already written the poem about being in here with him; peering at the skim of sky through the opening. What she hasn't anticipated is sitting here feeling as though the life's been scooped out of her, with vomit in her hair. The morning is pushing up through the sea, coming in at them in small bursts of purple light. He's still elsewhere, she can see it in him, but he has chosen to be elsewhere with her, she can't deny herself that tiny joy, despite the sharp ache in her stomach, her burning throat.

"Didn't you want to check?" she started.

"I walked to the top of the path," he replied. "When you were being sick. No one left on the beach now. They must have sorted it out themselves. Gone home. That's how it is in this place sometimes."

"Iestyn," she began, thinking about what Elin had been telling her over the past few days, dreamy eyed, down by the rocks. "He was acquitted, right?"

"Yes."

"And you're OK with him... being here?"

"He didn't do it. I never thought he did. It was everyone else, all these madwomen of the island; Viv, Mwynwen, they were the ones pointing the finger."

"But you were a child..."

"I wasn't a child," he barked. "I was eighteen. I knew my mother. I knew him. He didn't do anything. I know he didn't. Someone might have, but not Deian."

"So you do think she was killed, then?" she asks, wiping her mouth.

"Maybe. I don't know," he replies, his voice drying out.

He lifts a pair of binoculars to his eyes. She takes in his peculiar, wooden scent. It's like nothing she's smelt before. She realises that she doesn't need anything other than this. Just this small bird hide, the two of them. Let us never leave, she thinks to herself, starting to panic as the morning comes streaming in, lighting up their hair, their faces, their eyes. The reality of that boat is coming ever closer. She wants to put her fingers to the gap, hold back the light, stop it from happening.

"Will there be a boat, tomorrow, do you think?" she ventures.

"Today, you mean," he answers. Today. The word made her throat tighten again. So that was it. Today could take him from her. "Shouldn't have thought so. Should take a few more days yet for this to pass. I really need to go, to be honest. Found these bones. I've already sent them over to be checked out, but I'm starting to regret not going with them myself now. You can't trust anybody else to do the job for you, unfortunately."

"Don't tell me you've found a saint," she quips.

She isn't sure what to make of the look he is giving her now, dark and dolorous. She'll spend the next few days trying to capture it in words, trying to pinpoint exactly what it is that's changing between them, in the fetid air of the hide, as she tastes and regrets her own sour mouth.

The moment is lost when the wooden door is flung open by a sobbing Elin. A thousand thoughts scatter out, like a flock of birds.

"That's where you were," she cries, "I came back and you weren't, and it's been, just the most awful night and I..."

She falls into the bird hide alongside them. Today becomes another no-boat tomorrow, and even with Elin sinking into her arms, Mererid can't help but feel that the docked boat is secure, far away in Pwllheli. Deian rolls his eyes, and takes Elin's other arm.

23

s per usual, it could all be blamed on Sister Mary Catherine.
She'd loved the idea of the communal barbecue; to her it was
something akin to Jesus feeding the multitudes in Bethsaida.
As they set off, however, Viv was hoping for a miracle more like the
one at the marriage in Cana; for she would undoubtedly need her
water turned to wine if she was to get through the evening. Where
this endless theologising left them in terms of the sacrificial frozen
lamb that would be the barbecue's mainstay, she wasn't sure. Not
to mention that Howard's portion control was always inexorably in
favour of himself; hardly the most Christian of attitudes.

For the past few days, she'd allowed Iestyn to exist on the margins
of her consciousness; as someone who merely provided the backdrop
to her existence. She occasionally heard laughter outside the cottage
and peered her head out to see him among a crowd; his arm draped
occasionally over Elin's slim shoulders. She'd heard him fixing
something on the roof of Plas for Howard, and smelt the whiff of
fresh, white paint, when he'd given the window frames of the bird
observatory a new coat. Iestyn was like any other volunteer, she kept
telling herself, like those boys that kept being sent over by Gwyn
to serve their penance for something or other. She usually ignored
them, scowling with a peculiar kind of distaste at their bare-chested
dope-smoking, their sloppy Welsh as they hollered at one another and
turned up their radios. She would treat Iestyn with the same distaste.
They would co-exist, side by side, and he would serve his penance,
quietly, dutifully, until there was a boat to take him away. Then,
everything could go back to normal. She could go back to polishing
her plaque.

But the sisters had different ideas, of course. Even though she was now granted leave from the hermitage, they were still insistent on conducting daily prayer groups in her kitchen in order to offer guidance and support, their hands linked in a too-tight chain, with Elfyn trying desperately to force away Sister Mary Catherine's grasp with saturated licks, something Viv had spent hours training him to do. But nothing could deter Sister Mary Catherine in these moments of zealous clarity, in which she always emphasised that every day without a boat was an offering from God, who saw the need, she said, to keep them there to help Viv, and that the seas would never again be calm until Viv's inner tide-race had been stilled.

It sounded somewhat of a sensitive internal complaint to her; the inner tide-race, but she kept herself from saying so.

Viv had started to fear, despite their ramblings, that what the sisters were really praying for around that table was for the boat to stay where it was. They seemed to talk of their day-to-day existence on the island as a commonplace occurrence, as though their homeland isles of Caldey, Lundy and Llanddwyn were faraway, imaginary shores. They'd started making amendments in the hermitage, moving furniture around, making sure they got the best view during meditation and evening prayer. They'd taken to wearing the medieval gowns of the saint-shrine as housecoats. And as they forced Viv out of her cottage that evening, and down to the barbecue, they had even started to talk of establishing a rota for Church services. The implication being, that they could stay on a few more days even if the boats did resume their journeys, to make sure Viv was truly safeguarded. Viv fell behind, urging Sister Anna to follow her.

"Please tell me they're not serious about staying on," Viv said, taking Anna's hand lightly in hers.

"Don't you think it would be nice," she said, "all of us living here together? Supporting one another. Haven't we all struggled on alone long enough?"

"Anna, we're supposed to be hermits," she spat, hoping that her indiscretion would be lost to the wind. "Hermits don't live with other hermits! Otherwise we'd be…"

She struggled to find the antonym for hermits.

"You can look for it all you like, there really isn't one," said Anna, smugly.

"And why's that, do you think? We're not supposed to be anything other than what we are," she replied. She watched Elfyn bounding on ahead, comfortably lodged between Sister Mary Catherine and Sister Lucy Violet, his wagging black tail disappearing into their habits. Not Elfyn, too, she thought, sourly.

"This business between you and Iestyn," said Sister Anna, "it's all terribly exciting."

"Oh, well I'm glad it's entertaining," Viv spat.

"No, I don't mean it like that. I mean, Sister Vivian, you've been good to me, you've always listened to my ramblings about my daughter Arianwen, and you've given me solid, sturdy, if not occasionally controversial, advice. Now I think it's my turn to help you. Our turn."

"Anna, listen to me, don't let them brainwash you into thinking…"

"Oh I'm not, Viv dear, but Sister Mary Catherine is right, there is something symbolic about this scenario, something we can't ignore."

"Symbolic?" Viv cocked an eyebrow.

"Yes, of course. I mean, as Sister Mary Catherine says, if you don't see it, it's up to us to illuminate it."

"Illuminate what?"

"Oh come on, Viv. We all know Mary didn't always get along with Jesus," said Sister Anna, rustling off towards the scent of the sacrificial lamb.

They never noticed her slipping away at the foot of the path. She veered towards Solfach Beach as they trundled onto Henllwyn, and located a corner of the beach which kept her neatly tucked from view beneath a shadow of gorse at the bay's border. She knew that Elfyn had spotted her less-than-swift tumble into the shadows, but also that he'd keep quiet about it. She watched as the sisters entered the crowd, as their long black drapes caused the usual awkwardness among the short-sleeved crowd. Elfyn's head twitched in her direction, his ears cocked, ready for her command. They met one another's gaze – eye to dark eye over the dim horizon – and understood one another perfectly.

"Where is she?" she heard Sister Mary Catherine say, her voice rising above the flames. The three of them turned, looking right at her, while she hid behind some billowing blades of grass. Right on cue, Elfyn snatched Sister Lucy Violet's lamb burger from her hand and went hurtling towards the waves, dragging the whole tawdry scene behind him, as far away from Viv as he could muster.

She was waiting for her moment. She didn't want to be a spectacle. And her being in the same vicinity as Iestyn would undoubtedly be a spectacle. It was what Leri had been preparing her for, she now realised. She wouldn't yield. It was her against them now; from the perfect look-out, the upper vantage point. Or at least, it was for the first five minutes, until she remembered that Solfach Beach was often the nearest urinal for most of the wine-fuelled islanders. Its dark discretion made it so. She'd narrowly missed being doused in Howard's holy water. She'd witnessed a rather embarrassing fumble between two birdwatchers, and Elin, still in her wetsuit after a swim, crouching down, baring all, quickly followed by a laughing Mererid, smoking and urinating at the same time, the smoke and steam blending together. Leri had then walked the length of the beach alone, while Viv remained cloaked in shadow, watching her. All these had been and gone without knowing she was there. Her shadow empowered her.

But it didn't take long for the moon to force its way out from beneath the clouds, giving the bay a light silver shimmer, and her shape a little too much definition.

"Bloody hell Viv!" Howard had said, zipping his flies back up, "what on earth are you doing down there?"

"No need to shout," she'd said. "Are they gone?"

"Who?"

"The sisters."

"Who's sisters?"

"God's sisters, Howard, the nuns."

"I didn't know God 'ad sisters. He was an only child, wasn't he? I thought that was the whole point." He was close enough now for her to smell the mingling of whiskey, masticated lamb, and night-sweat.

"Are they still there, or not?" At this point, Howard came flying off the edge of the bank, knocking Viv sideways onto her back. Trying to steady himself in the soft sand, he soon opted for the more solid support of Viv's upper body. "Howard, in the name of God, will you get off me!"

A face she recognised as Mwynwen's came swimming into her line of vision, pale in the moonlight, the eyes bulbous and black.

"What do you think you're doing with my husband, Sister Vivian?" she said, her voice tingling with amusement.

She looked up to the rounded silhouette of Mwynwen's body against the night sky, and hooked at her waist, a splayed fan of baby hair.

Once she'd been assured that the sisters had left, she ventured with Howard and Mwynwen back to Henllwyn beach, where the barbecue itself was starting to die out. Strewn all over the pebbles were the remnants of things half-consumed, the barbecue dark and charred. At the far edge were the last few party-goers, congregated around some lilting flames; Iestyn among them. Mwynwen had assured her there was nothing to worry about.

"You never did anything wrong," Mwynwen told her, "and it's not you who should be hiding."

But while she nodded her head at Mwynwen's words it crossed her mind again, like it so often did these days, that perhaps Iestyn hadn't done anything wrong either. He was here, on this island, like everyone else. There had been no law preventing him from crossing those waters. She'd heard them say on the radio that it had been a baffling case. Delyth had never been found. Could still be alive, for all they knew. But then there was the small matter of no one having seen her leave. The impossibility of her being anywhere but here somewhere, melted into the landscape, trapped under the green, deep down, knotted up in weeds. The thought of bright-eyed Delyth being dead had never quite rung true with Viv. That peachy flesh seemed always too vibrant. Viv remembered the last day she had felt that skin, the clean palm leaving hers, Viv's lips aching, wanting more.

They approached the crowd slowly. Viv had taken the baby, which was warm and soft against her chest, while Mwynwen pushed the other two grandchildren in a rusted wheelbarrow, where they clung to one another like foetuses, under a blue blanket. Stopping short of joining the circle, they sat down near enough to gather some of the warmth of the flames. Howard fell at Mwynwen's feet, and after a few jolted snorts, fell into a deep sleep and proceeded to snore loudly. After so many weeks of silence, Viv allowed herself to get lost in the noises radiating from the night: the warm baby gurgling in her arms, one or two of the party-goers humming a quiet tune, a far-off seal moaning into the blackness, the sea gushing over the dark pebbles.

And with these sounds soothing her, convincing her that for once, things were perfectly normal, she allowed herself to look right over the divide, straight at her son. She felt her glance moving across the circle as if on tightrope, and trod the last, risky steps up towards his face. There he was. Right in front of her, looking back at her, trying out the beginning of a smile at the corner of his mouth. She tried one out on hers as well but found that it did not budge. He was coughing up the night in those tar-filled lungs of his, and it became enchanting to her, soothing. The simplicity of sitting on a beach with her son sitting only a few inches away from her, enjoying himself with his friends. It was what normal people did. Perhaps once it was quieter, once more of these party-goers had gone off to bed, he would come closer to her. They could have their talk. She could ask him.

But she lost that quietude, very suddenly. Nothing could have prepared her for the sight of Elin paddling in those black waves, facing them all as though she had just risen out of it, her hair disappearing into the night, her pale skin shining like death. She was wearing a red and white shirt that was all too familiar. She was, right now, young and laughing, the spitting image of Delyth. And seeing Iestyn reach for her, guiding her back in with his hands, it made her remember something she would rather forget. Suddenly she was back looking at Iestyn with the same horror she had felt all those years ago, when she'd seen what she'd seen.

She stood up suddenly, entirely forgetting what constituted the warmth in her hands. Its descent was somehow unreal, a clump of skin detaching itself. Mwynwen was quick to catch the baby, which then let out a resounding scream as it fell into the net of her cold hands. Viv was startled by the noise, stunned by her own carelessness. As she stepped backwards, her habit snagged in a spike on the wheelbarrow's handle, screeching the wheelbarrow along the stones, tipping the other two children out of their dreams and onto the pebbles. They banged their heads together, and hearing their baby brother crying, joined in, a chorus of wails which went on to wake Howard. Howard, half-asleep, started shouting at Mwynwen to silence the children, his voice like gasoline to the flaming wails. A chorus of wails, shouts and moans now sounded over the beach, startling the previously calm crowd. Iestyn got up and walked towards Viv. She could see him coming towards her. Deian sprang up and stood between them, pushing Iestyn back.

"What did you do to her?" Viv found herself saying over Deian's head, "what was it?"

"I didn't kill her," Iestyn said. "I didn't! Do you honestly think I'd have come back here if I had?"

He'd broken free from Deian's grasp now and was close; too close.

"But you did something, didn't you? You had that cardigan, the blood," Viv's voice petered away. She couldn't remember what was real now and what the radio had told her.

"I shouldn't have kept it," Iestyn said. "I know. But it reminded me that I hadn't, I hadn't done it," Iestyn said, his voice cracking. "Just let me explain properly, Mam, please."

The words winded Viv. The radio had implied as much. They'd said Delyth wouldn't give him what he wanted. That it had enraged him; he'd lost his head. But then, Viv had seen them, that one afternoon. Delyth hadn't seemed reticent to her.

"Just go, will you! Promise me you'll go when the next boat comes," she cried.

"But I've only just got here," he said.

His eyes were hard now. Hard enough for her question.

"Where is she?" Viv said, again, her voice crumbling away. "I know you know!"

"I don't know where she is," Iestyn said. "But she might still be here, Mam. Don't you feel it?"

"I don't feel anything anymore," she shouted. "Why did you have to come back here?"

"Because it's my home. It's the only home I've ever known. Because you chose it. You decided we'd all be better off living here, remember? To teach Wales a lesson. And do you think Wales has learnt its lesson, hmm?"

"Iestyn, I…"

"Oh, sorry, I forgot. You wouldn't know. Cause you haven't even been there to find out have you? All these years? Block it all out. You know, you used to have fire, mother…"

"God is my fire," she spat.

"Really? Him and your little colonised comrades? Reading the Bible to each other in English?"

She turned and ran. She could think of nothing else to do, even though much later, she realised that she should have stayed there, asked him again and again about Delyth, until she'd understood it all. *It reminded me that I hadn't done it,* he'd said. In her turning heel was fear, fear that her silence was forever gone; that there would be nothing now but this noise. He had brought his noise to the island. The thought made her limbs heavy as she ran, the night cloying about her, and she found it impossible to find her way, bumping into the tiny hedges until she finally saw the lime kiln beaming at her in the far distance, marking the crossroads. Steadying herself there, she finally heard the only sound she'd been longing for all night, the barking of a dog, comforting like a light at the top of the path.

24

Deian had dreamt about the bones all night. They had come at him in various forms, sometimes forming into a shining white hand, a creeping, eyeless creature playing havoc across his body; at other times becoming the cat claw that swiped at his face from a great height, a black paw whose hairs stood on end. He woke in a sweat, not knowing where he was, until he slowly identified the white, cold space as the spare room of the lighthouse.

Ever since he'd sent the bones over on that fishing boat, they'd been worrying him. He knew how careless fishermen could be. He should have waited; should never have let them out of his sight. The box had been hurled into a pile of others, despite the FRAGILE he'd spent ages bolding across the cardboard with a thin biro. He couldn't see them making their journey to the mainland, let alone to the university, or into Fran's soft hands. The note accompanying the parcel could be sodden by now for all he knew, his earnest plea a mush of ink and paper.

The bright sun was pouring in through the open shutters, the beige tiles shining back at him. Its neutrality comforted him; filling his own mind, flooding over the night's troubling images and swallowing them one by one, until there was nothing but this whiteness, this bright light, this colourless floor. Sitting up, he recalled the moment he stepped across the threshold. How he shut the door, put his head in his hands, and slid to the floor, hearing Mererid's steps pattering softly away from him. That was it now, he'd made his decision to sleep here, to lie here in a room of bone-hue, rather than follow those steps to a warmer bed, a room full of colourful paraphernalia, smatterings of fabric, books, pieces of paper patterned with scrawled, bright ink. He chose not to lie down with Mererid in the midst of all that. He chose this. Like he always did in life. The blankness. The nothingness. It seemed to be what constituted him, if Fran's eyes were to be believed.

Last night had been all too familiar. The shouting on the beach, it reminded him of how things could get when he and Iestyn were little; Viv and his mother drinking too much, arguing about politics; him and Iestyn throwing stones out into the water, hearing them plop into the night. Every now and then his mother's passionate reasoning would spill over into crying, and she'd be telling Viv, through stifled sobs; they'd turned their backs on Wales, that they shouldn't be here, where they couldn't change a thing. Every one would forget them, and there would be no point to what they'd done. Viv always shouted back at her that it was what the country deserved. They needed to teach her a lesson. Wales had forced them to do this, and they needed to stick it out. He always remembered wondering how an entire country would even notice if it was two women down, or how it was supposed to feel the pain Viv kept going on about, the slap in the face; the kick in the ribs. Sometimes, in his room at night, he drew diagrams of Wales's shape on the map bending over, twofold, being kicked by two angry women.

And in many ways, last night had been no different. Viv still had that old stubbornness in her eyes, even when she'd dropped the baby. He'd seen it, in a flash, the look that told everyone it wasn't her fault, that it was Iestyn who was making her act irrationally, that dropping the baby, kicking over the wheelbarrow (for it was difficult to tell what a leg really got up to under a habit) was her way of spiting Iestyn. That Iestyn had to be taught a lesson.

Hearing the crackle of the radio receiver echoing against the kitchen walls, he got out of bed, pulling his loose trousers about him. They would be making a decision about a boat today. All night the party-goers had watched the rhythm and shape of the waves, trying to predict what was going on underneath. He'd seen the white peaks stiffening, and knew it was unlikely. A boat would change everything, he thought, his stomach knotted as he heard Howard clearing his throat.

"No boat, today," gurgled an evidently hungover Howard. It's still too dangerous and Brian doesn't want to risk it."

"How's the head, Howard?" he heard a voice booming from the

dark. Viv's. He laughed. Viv never used the radio system sensibly.

"Listen Viv, don't you come over all nun-perfect with me, I've a good mind to tell those so called sisters of yours…" his voice trailed away in a rustle.

"Viv, stop mucking about, and get off the system," Mwynwen said. "There's no boat today. I repeat no boat. We might make a decision tonight about tomorrow's boat. There are a few other messages; there's been a call for Leri from some Clive Matthews, Gwyn is wondering how long it's to take to finish the survey so he can get moving with the pet cemetery, and there's been a call for Deian from the university. Some Francesca wants him to give him a call."

Deian bolted at the sound of his own name, and picked up the receiver, pressing his face hard into it.

"Hi Mwynwen, it's Deian. I'm down at the lighthouse. When did Fran call?"

"About ten minutes ago. Says it's urgent. You can come and use our phone if you want."

"No, it's OK. I'll ring her from my mobile. Is Viv OK?"

"Sister Vivian is fine," came a voice. "Elfyn and Sister Vivian are discussing how to wear the next couple of turbulent days without causing too much mayhem. I'm sorry about last night. Are the kids alright, Mwynwen?"

"You won't get much tougher than toddlers," Mwynwen laughed. "We've all dropped a baby in our time, don't worry about it. Deian, remember to ring that Francesca back, now. She sounded a bit desperate. Hope you haven't got a young woman into trouble now, Deian."

"Down at the lighthouse, eh? At this time in the morning," Howard's voice chipped in. "What have you been up to with those young ladies?"

"Howard, put that thing down," said Mwynwen.

The kitchen plunged back into silence. He stared at the radio, longing for one last voice. It had been ten years now since he'd heard his mother's voice over that radio system. He tried to hear it again in his mind but it always changed frequency – sometimes it was light, other times denser, harder; he was never sure on which side of neurotic it had been, although the many clippings he'd collected seemed to suggest that there had been a quiver in her voice that day; that another day without provisions had driven her over the edge. Most papers, of course, said it was Iestyn who'd been driven over the edge. A young man of twenty, in that heat, starved of girls for most of his life, it had been too much for him. Deian hadn't pasted those clippings in his scrapbook. They made him feel sick. He knew Iestyn would never have done those things.

Although, remembering his mother's restlessness the week she disappeared, he wasn't sure. Sometimes he thought he remembered Iestyn coming out of his house, tucking his shirt back into his trousers, and his mother coming to the door soon after, with a strange look on her face. But he didn't know what he was really remembering half the time. It was a memory of a memory, unclear, hazy. He couldn't recall whose half-smile it was that made him suspicious. Or whose gentle gestures he'd brushed aside, dismissed as nothing. In court, he had said as much. It was nothing. He had noticed nothing odd, that's what he had said. In those summers, didn't everyone look at one another in that way? It didn't have to mean anything.

Just like those bones didn't have to mean anything.

He walked out to the flagstaff with urgency, his phone pulsating in his hand. He watched it swim back into consciousness, and dialled Fran's number. She left the usual seven rings before she answered. Her voice seemed odd to him now, a distant relic from his previous life.

"Fran, it's me; Deian."

She gasped at the sound of his name.

"Deian, it's so good to hear your voice. Are you still on the island?"

"Yup, there's been no boat for a while."

"Look, I'm sorry what I did. I'm really, really sorry."

"It's OK, Fran," he said, impatiently. "Honest."

"No, it isn't. I mean, leaving like that. Swimming away, I mean it was pathetic, not to mention hurtful. It's just, sometimes, things build and you end up thinking so much about the right way of doing things that you end up doing the completely wrong thing."

"It's OK," Deian said, exhaling, realising for the first time that he meant what he said. A weight had been lifted. He no longer had to think about the things he couldn't give her.

"Look, about what the doctor said," he heard her twisting the cord. "It really isn't the end. I spoke to him and there are things we can still do, you know. There are still ways. Say something, will you," she said. "Please."

"Maybe it's for the best. It's been six years, Fran, and you won't even move in with me. You won't even share my toothbrush. The idea of us having a baby was just ridiculous, if you ask me."

"Don't say that," she said, quietly.

"You wanted that baby a hell of a lot more than you wanted me," he said, relieved to have let it out at last.

"That's not true… and as for living together, you know I just don't believe in that sort of thing and it was just…"

"Just what?"

"Just easier that way."

"Who for, Fran? Who for?"

"For me," she said, finally. "But I love you, Deian, I do. You have to believe that."

"Then marry me," he said, the words falling out of his mouth before he'd had a chance to stop them. He'd said it before, of course, countless times, but this time it was different. This time he knew he didn't really mean it. He listened on ino the abyss, watching some sheep gathering around him, their curious eyes fixed on him. Far off, he saw Mererid at the cottage door, in a shirt, sleepily raising an arm at him.

"Deian, I…" Fran started, pausing, the promise of a longer sentence in her breath.

"The bones," he said, cutting her off. "Did you get the bones?"

Fran hesitated.

"Yes. I got them."

He held his breath. The cat claw took another swipe at him.

"The report came back from the lab just now. They are actually human bones," she said. "Probably female."

He didn't feel the way he'd expected to feel. In fact, the first thing that entered his mind was that the find was a real nuisance. The whole survey could be compromised. His exercise in nothingness had gone horribly wrong, for if this were to get out, then the whole site needed to be excavated properly. The island could say goodbye to their pet cemetery. Gwyn, the island manager, would not be pleased.

"So what are we thinking?" said Fran's voice. "Saint Josephine? Saint Teresa of Avila? Santes Dwynwen? Any one of those missing a wrist?"

He held his breath. He couldn't believe she was laughing. She stopped after a while. For a while he could hear nothing but the far-off sea and the blood pumping in his ears.

"Deian, you can't possibly think that it's your mother."

He didn't like her tone.

"What if I do?"

"No, Deian, these are probably old bones. We're not talking ten years ago. More like two hundred years."

"Is that lab-proven as well or is that just idle speculation?"

Fran sighed.

"Speculation, I suppose, but you don't really think that...."

"There's no need to come to any solid conclusions, is there? There's more work to be done. I think you're being hasty. I mean, you and I know you've been wrong before, haven't you..."

"Deian, listen to me, you can't keep deluding yourself like this. And can we please get back to talking about..."

It was so easy to switch her off. One touch of a button and she was gone. The mainland snapped shut in a moment. He stared out to sea. He realised how strong a force it was, how much it kept away from them all. Fran couldn't get to him now. He wouldn't let her negativity spoil this for him. The fact was, he needed to get back to Cae Uchaf, get the team together again. This time he wouldn't need to lie. He had knelt there, his heart low, pummelling away at nothing, when all the while, there had been something, lying ever so close to him. She was there, had been there all the while.

He had been kneeling at her feet.

25

"The boat's coming over tomorrow." Leri had gone with Mwynwen on her rounds of the houses late that evening, filming the sentence rippling its effect over the islanders' faces. Mwynwen hadn't objected to her being there, more than she had acquiesced; she had merely tolerated the camera at her shoulder. She'd tried to shut a few doors on Leri in the process, of course, which could be blamed on the wind changing direction. Leri merely smiled sweetly at her, frowning into her yellow raincoat once her back was turned. She needed Mwynwen onside if she and Greta would be granted a few more days in Carreg Bach on the grounds that they needed to capture the atmosphere of a departure; its actuality and its aftermath, she told Mwynwen. "We really need to get under the island's skin," she'd said, regretting her choice of words as Mwywen's eyebrow formed a furry arch.

It was Greta who'd smoothed things over, as usual. It took only one little cup of tea and a slice of lemon cake for their extra and final week in Carreg to be sealed; and all the while Leri waited for her grumpily on the farmhouse wall, goading a goat. "It's all going to be fine," Greta had said, emerging from the house and looping her arm through Leri's. "Another week and we should be done, don't you think?"

She didn't know what to think. She'd filmed and erased so many sequences by now that she wasn't sure herself what was left of the documentary. For Greta it had unfolded in a neat, linear narrative, following the usual peaks and troughs. "It's just like the story's been handed to us," Greta had said one morning, after they'd finished a short interview with a stuttering birdwatcher. For Greta it seemed that these little snippets of the island's reality were enough; as if she had never sought anything other than this thin strip of narrative that linked people with birds, seals with water, saints with the earth. And the lack of boats, the power they had to suspend and change a story entirely, throw people together, drive people apart, thrilled Greta. "It's as if this last boat is staying away so it can push us all together," she'd said last night, her breath warm on Leri's neck, "so that by the time we leave, these extra days, these days of stasis will have bound us like a knot."

All the while, Leri thought about the undoable knot of Iestyn and Deian, annoyed that Deian would not budge, that the last boat had not taken him away, as she had planned.

Filming the departing holidaymakers seemed another wasteful endeavour. But although Leri was going through the motions, she found herself fascinated by the response evoked by those five words, which seemed to be the words that each islander half-hoped-for and half-feared as they saw Mwynwen's torch approaching in the far distance. Many of the holidaymakers who'd been downright irate at the first announcement seemed now a little subdued at the thought that their ordinary lives could resume their rhythm; that their children's elated shrieks would once more be boxed in between the greyness of suburban walls. The three nuns at Carreg were clinging on to one another as they entered the hermitage, as though Mwynwen was some kind of apparition, the camera's light a message from above. They squealed inside the dark kitchen as the news came, and Leri filmed their faces writhing with indecision. They asked if they could stay on. Mwynwen told them absolutely not; they had a group of Cistercian Monks coming. Sister Mary Catherine clapped her hands together, telling them that was wonderful news. They were bound to be Caldey's Cistercian Monks, with whom she was well acquainted. She was sure they could come to some arrangement. They could cook for the Monks, perhaps, clean even. Offer the hermit's helping hand. Mwynwen told them that considering the Monks' frugal diet, she didn't anticipate they'd be needing catering. Sister Mary Catherine then announced, rather sternly, that she really didn't think this was a laughing matter. Mwynwen said she didn't see anybody laughing. Sister Mary took a step into shadow; Leri backed into a door. Sister Anna Melangell tried to explain, in a series of silky sentences, that it was hardly a good time for them to be leaving, considering Sister Vivian needed them more than ever.

"What Viv needs is space," Mwynwen told them, and was soon up the field again, with Leri running after her, filming the back of her shoes.

The jubilant ones were those for whom the boat symbolised an addendum, rather than an extraction, hungry volunteers that had spent the weeks craving such delicacies as sausage rolls and pizza slices, raspberry muffins and gin from pretty blue bottles; all those things that, in their absence, had begun acquiring a painful appeal. One woman had been dreaming about bananas, anticipating their feel, colour and smell for nights on end. Leri herself felt she was missing nothing, except perhaps the abundance of red wine her flat offered, though Greta would sometimes keep her awake for hours talking about her imaginary roam through a supermarket, plopping fantastically ordinary things into her basket.

Iestyn and Deian, they found swimming in the low waters of the Cavern. Their shrieks and laughs were like those of schoolboys, Leri thought, and in the low light they looked as she imagined they must have looked all those years ago, suspended in time somehow, ignoring their mothers' far cries.

"Boat going over tomorrow boys, eight o'clock," said Mwynwen.

It was almost too dark then to see the look on their faces, but Deian sliced his way through the water towards them, and said he was no longer eager to leave. *Why is he still here?* Leri wondered, thinking of all she'd done to try and get rid of him. It had seemed a stroke of genius at the time, pilfering a few bones from the saints' shrine and planting them in the field; she was sure it would distance him from Iestyn, send him off the island, searching for answers. And yet he had not budged.

"Weren't you positively desperate to get off the island, Deis?" she'd asked him, zooming up close on his face.

"I haven't finished the survey," he said. "I've got to finish it before I go."

"Shouldn't *you* be going?" Iestyn's voice came at her, piercing the dark.

171

"I haven't finished my programme," she said. "I've got to finish it before I go."

Mwynwen's light was already moving away, falling into the jetty's cracks.

"Will you be going tomorrow, then?" she asked Iestyn.

He didn't flinch. She knew he wouldn't go.

"I've got a few things to finish off, too."

Before she could reply, Deian's voice, thick with salt water, was calling out for her to film something. He was moving his hand across the water, catching, in the moonlight, fiery tips at the water's edge that made it look like the water was ablaze. Iestyn joined him, swimming around him in a circle to create a thin ring of silver fire.

"Sea-sparkle," said Iestyn, breathily. "I remember this now. Deian's right, you should film this, it's only in a certain light that you can get it. Look!"

He looked right up at her at that moment; not with indignation or mockery or all those other things she'd convinced herself she saw in his eyes, but with a boyish, earnest expression, throwing up a handful of shimmering water at her. She wanted to tell him to shove his sea-sparkle up his arse.

The last port of call was the lighthouse cottage. She waited outside the small window while Mwynwen burst into the brightly-lit kitchen, watching the whole scene through a muted glaze.

"Sorry to spring this on you, girls, but Gwyn radioed me today to let me know that you'll be getting a new housemate. A Ben Mitchell. Bird Warden. They haven't got room for him up at the Obs. so he thought it might be OK to put him here, in the spare room. Any objections?"

"How old is he?" Elin had asked. "I mean, is he, is he...?"

"Twenty-something," Mwynwen had said. "Won't be here much, apparently."

"I think we'll cope Mererid, won't we?" said Elin, with something like anticipation glinting in her eye. Leri zoomed in. Clive was right. The balance could be tipped, just like that, and at that one moment, she allowed herself to believe that it wasn't all over, after all. It was the shift they all needed. The boat coming over could change everything, everyone knew that. They'd all be down at the Cavern tomorrow morning with their eyes wide open, their hands splayed, expectant; waiting for whatever that would be handed to them.

★ ★ ★

The next morning, they were all there to welcome the boat. The food orders arrived, along with some new holidaymakers, denied lovers, a few Monks, food parcels that had been long-craved-for and letters with their sentiments long-passed. The cargo fell from grasp to grasp, forming a neat pile by the boathouse, while the returning cargo made its swift descent in the opposite direction; bin-bags, recyclable goods, fishing rods, and the glinting, heavy gear of the Radio Society. There was excitable chatter from almost everyone; those hurtling their goodbyes, those elated to be arriving. There was the sound of a gear-shift deep at the island's core.

The three nuns walked along the jetty as though walking the plank, their gnarled hands clutching their crucifixes, grumpily and jealously acknowledging their Brothers, who were to take their place. Leri moved to get a closer shot. She caught Viv walking behind the sisters with a solemn look on her face, yet one which quivered on the brink of relief. She kissed the forehead of each nun as she bid them farewell, and eased their trembling bodies into the boat, with Elfyn barking gleefully at her heels. Acting right up until the final moment, she turned to wave one final goodbye to the sisters, who then seemed to applaud her performance as the orange curtains of the life jackets closed upon them.

Leri had been so preoccupied with filming the departure that she had little patience to look at what the boat itself offered. But there he was, dressed in a bright green jacket. Ben Mitchell. She saw Elin's eyes being drawn towards him almost immediately as he climbed off the jetty and onto the island, swaggering across the wood, refusing all help with his things. He was perfect, Leri thought, amazed by what Clive had managed to throw in at this last moment, so late in the game. He was exactly the kind of character that they needed, and it was evident from Elin's response that she would play straight into their hands; or Ben's hands, anyway. Iestyn frowned from a cool distance. Already, it was working, Leri thought. Already she could feel her documentary coming to life, exactly in the way it should.

She filmed the boat leaving the Cavern, and was saddened by some of the looks she found. Sister Mary Catherine, a rather robust creature, had begun weeping; the nun next to her had gently taken her hand, although she, too had a look of desperation on her face, as though she were clinging on to these final moments for dear life. The third and final nun had her eyes resolutely shut, holding on tight to the side of the boat, muttering her final prayer to the surrounding waves. Either that or she was on the verge of liberating last night's final feast all over the members of the Radio Society.

26

Mark has not come. Mererid waits until the Cavern has emptied; just to make sure. The sky is cloudless, the jetty clean, the sea widening her reflection. There's no Mark. She feels a sudden pang of guilt; as though she's made this happen. This empty boat, this still, noiseless Cavern is what she wanted. She tries to capture Mark's face in her mind, and finds that it is already hazy in her memory. The sides of his face are fading, somehow, and he becomes a floating, bobbing mass of features; plain, like a cork in the water. He's too far now to grasp, like the mainland: foreign like the thought of her own feet against concrete; the squeal of her rubber shoe against an accelerator.

She still feels weak after her exchange with Mwynwen. She'd gone to make inquiries about staying on as a volunteer until December. It would give her something, she'd thought, when Mark arrived, something real and solid to cling on to, to counteract whatever he had to say to her. She had felt so bold charging in through the farmhouse doors, as though the rest of her life were somehow sealed. She felt she had proved herself as an islander; that this love she felt for this tiny inch of land would be written all over her, scrawled onto her, the island roots all knotted up like a series of blue veins under her translucent skin. Surely Mwynwen would see it. She'd even taken some poems.

It was the only thing she could think of doing. There was no other way. She is due to leave in a week's time. The next semester is stretching in front of her like a prison sentence, and the antiseptic-soaked corridors of the university are already invading her dreams. She can't imagine walking down them again, knocking on Mark's door for them to go for lunch, going from conference to conference, from lecture to jazz evening to piles of marking to corridor-bantering and finally, towards reading-week drinks and then her dreaded wedding. How strange it seems that she should have had a mainland life that never looked out towards the periphery.

She can still hear the slightly condescending laugh that bounced across the table when she made her pitiful request, and sees Mwynwen bringing her teacup down like a full stop. "Look," she'd said, "it's gone to your head, '*merch i*. You've been here five weeks, and you've had one day of bad weather – one day. You've got your friends, and it's one of the best summers we've had for ages. But you wait until the skies start darkening, until the whole island starts being turned over by that sharp wind."

"But it's what I need," Mererid had said. "Some solitude to finish my collection, and my contract with the university isn't…"

"Aren't you supposed to be getting married in October?" Mwynwen asked. Mererid had never mentioned this to Mwynwen. Very suddenly she felt naked, the way you do when you're being told something about yourself that has become common knowledge. She can imagine herself becoming an object in this very kitchen. *That girl*, they would say. *That Mererid, you know, the so-called poet. Doing no work. Haven't seen a poem, yet! Getting married, apparently. Spending all her time up at the dig.*

"The wedding can wait," she'd said. "Mark is very understanding. My work comes first."

"Ah yes, your work," Mwynwen had said, dragging the last word across the table.

"I brought you some poems," she'd replied, hastily, hoisting out her slim manuscript, wishing it were bulkier. She sat in silence as Mwynwen flicked through the pages; her eyes dulling as they deciphered the poems.

"Very pretty," she said, sliding the paper back at her across the table.

"Look Mwynwen, I really think…"

"It won't work," Mwynwen had said. "You're a nice girl, Mererid, but you don't belong here. You can have your summer with us, write what you like about it, but you're no islander."

The final words were sharp pricks to her skin; she knew Mwynwen was right. Walking back in the dim light to the lighthouse, she could feel the wind sharpening around her. Even the smells were different, the air gathering a moist dampness, eluding the spongy sweetness of summer. Soon everything that made the island for her would be gone. The cottage would be empty, its eyes looking out at no one, apart from the odd sheep. What she wanted desperately to hold on to had to be captured in other ways.

And knowing this, she has her little silver phone in hand, and is walking towards the flagstaff, ready for anything Mark will throw at her. She wonders whether she should be the one doing the throwing; he has not come, she has every right to be annoyed. Then again, she can't use this against him, for she can see the long chain of events that have led to this strange morning, and her first pang of loneliness since arriving on the island. She hasn't touched the phone for three weeks now. It's become a ticking time-bomb to her, sitting on her windowsill untouched, every now and then being brought to life by something the islanders call the phantom phone signal, the unreal, green glow that is some kind of hologram of life. It is at those moments that she switches it off, suddenly, afraid that there is a way, after all, for people to reach her. Afraid that Mark can be transported to her in some way through the phone.

Message after message comes hurtling into her inbox, the little envelope twirling in the green space. It opens invitingly, a small triangular wave of hope. Most messages are from Mark, asking her to get in touch. The last one has a fraught tone. *Any news on boats? Starting to get sick of waiting now. RING ME.* No kiss. She cannot bear to listen to her voice messages. Voices are something distant to her, now. She doesn't want to hear her mum's voice, or her sister's, or Mark's, or any other frequency that carries all the smug modulations of the mainland.

Breathing hard, she dials Mark's number.

"Hello?" He answers as if he doesn't know it's her, even though her name must come up on the screen.

"Hi Mark, it's Mererid."

"You're alive then." His voice is limp, deflated.

"Yes. I'm sorry I haven't been in touch." She wonders at her strange formality. She feels that next she will say something like. *Anyhow, we need to liaise about the wedding.* Instead she says, "It's been an awful couple of days. Awful. With the boats not coming. People have been stranded here for days. I mean there really was no way for people to get over…"

"I know, Mer, I checked." His voice is colder than before.

"How are you?" she manages, a strain in her voice.

"Fine, considering…"

"Considering, what?" she asks.

"Considering I had to spend the best part of this week cancelling our wedding."

She hears a clutter of plates behind him, a muffled cough.

"But…" Mererid pushes the word out to sea and watches it drift off.

"Are you going to tell me that's not what you wanted?"

"Mark…" her voice carries tears with it, but she can't force them out, they're not real. It makes her think of an artificial beach they once saw in Ohio.

"I'm not stupid, Mererid. Ever since you've been on that island you've been different. You were awful when I came over, just awful. So nice to me, so compliant, so willing to do anything I wanted, and yet you felt nothing. I could see it in you, nothing at all." So he had known. The whole day she had been acting, succeeding, she thought. And all the while it had been transparent. "You let me make love to you like you weren't even in the same room," Mark charged on, as if he'd been practising the speech for weeks, and it was his opening night. "You were cold, Mererid, cold and mechanical and plain strange. And then afterwards, I hear nothing from you. Three weeks, and nothing. I rang the farmhouse, just to check you weren't dead. You weren't. They said you seemed to be having a whale of a time. *Do you want me to get her?* that woman asks me. *No,* I told her. *Leave her. She obviously wants to be left alone.*"

She has the sensation of something crumbling inside her, though it's not entirely unwelcome. She thinks of searching for a trite excuse. Something about having no battery, no phone, not remembering his number well enough to dial from the warden's house, anything to get her away from this, from his *knowing*. Everything he's saying is true, she can see it, feel it. Never has she so desperately wanted Mark's approval, wanted him to love her, even wanted him to say that the wedding is back on, for this not to be her fault.

She hears the clinking of glasses. A familiar female voice calling Mark to the table.

"Margot's there, isn't she?" Mererid whispers, imagining the voluptuous form of their fellow lecturer standing right in front of Mark, hands tea-potted on hips.

"So what if she is? I think I at least deserve a friend right now, don't you?"

Mererid pictures Margot mouthing sympathies to Mark. She wishes she had not let Margot be right about her. She can imagine the consoling bottles of red wine they will drink together tonight, how they'll talk long into the night, listening to album after album change itself in the machine, and how finally, when Mark is on the verge of passing out, how a lunge from Margot will seem warm, wanted, secure.

"We can talk about this," she says suddenly, even though she knows she doesn't want to.

"What's the point. I've told everyone it's over now."

"Everyone?"

"Everyone who needed to know. Don't start telling me different now, it'll just confuse everyone."

More clinking, a shifting of a chair, a muffled, impatient sigh.

"My stuff."

She thinks of her books, her clothes, everything strewn around the house. She thinks about Margot placing her feet on her pile of beloved Derek Walcott books that she has never, despite Mark's repeated requests, moved from the corner of the living room.

"Look we can talk about it again, Mer, I've got to go now."

He's held out for so long, but on the last syllable, there it is; a slight crack in his voice. It sends ripples of disappointment through her, and she has never needed Mark's love more. She wants to say something to bring him back to her, to make Margot go away. But she can't. She lets him terminate the call, and she sits there, in the flagstaff, wound up and unable to cry.

She walks back towards the cottage as though trudging through tar. She does something she does frequently to get her through things, focuses on her feet, on their forward movement. She's realised recently that this can get you through most things, this focusing on the feet, the gentle movement – the notion that no matter how bad things get, no matter how nervous you are, or what insurmountable task lies ahead of you, that even small, size three feet, are perfectly capable of getting you through it. This is how she would have eventually married Mark, she suddenly thinks, one foot in front of the other, all the way down the aisle.

27

I estyn was pacing the room, smoking as if smoke were something to be swallowed. He wouldn't accept the cup of peppermint tea, or Elfyn's soft requests to rest his head on his knee. Viv felt that the only thing he relished about being in her house was being near her all-seeing, all-knowing window. He sat down purposefully by it as if it were a television screen, his eyes skimming the top of the island. They watched together in silence as Elin and the new bird warden came into view, backpacks on their shoulders, disappearing off into the far distance, walking closely together.

"She's too young for you," she ventured, wishing she hadn't, as those two black marble eyes rolled towards her.

There came a clunk from the shadows, as Leri's clipboard slipped to the ground.

"Sorry," Leri said, "nearly there now." Leri shifted the tripod around once more, while Greta scribbled down some notes. "I want to get as much of the island into the shot as I can. We need to give this a context."

To Viv it seemed that there was no difference at all between her recently-departed hermit entourage and these two girls in the corner of her cottage; if anything, the nuns were a little more decorous in their use of space. The camera crew's gear seemed now to be everywhere, miscellaneous black objects cluttering every single surface, jutting out in jagged angles. But she'd grown so accustomed to invasion; to the feeling that she would never again be able to shut her cottage door, that this seemed the normal routine life of any hermit. Get up, feed the dog, have breakfast, decide whether to allow ex-convict son back into your life, allow an infinite amount of busybodies into your house. She'd long struck the ritual morning prayer off her list; feeling that if she wasn't high up on God's list of priorities then he wouldn't be on her list, either.

Consenting to be filmed for national television seemed to be the next logical step, somehow. She was exhaustingly resigned to it all; and upon hearing of Iestyn's sudden request for the 'conversation' with her (a word Leri had curled between her thin fingers), she had no energy left to refuse.

She sat, therefore, in the only place left for her, waiting for the pantomime to commence; facing her preoccupied son. There was something strangely comforting about it. Certainly there had been none of the forced politeness she'd feared, he just stared out to sea, his face blank, as if he'd been sat here for the last ten years. It made her feel almost like a normal mother again. Just a plain old mother around the table with her son ignoring her.

She'd already said there were certain things she wasn't ready to discuss – the court case, for example, or anything to do with his time in prison. "That won't be necessary," Leri had chirped, "we only want to know what his boyhood was like here. Mother and son talking to each other in a frank, honest way. Hold this, Greta."

Viv saw something between them as Greta took the clipboard. The slight linger of Leri's palm against Greta's back, Greta exuding a bright smile. Viv wanted to ask them if it was worth it, what they'd done, the one thing she and Delyth had never dared to do. She thought back suddenly to that day when they'd reached the summit of the mountain, when they'd turned to one another. It had seemed so possible, nothing but the pounding muscle of sea surrounding them, the wind blowing their long hair into one another's faces. She'd reached out a hand, without knowing where it was going. And Delyth had moved away before it had landed. Viv had turned her outstretched hand into some surreal wave on the wind. Delyth had laughed and taken her arm. That had been it. She shook the memory away suddenly, banging her knee against the table.

She saw lovers here all the time; ones that would never have looked twice at one another on the mainland. Even a misunderstanding sometimes made its way towards a kind of truth. She remembered how Mwynwen said something to Howard all those years ago that

182

she hadn't really meant, not really, and once she saw Howard coming towards her, all bold hands and broad intentions, she'd succumbed to it; she'd realised that it *was* her truth somehow. "It's like from the moment I'd realised he'd misunderstood me, I started thinking that maybe that's what I meant after all," she remembered Mwynwen saying, biting her lip.

She'd seen it happening, over and over. She knew it had happened to her, too, with Delyth, almost without her knowing, creeping up on her in the middle of the night, the beginning of afternoons, the bitter, argumentative ends of each evening. She wondered if Delyth knew. Whether she was right about that strange look Delyth gave her in the door that afternoon she disappeared, the "Oh Viv" that had come at her like an apology before she had reached out and planted that one solitary kiss on her lips, that had ignited so much in Viv, a kiss that still tingled, even in memory. Before Viv had even been able to lift her eyes to look at her properly, she was already climbing the mountain path, the peaks of her red and blue headscarf flapping behind her, waving goodbye.

She saw now that these two in her kitchen thought they knew one another, just like she'd thought she'd known Delyth. They probably thought that the experience on the island would bind them forever. It wouldn't.

"OK then," Leri ventured, trying to draw Iestyn's attention away from the window. "Maybe we could start at the beginning. Try to make it seem natural. Just try to pretend we're not here." Viv listened to the purr of the camera and wondered what was natural about any of it. She was sat face to face with a man she half-recognised, who people kept telling her was her son. "Iestyn, you start."

"OK," he said, clearing his throat. "So, Mam; can I still call you that?"

"What else would you call me?"

"Sister Vivian," he said, not looking at her. "It's what everybody else calls you, isn't it?"

"Not everybody," she said. "Some people know that the title just isn't me."

"I asked the chaplain about you," he said. "In prison."

"You talked to a chaplain?" she asked.

"Don't sound so surprised. She had beautiful Welsh."

"A she?"

"Yes; Luned. She'd heard about the island. Said she'd been here. The isle of twenty thousand saints, it's all anyone ever knows about this place, isn't it? She wasn't surprised you'd become a nun after everything, she says it's often what people do when they've... been through something."

"I'm not really sure I want to be Sister Vivian anymore," Viv replied.

"Why not?"

"Because God's a bit elusive, isn't he? Never there when you want him."

"I thought the idea with God was that he was everywhere," Iestyn said, his gaze finally moving away from the window.

"Yes, but if you're everywhere, you can't really be anywhere, can you? I mean they say if you want something done, ask the busy person, but I mean, when you're *that* busy, you're really no use to anyone."

Iestyn burst out laughing. It surprised Viv, this sudden burst of sound, but she recognised it as the same laughter that had warmed her all those years ago; laughter that lit the shadow between them.

"So you're not a nun anymore," he said.

"Never really was. Didn't really ever qualify," she said, smirking.

She'd forgotten all about Leri until she heard her voice from the shadows:

"Look Viv, Iestyn, this is all very nice but... this really wasn't what I had in mind."

Leri made them change places. The light was catching too much of Iestyn's face, apparently. She wanted him cloaked in shadow, and Viv lit like a beacon.

"Ask your mother why she came here, Iestyn," she said. "In 1979, wasn't it? The referendum?"

"All seems a bit silly now, doesn't it Mam? Considering they've got their Assembly now, and you're still here," Iestyn spouted, his smoke filling the room.

"No it doesn't. It still makes sense to me," Viv snapped. "You wouldn't know what things were like, you were only two at the time. Things weren't really working out between me and your dad. He voted no to spite me more than anything, just like Jeremy, Delyth's husband, did." She managed a weak smile. "Me and Delyth wanted so much more than an ordinary life in Mynytho can give you. The referendum meant everything to us, everything. And we couldn't believe it when the news came that they didn't want it. I mean, that they'd colonised us so well that we'd started believing we didn't want our own freedom. You can't stay in a country that doesn't want its own freedom."

"It didn't want its own freedom, *then*, Mam," Iestyn said. "But things changed."

"You're telling me things changed!" Viv was surprised by the bitterness in her voice, bolting over the table at Iestyn, making Elfyn's ears rise in velvety peaks. How was she supposed to go back, with Iestyn in prison, Delyth dead in the water somewhere, how could she ever go back?

"We moved here because it seemed to be so separate somehow, from all the rest of it. An island that governed itself, even if it didn't politically. Where everyone spoke Welsh. I didn't want to be in Wales, but I couldn't leave it entirely. It seemed plausible enough at the time. It seemed like the only option."

"It was a happy option," Iestyn said. "For a while, wasn't it? We were happy here."

"Yes we were," she said, feeling something tugging at the root of her. She saw Iestyn and Deian running towards her as little boys, breathless, arms full of their south-end finds, Delyth calling at them from her cottage that dinner was ready. Howard calling by with some strips of bloodied rabbit wrapped in paper. "I suppose so. It seemed like there was only one piece of land where all the usual things hadn't happened, where colonisation hadn't yet hit, and maybe would never hit. It seemed the only possible place for you to bring up a child speaking Welsh and for them to be safe from everything else."

"And do you feel it is safe now?" Iestyn asked.

"I thought it was. Until one day you notice a little thing here, a little thing there. Wardens, coming and going. Birds attracting people from all over the world. Bilingual signs going up. Before you know it you're in a minority again. Especially when you haven't got anyone to talk to, I mean to really talk to."

She nearly said Delyth's name. But couldn't bring herself to do it.

"Like Delyth you mean," Iestyn said.

"Yes," she said, her vowels trembling in her mouth. "Yes, like Delyth."

"Is that why you made her a saint?" Iestyn asked. "That plaque in the cemetery, it seems kind of... misplaced."

"She was a saint," Viv said. "She was taken from us."

"She took herself away," Iestyn said. "Killed herself, Mam."

"She never! Don't you dare say that!"

Iestyn rose to his feet.

"So you'd rather believe that I killed her. You'd rather testify in court that I'd been acting strangely for months, for *months,* Mam, that I was fixated with her, or some rubbish like that, than believe that she actually killed herself? That she didn't want to live here with you?"

"Iestyn, sit down," Viv pleaded with him, feeling the air being sucked out of Leri's lungs, the camera whirring its approval.

"No, I will not sit down. I've been sitting down for ten fucking years in a cell in Cardiff because of you. And because of her! For all I know you both plotted it! Send him to prison, and his Welsh will improve twofold! She's probably waiting for you in some bloody retirement home over on the peninsula."

"Iestyn you are being ridiculous," Viv said, her motherly voice gathering strength.

"Am I?" Iestyn said, hurtling into the corner of the room, out of the camera's reach. "Like you were, when you decided to turn your back on me? You'd rather believe that I killed Delyth than believe anything else, *that's* what's ridiculous."

"There was evidence, Iestyn, they convicted you," she replied, trying to reason with herself. "What was I supposed to think?"

"One fucking cardigan," Iestyn spat. "And I just so happened to be the last one to see her; well big deal..."

"Her prints were on you, you'd... been together," Viv said, the words sour in her mouth.

"So? It doesn't mean I killed her," he spat.

"But you seemed so cold in court. Showed no remorse," she said.

"That's because I hadn't done anything!" Iestyn said, banging his fist against the table. "I couldn't believe it was happening."

"She wouldn't have killed herself..."

"You and I both know how worked up she could get about living here. About being forgotten. About life passing you both by... Wales passing her by."

"She was happy here," Viv said. "It was our dream."

"*Your* dream, Mam. Yours. The day she disappeared," Iestyn said, "she was being spiteful, refusing me."

"Delyth wasn't like that," Viv replied sourly.

"Oh here we go," Iestyn said. "Well she certainly wasn't like you, Mother. She didn't want *you*, did she? Is that what all this is about?"

Viv couldn't believe he'd said it. She pushed the table away from her and got up.

"That's enough filming for now," Viv said, standing in front of the camera.

"But," Leri said, "that was great."

"We understand," Greta said, tugging at Leri's sleeve. "Come on Ler, time for us to go."

"I really think we should stay," Leri said. "I mean it feels like we're really getting to the crux of something here."

"I'll give you a crux if you don't leave this minute," said Viv.

She shoved them out of the door, hurtling their gear after them. She walked back to the table to face her son. He was still that two-year-old at the top of the stairs, wrapped in the Laura Ashley curtains.

"I don't want to die not knowing what happened to her, Iestyn," Viv said, "surely you understand that. I loved her. We all loved her."

"She wasn't a saint," Iestyn said bitterly.

"And who was?" she replied. Tentatively, she put one of her hands on his. They were soft, warm. The hands of a boy. "Delyth's one of them, now. One of the twenty thousand saints. No matter how she acted. She has to be a saint. It's the only way I can see her, now, please try to understand."

"Deian says there aren't any saints here, only bones," Iestyn replied.

"He would say that, he's an archaeologist," she said. "They're only interested in solid things, real evidence; not something as inconclusive as a saint." The sea was starting to awaken, far off in the distance. Iestyn's eyes were still drawn every now and then to the top end of the island. "Do you have any idea," she asked tentatively, "what happened?"

"I'm not sure," Iestyn replied. "I've had ten years to think about it. About the last time I saw her, tracing those steps, wondering, over and over again where she was going, what she was up to."

"And?" Viv looked into his eyes. She was afraid, after all these years, that she would finally be given an answer. She was afraid of it being the wrong one, the unsaintly answer, something that would make her stop polishing her plaque.

"And I don't know if I'm right."

For the first time in years, she thought it would be better if she never knew. She wanted nothing more at this moment but this, her son at her table, his eyes wandering away from her, his palms smoothing themselves against her mahogany table. She wanted Delyth to be gone, to be at peace, to stop rearing her beautiful head between them. Hearing a sudden knock on the side window, she shooed Leri and Greta away as though they were two verminous seagulls.

28

They'd been shovelling for four long, sweltering days, and had found nothing. Deian had done most of it alone; having long lost his power over his harem of volunteers. It was primarily his own fault. He'd banned Leri from filming the dig, he'd finally given Mererid (or so the others joked) something to write about, and Elin was blaming her new-found interest in ornithology on him not encouraging her archaeological flair, as she flounced off toward the Bird Observatory. The only two who stood by him were Greta and Iestyn. Greta seemed only to spend time with Leri when it was necessary these days, spending most afternoons working diligently by his side, urging him on through the heat, the sweat pouring down her face in tiny streams.

Iestyn worked like never before, overturning the soil with relentless gusto, anything, he said, to take his eyes off Elin trying to extract herself from him in a series of back-turning brush-offs, so that she could start a relationship with Ben Mitchell, bird warden and bulk-of-biceps. "She won't tell me straight," Iestyn had said, staring into the soil, "because that'd be saying it's her fault. Nobody round here takes the blame for anything; you noticed that? It's like everyone's saying it's the island's fault they do anything. Not that I care. I mean it was only a fling, wasn't it?"

The field lay naked and exposed before them; the survey complete.

Deian now had to decide what he would tell Gwyn. He either told him about the bones he'd found, demanded that a proper excavation be carried out, or he said nothing, and allowed a whole lot of Bardsey pets make their bed at its core. Fran's words returned to him again and again. "More like two hundred years, Deian," and he knew she was right. He had known from the moment he'd seen those bones, although something inside him had let him believe that maybe this time he'd actually struck against exactly what he'd been looking for.

He decided to tell Howard to come and fill the whole field back in, and tell them to proceed with their arrangements for the cemetery. No one need ever know about those bones. The last thing he wanted was for people to get into some frenzy about another saint, for there to be more camera crews here, more clipboards and speculation. No, he would keep the bones to himself. They could go into his private collection, become his own patron saint. It probably wasn't even a saint, anyhow, he thought to himself. He always did think that was just a far-fetched marketing ploy. The wrist probably belonged to a wench from one of the pirate ships, knowing his luck.

Iestyn hadn't been sleeping well. He'd woken Deian up several times in recent nights, thrashing about in his sleep as though he were drowning in his sea of blankets. Deian recognised his mother's name peaking above the tempest every now and then.

One morning, Deian awoke to find his friend peering over his bed.

"We've got to go around the back of the mountain," he said. "Today."

"Why?" Deian asked, half-asleep.

"Because I need to see it. One last time."

"OK, well go then," he replied.

"You have to come with me," he said.

"Why?"

"Because you have to."

The back of the mountain was one of those places you didn't go; not if you weren't completely well-versed in its dangers. It was somewhere they hadn't been together since they were boys, when they had been fearless enough to ignore the peril of its sharp gradient, a green angle that shot straight down into the rocks beneath. They'd scurry down there every summer to see the Seal Cave, squeezing into that tiny fissure of rock where you could see the seals close up. Deian remembered staring down at their moist heads from that tiny ledge, holding his breath. He also remembered Iestyn throwing down clumps of dirt at them, disturbing the tranquility of the moment, the fleshy mass segregating, throwing them their icy stares as they slunk away.

Deian had attempted it alone, a few years back, becoming dizzy as he descended down towards the cave. But he lost his courage completely in the end, clinging to clumps of grass as though they were safety ropes, feeling as though the entire world was sliding away beneath him. The back of the mountain had become too painful for him, chafing him with memory as he clambered his way back up. Police had searched there, all those years ago, moving along the outline of the rocks, looking for his mother. He remembered sitting at the top of the mountain in the deep dark, watching them pull an object out of the water and shining their pale torches on it.

He thought Iestyn meant it as a kind of pilgrimage for them both. A final journey of discovery, perhaps, before they parted ways. But when Deian turned up to meet him at the bottom of the mountain path, he saw it had turned into a Sunday school trip, complete with hats, sandwiches and large grins, with Mererid, Elin, Iestyn, Greta and Ben Mitchell back-packed and all bound up in hiking boots.

"So, Iestyn says you're going to show us this Seal Cave," Ben Mitchell enthused, his white teeth grinning back at him.

"I'm not sure that's what I..." he looked to Iestyn for salvation.

"I told them all about the Seal Cave," Iestyn said, his face yielding nothing. "It's a great place to see seals, just behind the mountain, isn't it Deis? There's a little ledge for you to sit and everything."

"Yes, but it's really not that safe, taking such a big crew around the side of the mountain," Deian protested. "I mean, Gwyn really wouldn't approve."

"Well, Gwyn's not here, is he?" Iestyn said. "If Ben wants to see the cave, we should let him see it! Come on, this way, everyone."

Before he could argue, Iestyn was leading them up the path, ensuring that their five companions provided the breakwater between them. All the way up Deian felt sick, feeling the precipice creeping ever closer in clumps of purple heather, dreading the mass of roaring sea that would be laughing up at them once they reached the summit. Deian found himself wondering whether Iestyn had planned the expedition as a kind of bizarre prank; to drive Elin and Ben apart once and for all. Elin, it would seem, was still undecided. When Deian looked up the first time, he saw her and Ben with their heads bent close together over a wild flower; the next minute, her arm was sneaking its way around Iestyn's waist. Iestyn would occasionally draw her in, then shuffle her off again. Ben didn't seem to mind this, and when Elin fell behind, he was trying to interlace his fingers through hers. Mererid and Greta were noiselessly conversing about the whole saga, their awe bouncing off their sunglasses. It really wasn't the ideal atmosphere for sliding down the side of a mountain, Deian thought to himself, peering back over his shoulder. He had a strange sensation they were being crept up upon by something, or someone, but when he turned to face his fear, he saw nothing, just a mound of mountain hair swinging in the breeze.

When they started their descent, he found himself assuming a stern, fatherly tone.

"Don't lean into the wind," he told Mererid, seeing her small frame grappling with the air's angles, "lean back into the mountain if you can." He had visions of her tumbling to her death right in front of him, breaking her teeth on the rocks. Elin, hearing this advice, let her whole body fall back into the mountain side, giggling as she fell against Ben, pulling him down with her. They both slid forwards cautiously on their behinds, sliding down towards the sea on the pale yellow grass.

"Get up," Iestyn told her, trying to grab the back of her coat.

"No," she said to him sternly, "Leave me alone."

Iestyn, of course, refused to lean back, nearly toppling over.

"Cut it out will you?" Deian snapped into the snarling face of his friend. "You'll get us all killed."

"Come on Deian," Iestyn said to him, in Welsh. "You and me used to do this all the time. We practically rolled down here."

"That was when we were two foot nothing and totally fearless," he retorted, "and I don't know about you, but I'm shitting myself now. We shouldn't have come here. I don't think the girls can handle it. And I hardly know that Ben. I don't want to be responsible for the death of a stranger. It would very irritating." A wide smile slid across Iestyn's face, revealing his crooked teeth. "What?" Deian said.

"Welcome back," Iestyn said, slapping him on the back. It wasn't until then that Deian realised he'd said the whole of the last sentence in Welsh. He felt something, right then, on the edge of the mountain, the sea beneath him laughing, the language rolling around in his mouth once again; a curious moment of balance. But just as suddenly as it had come, it had gone. He found Mererid by his side, her pale cheeks turned a proud purple – and yet he could say nothing to her in her own language. At that moment he was nearly knocked flying to his death by the sliding behinds of Ben and Elin.

"Will you watch what you're doing!" Deian howled. "I go in front, the rest of you follow, those are the orders."

"Yes sir!" the three of them had saluted and smirked. Deian shook his head, walked on, and did not look back.

After some painful manoeuvring, they finally reached the entrance to the seal cave. Deian walked across to its entrance, a small opening on the side of the rock. He didn't remember it being so small, he thought, realising that he was probably too thick-set to get in. Elin and Mererid would be alright, with those narrow hips of theirs, perhaps he could get them in first. Pondering this, he caught sight of another figure, descending from a different direction. It was evident from the way she shuffled backwards a little when they saw her that she hadn't wanted to be seen. He realised that his feeling of being watched had not been ill-founded, as Leri came clambering down towards them, camera in her hand.

Deian was annoyed. Someone must have told Leri they were coming. Someone had leaked the information. He shot Greta a look, but far from complicity, saw something else entirely pressing itself into her pale face, something like shock. He saw, in the way Iestyn gestured to Leri, that it had been Iestyn who'd told her. He wasn't surprised. He'd seen Iestyn's reticence to be filmed fizzling away over the past few days. He was becoming reckless, showing off, enjoying being the centre of attention again.

"You shouldn't be here," he said sternly, to Leri. "It's not safe. There are too many of us down here as it is."

He wanted them all gone. He wanted there to be no one but him, like all those years ago, staring out bleakly to the water and wondering, if he stayed there long enough, whether he would eventually become part of the island's very fibre, fossilized within.

"Look, I won't interefere," said Leri, zooming in on him. "I'm happy just to get a feel of the place. Would you say something about what you're doing now, Deian."

Deian sighed.

"I'm not sure I know what the hell we're doing down here, to be honest," he said, throwing Iestyn a look.

"You've come to see the seals, haven't you?"

Her clipped accent was really getting on his nerves.

"Do you really think any seals are going to come near this cave if they hear us? Can we all be quiet please, so I can get people into the cave. Then you can see what it's all about. And that," he said, pressing his finger right into the camera screen, "is not coming anywhere near the seal cave. You can film people going in, and that is it. Look, can we just get on with it. The tide's against us," he said, watching the swell of blue encroaching.

He gestured towards Elin first, instructing her to crawl in on her stomach. "Who will catch me at the other side? Will there be something to hold onto?" she asked nervously. He told her to trust him, lowering her in gently. Soon enough, he heard her gasping from within, her voice echoing around the cave. "Why it's beautiful! It's so..."

"Elin, shhhh," Deian whispered into the gap. "Quiet."

Next it was Mererid's turn. He thought of asking Iestyn to help her in, but knew that his reticence would betray him. Already people on the island had started to talk about them, in the way only islanders could, sustaining a piece of information for days, feasting on it like hungry moles. This one gesture of his of asking Iestyn to take over, just so as not to have to touch her, could dominate an entire evening discussion. No, he had to act normal. She paused before coming towards him, as though she were waiting to be asked, he thought, as though she *knew*. He was extra cautious with those frail hips of hers, watching her black mac submerging under the beige rocks, and holding on to her legs for a moment longer than he had with Elin, just to make sure. The second after she disappeared, a white hand suddenly hurtled once more through the opening and grabbed his – a gesture of thanks, he assumed, yet it had sent an electrifying surge through him.

He then made his own way to the opening. He sensed Leri behind him and quickly turned around.

"You are in no way allowed to film me going in," he said, imagining his bottom appearing on the documentary. "You haven't got my consent to film anything, and I won't have you in there, disturbing things."

"But Deian…"

"No," he said firmly.

"We have to get the shot of…"

"Later," he said, reluctantly. "I'll take you lot in later. For now you can stay there, and behave yourselves. Don't wander around. And be quiet – or you'll frighten the seals."

He dropped to his knees and made his way into the cave. He just about fitted, though he'd had to pull a little harder on the surrounding rocks to hoist his waist through. Mererid and Elin were already sitting on the ledge, the pale blue water flickering on their faces. He grappled his way around the corner of the cave and sat between them. He made sure he didn't lean against Mererid.

"Ben," Elin started, "I thought he was…"

"There isn't room," Deian asserted, motioning for Elin to be quiet.

The three of them sat there for several minutes in complete silence. They waited and waited, watching the reflection of their dangling legs in the water until eventually, the seals came. One by one, they came sloshing into the cave, unaware of them at first, and then later, when they saw them, staring up at them with a docile curiosity, their dark eyes dancing in the shadows, their white whiskers grazing trails across the water.

Then, they heard something. Something they tried to ignore at first, so indecipherable was the sound. Deian tried to ignore the sounds that followed too, those sounds that came spiralling into the cave, of raised voices, the sound of something being hit, something cracking. The noise didn't seem to disturb the seals; and the purity of the moment remained. Until Elin spoke.

"I think I'll go and, you know, someone should check what's going on."

Her voice boomed off the walls, and two seals swam hurriedly out to sea once more.

"Great Elin, thanks for that," Deian said bitterly.

"I want to... something's not right and...." Elin rose to her feet and cautiously manoeuvred her way across the strip of a ledge, back over to the opening. As the cave emptied, he found himself sitting right next to Mererid, wanting now, more than ever to reach out and touch her. She looked up at him and smiled, a welcoming open, smile, which seemed to be some kind of invitation. *Just do it,* he thought. His hand embarked on some kind of journey. It had lifted itself up as if independent from his body and as soon as it set sail, he knew it would have to land somewhere.

Just as the tips of his fingers touched Mererid's black-silk hair, and he had enough courage to bring his other hand up to greet the other side of her face, they heard the sound of sobbing coming from outside. It wasn't one they recognised, it was deep and throaty. Mererid's hair bolted away from his hands. He still wanted to ignore the sound, to coax the scene back into existence so that he and Mererid were face to face, her hair in his hands, but he couldn't. Mererid was gone – she had already wriggled her way back up through the cave entrance.

He squeezed himself back into the scene, away from the darkness and into the light. He found it hard first of all to reconcile what he saw in front of him, which was Mererid with her arm over Leri's shoulder, Elin's eyes darting off into the distance, as though she were looking for something, and Greta sitting on the grass bank, staring down into the waves below. It seemed as though nothing had changed, apart from the absence of Iestyn and Ben – one of whom he could make out at a further distance up the mountain, running away from the scene.

"What did he do?" Deian asked, knowing that it had to be Iestyn.

"They started fighting," Greta explained. "When they were climbing into the cave. Iestyn pushed Ben forward and he came back and tried to punch him."

"Tried to?"

"Yes, he tried, but, he missed. Ben fell into Leri and, everything happened so fast. I didn't know what he was doing, and then he was just gone."

"And it's all my…" Elin sighed.

"Where is he, then? Where's Iestyn?" he said, suddenly recognising the runaway bottom as that of Ben Mitchell.

Leri looked at him, her eyes rimmed red. There was something wild about her now, something desperate. She'd been hit on the side of her face with the impact of Ben's fall, causing a gash. She didn't seem to be in pain, just vacant, as the blood dripped out through her fingers. Suddenly he saw what she was staring at. At her feet, in a million mangled pieces, was her camera. It was entirely snapped in half, combusted almost. The tape deck was open and the tape had been damaged too, or rather looked as if it had been pulled out. He could imagine Iestyn mangling it in front of her.

"Where's Iestyn?" he asked them again, searching the four corners of the mountain frantically for his friend.

"He's gone, Deian," Greta said, her voice hoarse and raspy. "It was so quick. He just ran. Then he was gone. It wasn't like he jumped or anything, though I suppose he must have done." Her voice trailed away into nothingness, pointing towards the rocks. Deian walked in the direction of her finger, and stared down. He tried to steady himself as he confronted the dizzying distance. The thrashing waves made him think again of Iestyn in his bed last night, submerged in his own sweat. He shouted Iestyn's name.

"Where is he?" he asked again, turning around to greet the pale faces behind him, hating the sound of his own thin voice, echoing deep into a darkening afternoon.

29

Elgar's cave was cool and empty, like Leri soon hoped her mind would be. This side of the mountain, facing inwards towards the island, felt much safer to her. She'd crawled in as far as she could on her hands and knees, and when she could get no further, she lay down, her breath hot on the damp rock, inches from her face. She fumbled for a lighter in her pocket. It felt like the only thing she had left, and it was enough knowing it was there, though she didn't know what she'd eventually end up doing with it. If she made a fire, they'd know where she was. And she didn't want anyone knowing where she was until she'd had time to think things over, to stop her heart ricocheting in her ribs. Instead of tears, there were droplets of sweat pouring from her eyes. Though she longed to close them, she couldn't bear the sting of dark that lay behind her lids. The open-eyed dark was better. As long as she saw the stone directly above her, she felt safe.

It had been so much easier to let Deian believe that the mangled tape had been Iestyn's doing. Leri wanted to believe it too. If she convinced herself hard enough, then telling Clive didn't have to be an ordeal. It would just be one of those things. Like when cameras got blown up in war-zones or wildlife footage got destroyed underfoot by charging elephants. Technology was vulnerable – it was the price it paid for its brilliance, simple as that. And if you put yourselves in volatile situations, that's what happened. She had other tapes; there were fragments that could be assembled with some clever editing. No money had been wasted; and that was the main thing, the company never cared about wasting time. They wouldn't care about having wasted her, either.

She would have to tell Clive it had been his fault. *We pushed him too hard,* she'd say. *It backfired on us. Ben Mitchell was a step too far.*

Walking back from the back of the mountain that afternoon, the life had drained out of her along with the blood on her face. Greta had torn off a piece of her shirt as a tourniquet, but it hadn't stopped the bleeding, or helped with the pain. As her wound pounded onto the material, her story went with it, and she felt as though her whole career was nothing more now than a viscous drool on this one cloth, which may as well have been her cleanly-pressed BAFTA dress.

Once they were over the peak, the whole island had come into view. She'd seen everything from this great colossal height, exactly as she had done with her camera, seeing the lighthouse in front of her, a gleaming promise, seeing the houses ingrained in the mountains, the people coming and going. She saw Mwynwen, in the distance, swinging a grandchild around in her garden, and thought about the interview she'd had with her that morning which was now no more than a strip of tape trapped by a blade of grass. It had been the best piece to camera so far. Mwynwen's eyes averting hers when she started opening up about the island; letting things slip about Delyth without knowing it, almost. No one ever killed themselves here, she said, it just wasn't what you did. It was too easy, for one thing. That vast ocean surrounding you, day in, day out, always waiting to engulf you, a silver invitation that goaded you each day. "You don't go with it," Mwynwen had said. "Even though that's what you feel like doing at times." Her fingers reached to wipe the sentence from her mouth, almost as if she knew it would be the perfect end-of-part for the documentary.

It had been her final tape. The clincher. Even from a distance she'd been able to pick up on the tensions between Ben and Iestyn, had caught Elin loitering in limbo between the two. She even captured Deian all irate and tetchy, twitching by the cave entrance. Not an islander, not an archaeologist, just an irate man at the bottom of a mountain, while Mererid gazed at him, the poem she wanted to write already far better than the poem itself would ever be. They'd all come alive for her, becoming themselves, somehow, or at least the selves she'd always wanted them to be. The selves they would never be again, after this moment. She remembered Iestyn's words, clear as a

Bardsey morning. "I have to go around the back of that mountain," he'd said. "I know I'll find what I'm looking for."

That morning he'd told her he was ready to do it, at last, and wanted her to come. To film whatever he was about to do, which, according to him, would give her the closure she wanted, and would change everything. Careering down that mountain, she was a burst of ambition, knowing each step took her closer to her masterpiece, to the look of approval in Clive's eyes, to the feel of a trophy cool against her hands.

She knew Greta would be with them. Greta snuck off on her own with the camera these days, filming what she thought was right, she always said, insisting on clinging on to certain tapes. She'd allowed her these few concessions, thinking that perhaps she'd be able to make use of some of the material in the long run. The documentary would need careful pacing, after all. She may well end up needing some of the more ordinary, boring moments that she imagined Greta had been capturing. Elin's countless swims among seals, Mererid's early drafts being scrunched into balls, Deian's indentations becoming deeper each day. These could all find their place.

The day on the mountain had been crucial in every way. Its dangerous angles, the fact that the wind was against them, it was a drama gently unfolding. Deian had been restless, seething, wary of everything. She had hoped she would have been able to follow them unnoticed for much longer, but there had been nowhere to hide. The mountain side was bare, naked, honest. Treeless, just like the rest of the island.

But then, at the last minute, her focus had been wrong. She'd stood in the wrong place when Ben and Iestyn had embarked on their fight. Her last shot was Ben's hand launching through the air towards her. For the first time in her life, she lost control of the camera, watching it being lifted into the air by the impact, before landing on those rocks outside the cave, fragmenting into several pieces. The blood came away in crimson patterns in her palms. She felt weak. A smile wriggled itself onto Iestyn's face. "You're buggered now, aren't you?" he'd said, laughing into the wind.

"Iestyn, please," she'd said. "We can get another camera out here

200

in a few days and…"

He'd laughed right into her face.

"Do you really think I can't do anything unless you're there? I was going to give you this one last gift, Leri. But you've gone and fucked it all up now. See you around."

She hadn't got up when she saw him go. She just stared at the empty space in front of her, while the blood kept coming. There was too much being taken out of her for her to take anything in. Greta had run towards the precipice, screaming.

"The tapes," she mumbled. "The tape will be alright; is it alright, Greta?"

That moment, she felt everything changing. Greta's eyes were darker than they'd ever been.

"The tape," she kept saying, "get the tape out."

"How can you be worried about the tape?" she'd screamed at her. "Iestyn's just gone and killed himself!"

The mainland swung at her like a big pendulum, making her drowsy.

"The tape," she said again. "The tape."

She didn't remember how long it took for Greta to return to her side and hold the tape up to her face. Through the one eye that hadn't yet closed she could see it was intact. Or at least, it was for that moment.

Her eyes failed her, but she had registered the noise. That peculiar fluid scratchy sound of a tape being mangled. She'd done it before herself when her projects had gone wrong. She knew what was happening. Greta was pulling out the tape, making ribbons of it, doing it so calmly and methodically, undoing her story in front of her.

That was when she'd let out that desperate cry that had been locked inside her for so long, and let it resound, hearing somewhere in the far distance, beneath the whisper of ribbons taking to the wind, the sound of seals sloshing away. She let them carry her to a place she'd never been before. Where there was nothing but blackness.

From the moment she'd come to, she did nothing but crave the calm she'd experienced during that one moment, where there was simply nothing, her mind perfectly empty. She'd never fainted before, and had found it positively exhilarating. Like being dead, only better, because you got to wake up and do it again. When she'd tried to get up, she'd gone floppy, as though she were hoping to fall back into the place she'd just been. "Make an effort, Ler," she'd heard Greta saying, her voice sounding strange to her ears. But she couldn't. All she wanted now was that darkness, again and again and again.

She still couldn't really remember the moment it had happened, how she'd found her way to the small white cave. She couldn't quite pinpoint when she'd realised that it was in her power to leave them; to get here, to shroud herself in the darkness that she sought. It had happened too suddenly. They had finally got her up over the top of the mountain side, and were urging her to walk a few steps alone. She felt her entire body weighed down, as she made her silent trudge towards the rest of her life; Elin snivelling behind her, Greta in front, facing the wind, and herself in the middle, knowing her story had gone. Even Iestyn had gone. And she had that strange sensation that something in herself had gone too. The essential, congealing part of her, that held everything together, was somehow broken. The join was now a mass of weak ribbon, nothing held itself in place anymore, not like it was supposed to. Her legs were heavy, her brain would not start up again. But she knew that there was a way of saving some small part of herself; or at least, to keep everything together until she had the freedom to fall apart. Even if her body was weak, her brain defunct, she still had her will. And her feet.

And that's when she started running. It was brave, considering her legs were so weak, but she'd somehow gained strength in the very endeavour, until her limping canter turned into a bold charge, sprinting away without any desire of stopping. Away from those two voices behind her, away from the path, an ungraceful, stumbling sprint away from them all. All the while she'd been terrified of stopping, of looking behind her, and it was only when she finally did, that she realised what she ultimately feared: that they wouldn't be chasing her. Only since she'd grappled her way through the green, thrown herself down her own path and then to the cave; only now did she feel truly alone. And she didn't like it.

No more than she had liked shivering by the cave, still in her shorts, with all manner of small creatures writhing in the dark around her. It was September now, with an Autumn lingering in the air, biting at her ankles. The walls of the cave offered no warmth. After a while, however, it hadn't seemed to matter. She'd just lain there, staring at the ceiling of the cave, flickering her lighter on and off, on and off, until its flame had dwindled to a scratchy spark. It had felt like she was waiting for something, though she didn't know what it was. It wasn't for Greta. Greta had ruined her tape, had shown her what she thought of her. It wasn't for Iestyn; Iestyn who had just disappeared in a flash of blue, to spite her. It wasn't for Clive either, for Clive would never come and get her. He would let her deal with what she'd been given. Her name was being erased from the credits; the documentary was being erased from the schedule. Very slowly, Leri herself was being erased.

And lying on her back in this tiny, cool cave seemed the best way to seep into such erasure, becoming the dark, the dark becoming her. Her life being shrunk to this one, tiny, circular view of sea until the light gave way and even that, too, had gone.

30

Mererid stays the night in Deian's loft. It isn't how she's imagined it would be. It's a night tense with trauma; the door opening and shutting, the light flashing and waning, the scuttle of goats echoing between footsteps. Deian goes up and down up and down the wooden stairs, which creak and moan, creak and moan. People come and go in the goat yard, and she hides from hushed voices without knowing why. It's one of those nights where nothing is the same; it reminds her of the night Mark's mother died, the lukewarm cups of tea that would never be drunk, the phone ringing its endless valediction, the shape of Mark's fist in the living room wall. Except here, because everything is already disordered, the events establish a kind of order. The children are ushered off to bed at an appropriate time, the radio system becomes a practicality; voices are silenced after dark, lights are extinguished, one by one.

They seem to think Iestyn is dead. She hears Mwynwen berating him in the shadows, saying that it was selfish, to end it like this; that this must have been his plan all along. She hears Howard clearing his throat and saying something about knowing all the facts before they notify the police. He'll take the lifeboat out tomorrow. Deian can come with him. Then comes the news that Leri, too, has not returned with the others. Howard says that Leri's made her own bed, and she can find her own lifeboat. Greta's voice is strained, and fading. She'll wait in the cottage until the morning, then. There's nothing more she can do.

Out of the tiny window Mererid then sees Viv walking away, dog at heel, her face still as ever. She hadn't realised she was even there.

The darker it gets, the less she can see from the small window, the more she wonders what Deian is still doing down there, in the goat yard, when the voices are long gone, his gas lamp tinkling in the wind. When he finally comes to her, closing the door for the last time, she puts a blanket around his shivering shoulders, laying it gently upon him; a white film in the grey light. He looks like a little boy, his mouth down-turned by the heaviness of his face. She wants to kiss him; not passionately, but like a mother would, a kiss on the forehead, a ruffling of hair. When she does, it's awkward, like a distant grandmother's grappling. He says he wants to be left alone; then as she turns to go he reaches for her hand and says that doesn't mean he doesn't want her here. He looks as though he may cry; and later on she cries for him, in concealed streams of dark, their salty ends disappearing in her mouth.

She lies in his bed, inhaling his aroma thick on the duck-down duvet. He lies on the floor next to her, tracing Iestyn's shape in the rumpled bed with his palms.

"I should have seen it coming," he keeps saying. "Maybe he planned this all along. He'd had enough time to think about it, hadn't he? Maybe this is his revenge."

"But he didn't seem to want revenge," she says, thinking again of that descent over the precipice. Even though she could only see the back of his head, she was sure he had been smiling.

"It'll prove to us that we cared about him. That we never really doubted him. We'll be making him a saint soon enough, and no one will ever remember the truth of it."

"But what is the truth of it?"

"You tell me," he says, turning around to look at her. "You saw what happened. I didn't."

She tells him again all she remembers. Squeezing out the cave's tiny pout; seeing Leri fly past her. Ben in the distance, and then Iestyn drifting over that precipice, smooth as anything, as though he were holding onto invisible threads, gearing himself through the air. His grey-peppered hair against the clear sky, like a Manx Shearwater's confident descent into the warm, accepting breeze.

"Except Iestyn's not fucking Icarus," Deian says.

The night begins and ends with them both sitting up in their beds, staring at the light pouring in through the loft, like they did in the bird

205

hide. She finds some kind of excuse to slide down to the floor, next to him. She knows this isn't the time — and that he will tell her so — but now more than ever she wants to be right next to him, breathe in that earthy smell and pull him onto her, inside her, even. She ends up reciting a poem about loss, in long, dulcet tones, hating the pretentious gesture even as she's doing it. It's like something Mark would do.

Deian says he'll go back down the mountain, once it's light, and search again. She says she'll come with him. Except when it finally does become light, Mererid falls away from herself, and into deep sleep.

Her dreams are cluttered with visions of the mountain, of herself and Deian, of Iestyn's sudden lunge over the rocks. The next second Deian is inside her, her hands roaming the map of his beard, his chest pushing down on hers, but when she looks up again she finds Iestyn there, a frenzy of sweat. The next moment she and Elin are rolling down the mountain like little girls, rolling on their sides with a childish abandon, shrieking into the wind, regardless of the rocks lying in wait. The next minute Greta is binding her in thin tape, around and around her naked body. The next moment she is swimming among seals, right in the middle of a circle of eyes, hovering, her arms unmoving, nothing but sheer will keeping her afloat. The next minute, Deian is hoisting her out of the water and they are back on their ledge, where he finally kisses her. The seals swish by her feet.

Then she wakes and finds the room is white with daylight. Deian is gone. She opens the door and inhales a million childhood mornings; the air damp and fresh and green. She creaks her way down the wooden stairs, and feeds the goats, as Deian asked her to do. She relishes this moment of aloneness with the two bobbing heads; and takes some solace in the fact that she has provided for them, even if she cannot provide for anyone else. For one solitary moment, from when the goats first chomped their way through her offering, to when they flick her hand away, is the one time she truly feels like an islander.

Standing alone in the goat yard, she feels abandoned. She knows there are people about, somewhere; that Deian must be searching the mountain; that Viv, Mwynwen, Howard are probably surging out into the morning in that red and white lifeboat. That Greta is huddled by the window of Carreg Bach. That Elin is waiting by the radio in the lighthouse kitchen, just in case, while Ben stays in his room, his door resolutely shut. She knows there will be tens of birdwatchers, dolphin–observers and holiday–makers who won't even have heard the news yet, who are waking up to another Bardsey morning. But just for one moment, with Deian gone, with Iestyn gone, and even Leri now missing, she has this strange feeling that the island is in fact swallowing them up, one by one. Gobbling them up in tides of turf, pulling them down, deep into the roots. Soon it will be her turn. Thrust down into the soil, one of the twenty thousand saints. She finds herself wondering what Mark will do when he hears of her disappearance. She imagines him and Margot and their tortuous, strange lovemaking that night, Mark calling out her name.

She allows herself to imagine that she is the only one left on this island now; roaming around the ruins, looking for something, for someone, before realising that there simply is nothing, no one else. She is utterly alone, and this land is hers, to make of it what she will.

31

The radio presenter on Radio Cymru announced that it had been ten years since devolution in Wales. Viv dropped her cup, letting it smash into a shower of blue and white on the floor. There was further speculation by an academic and a journalist about where the country was bound in terms of self-government, about how these next four years would be crucial in securing a Parliament for Wales. That the Welsh had to really want it, because it would be an absolute disaster otherwise.

Then she heard more familiar voices. It was one of these endlessly fashionable reunion programmes, where some of the campaigners of the 1979 referendum had come together to discuss what that first disappointment had been like. She recognised one voice intimately, and it shocked her. It was the gravel-like voice of Lewys, the man who'd helped her and Delyth during their campaign. He'd been more than that once, for she remembered that they'd kissed several times, during those long nights spent at the village hall making placards. She remembered it clearly, how they'd been all heated against the wall, his hands searching for the clasp of her skirt. When we win, he'd said to her, we'll move from here; somewhere where we can really see things changing. She'd agreed to it at the time, but had never intended going with him. It was more to get him off her, to get the waft of garlic breath out of her ear. "If we don't win," she'd said, "I'm going to live on Bardsey." "Oh, and I suppose you'll become a nun, too, will you?" he'd said, laughing.

She hadn't seen him since the news had come through that morning; since she'd seen him clutching the rusty gates outside the village hall, his hands red, his face crumpled. "They haven't heard the last of this," he kept saying, beating his head against the railings. "Well they've heard the last of me," Viv had replied, coolly stripping one of her posters from the notice board outside, trampling the green cardboard underfoot. She'd gone home and taken the postcard of Bardsey out of the top drawer, smoothing it with her hands. "It's still Wales," he'd shouted at her down the phone when she'd told him. "You're not escaping anything. You're just turning your back on us all." It wasn't Wales, she'd told him, it was better than that. It wasn't some pathetic colonised nation. Wales was attached to England, and Bardsey wasn't. You only had to look at a map to tell, she said, putting the phone down.

He was an Assembly Member now. Viv was stunned to hear her name mentioned on the radio. He talked about her with precision. She had obviously become a mere fact to him, an historical appendix. He said something about political extremities, about a political situation pushing someone so far away from themselves, that there was no way back for them. In this case, he said, this particular individual wasn't politically astute enough to see how things would pan out. "You weren't that worried how things would pan out when you were shoving your hands down my tan tights," she barked at the radio, rousing Elfyn from his nap.

Next, it was Delyth's turn to be dissected, laid out on the cold slab above the commentators. She was surprised they still remembered them both. Though she knew that she and Delyth made a splash of it at the time, wanting the press to know why they were leaving, she didn't think it would stick, somehow. But she realised it was precisely because of what happened to Delyth that they all remembered, not because of what she had termed so dramatically at the time as her sacrifice. She listened to Delyth's name being bandied about by those who had never laid eyes on her small, soft, frame, had never heard that quiet voice with its undercurrent of strong vibrations. For them it was a fiction, a fascinating story. A disappearance makes people remember you like nothing else, she thought.

And soon enough, Iestyn would be remembered in the same way. The thought had sat in her mind since she'd heard last night. An accident, Deian said, though she knew differently from his eyes. The first thing that struck her was the fact that she would have to get the plaque amended. It was all a bit of a nuisance, considering it had taken her years to get it erected in the first place. They could forget about taking it down and shipping it over, she would insist that the engraver would have to come to her, this time. It couldn't be good for her at her age, she thought, all this toing and froing, all these reappearances and disappearances. It played havoc with her bowels, for one thing. And that was the last thing you needed with a compost toilet.

Iestyn's name would have to sit next to Delyth's. Underneath, she supposed, though people wouldn't necessarily like the look of that: it would make them seem as though they were a married couple. She'd have to make it plain enough, by adding the dates. But then it could still seem like some sort of inappropriate arrangement, and she couldn't afford to add more words to explain otherwise. She didn't want historians in centuries to come thinking it was some kind of island of debauchery, with the twenty thousand saints seeming some far off myth, a cover-up, even.

No, Iestyn would have to have his own plaque. It was the only way. They would have to lie side by side. But you couldn't make one of them a saint and the other a mere mortal, so Iestyn would have to be duly appointed. She saw it there in front of her eyes, laughing back at her: St Iestyn. It seemed like his final joke on her somehow; his finest gag to date.

She turned the radio up. Two commentators were discussing the possible legislative powers of the Assembly. She tried out the word for measure – Cynulliad – shoving it into the back of the mouth, before then attempting the mouth-widening Senedd, as they had now apparently named the building that hosted it. She tried to envisage it in her mind, from what she'd heard on the radio, the glass panels, the angular face, but it remained no more than an untidy scattering of parts, like a bed she'd once ordered and had never succeeded in putting together. It was no mean feat, assembling the Assembly, she thought, laughing to herself. Elfyn tilted his head in confusion.

She wondered whether Howard would allow her to come with him in the lifeboat this morning. She would have to insist upon it, she couldn't have him doing it his way. She remembered how useless he'd been when Delyth had gone missing. His idea of carrying out a thorough investigation was taking a stick along to poke in the water, before combining the search with some lobster-baiting. She would wear her habit. That usually got him to take her seriously, to forget that she was nothing more than a mere woman. She wondered what they were going to do with Iestyn's body, once they found it. At least if they found him today he'd be well preserved enough for her to have a good look at him. But then the death would have to be registered, which would be a nuisance. Such things usually involved the mainland, peppery-smelling buildings, overbearing bureaucrats. She couldn't do it. Not again.

Unless they buried him here. She didn't know if they're allowed to bury people here anymore, though perhaps they could make an exception. Perhaps they could stick him in the pet cemetery in Cae Uchaf and be done with it. Deep down enough so that Elfyn could go on top of him. In centuries to come archaeologists might think they'd found some strange saintly crossbreed.

But she'd never get away with it. A disappearance wasn't what it used to be, she thought, remembering how quickly life had resumed on this island after Delyth had disappeared, and after Iestyn was taken away. How soon it had all gone back to normal. These days, disappearances were dragged on for weeks on end, with everybody and anybody, it seemed, staring into the abyss, speculating on the absence, the nothingness, the pure silence. Only this week she heard on the news that two schoolgirls had gone missing, and the longer they remained missing, the more of a story it became.

After the news bulletin, the chattering on the radio returned to the lively debate about Devolution in Wales. What struck Viv was how much the contributors cared about what was happening in Wales. Their voices were lit somehow, on fire, bursting brightly out of her transistor. Their Welsh was slick, urban, rhythmic, so unlike her own. Every ten minutes, a lively jingle announced, yet again, the tenth year anniversary of devolution. And it was this ten years which made her shudder. Not ten years since the crushing blow of 1979, since setting sail to the island, but ten years since everything had changed. Ten years since she'd been given exactly what she'd fought for, and she still hadn't returned. Why? Because it hadn't been her struggle? Because other people had secured the success for her? She still didn't know. For those ten years, her son had had more experience of Devolution that she had; even in Cardiff prison, such changes were visible.

Sometimes she thought she stayed on because of Delyth, because she still felt that somehow, Delyth was here. But then another part of her felt that Delyth was on the mainland, at least in spirit, peering through the glass-encrusted walls of the building she had heard so much about. Another part of her thought Delyth was nowhere, just like herself, had almost never existed. And there was a remaining part of her which believed that she used Delyth's name as an excuse to do very little at all, to retreat from the world. To wear her habit. To have her way.

She was so engrossed in the debate by now that she didn't notice the door opening, and Iestyn sneaking in. She only noticed him when she heard Elfyn licking his face. She saw everything as if through a thin film, and wondered if he was really there at all. Something made her turn the radio up.

"It was because of me, wasn't it, that you never went back," Iestyn said.

The instinct in her was to rush towards him and gather him up in her arms. He was still the two-year old at the top of the stairs. But she didn't. She reached for a brush to sweep up the mess of china from the floor.

"No," she said, wondering if that was true. "Everything changed when you went into prison, but I could have gone back, I should have gone back. Instead, I decided to become Sister Vivian, pillar of the community," she smiled weakly.

Iestyn started rolling a cigarette. As though nothing had happened; as though he hadn't just walked out of the sea. My boy, Viv thought, watching a ray of light illuminating his wayward fringe. She wanted to touch him, but she couldn't. She was afraid her fingers would go straight through him, finding he wasn't really there at all.

"You should have gone back. I'm sure that's what Delyth would have wanted you to do," Iestyn said, lighting the cigarette. "I think…

I think it was her plan all along. If she wasn't here, you'd leave. She believed that."

"No, Iestyn," she added, feeling a sob somewhere deep in her throat, spiralling its way towards the light. "Delyth must have been ill…"

"She wasn't ill. And she didn't kill herself," Iestyn said. "Not like we think she did, anyway." She stared at Iestyn. She didn't need to know where he'd been. It was all there in his eyes. She saw caves, crevices, dark tides, things she knew had been there all along. She saw Delyth, just beneath the surface of his eyes, laughing back at her. "I went down that mountain to find out. That's where she was last seen, wasn't it? I needed to know, Mam. Whether it was possible to kill yourself down there."

"How could you do that to Deian?" she said, her voice high and sharp, as though she were telling him off for stealing from the island shop. "He was worried sick! He had no idea where you were. He thought you were dead."

"What about you?" he asked. "Didn't you think I was dead? Didn't you care where I was?"

"I thought you'd killed yourself," she said. "To spite me."

"That's right, it would have to be about you," he replied, his voice hardening. "Everything was always about you, wasn't it? You said we all had to stay put, and we all listened. I mean, I was twenty years old, and I was still here. I had no concept of anything beyond this island."

"I wanted what was best for you," she said, trying her best not to look in his eyes, knowing how restless the dog became when she cried. "This island was going to be our chance to govern things in the way *we* wanted; keep us all safe, keep our language safe. It was for the greater good, please try to see that."

"But it wasn't safe, was it, Mam?" he said, coming closer to her. "It was safe for a while, when me and Deian were boys, but you know how things change, how they always change. There was more English being spoken here than Welsh by the time I was arrested, and it was as if you hadn't noticed; either that or you didn't care."

"Don't you dare tell me I didn't care," she spat, banging her fist against the mahogany, springing Elfyn from his basket. "After everything I'd been through; of course I cared. But there was little I could do about it. I wasn't going to change my mind again, leave, tell everyone I was wrong, was I? I'd got used to this island. I loved it, I still love it."

"Well, you used to love Wales, you used to say it was all that was worth fighting for, that its weaknesses made it what it was, made us who we are," Iestyn recited back at her. She remembered these words perfectly, standing atop the mountain, Iestyn's hands in hers, staring out across the water towards the mainland. She'd always intended to go back, someday. "What happened, Mam? Did it get too powerful for you? Was it not flawed enough for you in the end? Delyth wanted to go back didn't she? She knew more than you did, she'd been going back and forth to Aberdaron to see how things were panning out. She knew you'd scrape through that second referendum, and so did you."

"Yes, and scrape through we did," said Viv bitterly, remembering how she'd turned her radio off, and stared into the dark morning. A measly one percent. A bittersweet triumph. They'd got what they wanted but the battle was only just beginning; Wales was still full of all those hateful no-voters, she couldn't go through that again. The likes of Jeremy and her husband.

"Delyth knew you wouldn't leave. The day after the referendum everything was so placid here. Like nothing had changed. She didn't want to go without you. But she knew that if she stayed, she'd be forgotten completely, swallowed up by this place. She had to do something drastic."

"I don't understand what you're telling me," Viv said, even though she knew full well what he was telling her. The thought had passed through her own mind, a hundred times.

"When I threw myself off that rock yesterday, I was prepared for anything. Prepared to die, even, if it meant it led you to her. For one strange moment there in the air, I felt like she was with me. When I hit the water, I felt like I was going to her."

Viv saw it unfolding in a succession of scenes. Delyth on the rock looking down. Delyth in the water.

"So that's what you're saying she did," Viv said, breathless by now.

"All I know is that it's lethal there; a whole lot of rocks waiting to split you open. Good thing I had the sense not to go head-first. I really knackered this knee though."

She looked down to the rip in his jeans, seeing the dark trail that had been oozing its way to the door. Elfyn was silently lapping it up, his pink tongue darkening. She reached for her first aid kid and took out her bottle of TCP.

"So she knocked herself out, is that it?" Viv asked, pouring the yellow liquid onto a cotton wool bud. "Bled to death," she said, almost tasting the blood herself.

"No, Mam. I'm saying we can rule it out. If she'd done that, she'd have been floating right there in the water. We would have found her, easily. Ah!" Iestyn winced as Viv pressed the cotton to his knee. She ripped away the fabric. The wound was deeper than she thought.

"But she could have drifted out..." Viv replied, wiping the blood clean, getting to the heart of the wound.

"Ah yes, the drifting theory!" he said. "That's what I tried next. Just drifting, pretending to be dead. Do you know what happened? Bloody seals came and got me. They came to rescue me. Carried me back. Wobbled me over to dry land as though I were a pup. Put me as high up as they could."

"I've heard it all now! So you're using the seals as evidence," she said, as Elfyn sniffed at her hands. "You'll have a hell of a job getting them to testify."

"What I'm saying is that she never did any of those things. For her it wasn't about ending it all. It was about starting something. She never wanted her body to be found. She never wanted anyone to see it as her killing herself, although, it seems to me that we could struggle to find another word for what she did."

Looking at her son now, watching the stray bits of tobacco fall away from the casement of paper and land haphazardly on her table, Viv couldn't quite reconcile the image with what had been here a few weeks ago, those blank moon faces of Sister Mary Catherine, Lucy Violet, and Anna Melangell, all huddled around staring at her in earnest.

She shuddered to think that they had been her family.

"I think she wanted to be a martyr," he said.

Viv stared at the wound. It was like a gaping, fleshy eye, pumping red tears.

"Think about it Mam. Think about everything that happened afterwards."

"She wouldn't have left me."

"In her eyes you'd already left her. She wanted you to go back, so badly, but you wouldn't go. You were a team, once, remember? You were always the notorious one in those campaigns, the front woman, the figurehead, and she enjoyed being behind you, amending your speeches, urging you on. For her, you were the only one who could really change things; but you always had to be spurred by her, didn't you? That's why it drove her mad, at the end, that you wouldn't budge, that she couldn't make you change your mind. Not for anything. Despite all these changes."

"She could have gone back. I didn't stop her," Viv said, her voice breaking

"You did, remember? All those times she tried to leave and you persuaded her not to. Because you were stubborn and you'd got used to it. She gave in so many times. So she had to think of other ways. Even if it meant alienating you, upsetting you. She probably thought it was for the greater good. God knows, we both know this place gives you funny ideas, at the best of times."

"You and her," said Viv, afraid of letting her memories back in. "That's what that was all about?"

"I didn't realise at the time, but it must have been. She must have thought it would get to you, make you want to leave. It was her last attempt. All these years I've thought about what she'd said when we were last together, properly together, you know. 'Why do you think I'm doing this?' she said. I just stared at her then, didn't have a clue what she was telling me. I was twenty but I was so sheltered. Prison knocked that right out of me."

"You were still a boy, in so many ways," Viv said, trying not to think about that day she'd seen them, over at the south end, Delyth sprawled on her back on the smooth rock, Iestyn pounding away, crying with pleasure. Delyth had looked right at her. "It was easier for her."

"You did know, then. She always said you knew. But you never said anything. You never punished her, by leaving, like she wanted you to do."

"It would have passed," Viv said, remembering that pang still.

"It had already passed. I got so fucking angry with her when she refused me. That's why I hit her. I didn't mean to. A few days before the referendum, before she went missing. She told me she didn't want to do that anymore, that there was no point, and I hit her across the face. She fell back, and hit her head. That's when I... oh God when I..."

"When you what, Iestyn?" Viv asked, her throat tightening. Delyth was now lying in front of them both, on her back in the grass.

"I didn't do it. I thought about it, but I couldn't. I... I pushed her back down, ripping off her cardigan, pushing up her dress. She looked so scared. I wanted her so badly, and wanted to hurt her so much, but when it came to it, I just couldn't do it. I saw that look of disgust in her eyes and I just burst into tears and ran away, that cardigan in my hand. I slept with it for nights afterwards, just smelling her."

"You should have told the court," Viv started, remembering the small graze on Delyth's head that day, the drying blood. *Let me dress it for you*, she'd said to her.

"I couldn't tell them all of it," he said. "Not with Deian looking at me like that."

"You could've told them part of it," she said.

"What, that I nearly killed her? Or worse?" he said. "That would have gone down well. No I couldn't. I just couldn't work it out when she went missing. You and I know she didn't want to die. But she wanted something *more,* didn't she? That's why she did it, I think. So she could be something more. Something more than a temptress or a lover, something she'd become when you'd first started campaigning. Something you'd drawn out of her. She wanted to be remembered. She knew you wouldn't let anyone forget her."

The plaque, Viv thought. Delyth must have known she'd fight to get that plaque.

"Think about it, Mam. She didn't want to be some tragic suicide victim. It would have been such a negative slant, the papers would have loved that, she couldn't have done that to you. She wanted something that would draw attention to the island, to you and her, to the reason you'd come here in the first place. Something that would have the feel of a legend of some sort. It worked, didn't it? It all worked out, apart from that you stayed here."

"How do you mean?"

"I think she thought that if she went missing, you'd lose faith in this place, get angry with the island somehow. And you'd go back, start fighting again. She probably thought all three of us would go together. That me and Deian would be your support system, that we'd be the ones writing your speeches. I think she'd imagined us all fighting for independence, in her name. OK, it was far-fetched, but she was far-fetched, Mum. She wasn't to know that that plaque would be where it ended. She wasn't to know that her own son would end up forgetting his Welsh. That I'd get put in prison. She just didn't think it through."

Viv steadied herself by the kitchen table. She sat down and imagined the body of Delyth, drifting in the bottle of antiseptic.

"You can go on all you like," she said, forcing his shuddering knee to stay still. "You still can't know anything. Not for sure."

"Listen to me," he said, grabbing her shoulders. "Down the side of the mountain, along the water, there are a series of tiny, tiny crevices, like caves, where the water's been grinding down the rock. Only they're less like caves, and more like pods," Iestyn said. "They can't be reached by boat, you have to swim into them, and once you do, it's only a matter of time before they start filling with water. I swam out into one of them, and pulled myself in. I lay there for ages, letting the water get to me, being pushed further and further into the rock. A few more inches and I would have been trapped. It was like lying in a chute, waiting to be pushed on into another world. She wanted somewhere no one would find her."

"The police would have found her, surely..."

"No," he said. "Not if she pushed herself right into the rock. You remember how slight she was. She would have got much further in

218

than I would have. They never would have found her. When I think back, it's obvious. She was trying to tell me something that day, trying to tell us all she was going to do it. But we all took it the wrong way. We thought she was just rambling, as usual. We thought it was the referendum and everything. But it signalled a kind of end for her. Now or never, she thought."

Viv felt sick. It came back to her now, Delyth in the door that day. Saying how she was fed up of being invisible. She'd had that funny look, going through the gate, and the kiss, that one kiss, she saw it now as the kiss goodbye. The kiss had been the final part of the plan. It had sealed everything. Viv was supposed to know what Delyth was telling her.

"But you can't know," Viv said, pacing the room, Elfyn moving back and forth with her. "You can't! This is just some convenient story you've had a chance to dream up these last ten years. Can't you just accept we may never know what happened to her?"

"I found this," he said, reaching something out towards her. "Tied to the rock. It was so far back I almost couldn't reach it. I almost drowned trying to get it."

The head scarf was unmistakable. Weathered by the rain and the storm and countless nights that had eaten away at it, but nevertheless, it was the unmistakable headscarf of Delyth's, the red and blue one she wore on those sweltering summer evenings. Touching it was like allowing the tide-race to come flooding in to Viv's own crevices, filling her up, whirling around her until she was full of it.

"How do I know," she said, looking right into his eyes. "That you haven't just been hoarding this, all these years? Waiting for this moment. How can I possibly know?"

"You'll never know," he answered. "But if you don't accept what I'm telling you, where does that leave you? It leaves you with nothing, all over again; with a disappearance, with all these questions. Either way, she got what she wanted. To stop being invisible. She wasn't to know that by doing it, she'd make you invisible. That you'd be the one hiding behind her all these years."

"Deian needs to have this," she said, her hands shaking across the red and blue fabric.

"I'll go and find him," he said. "When I'm ready."

She realised now, more than ever, that his eyes held things she'd never seen – the newly paved streets of Cardiff Bay, the peaks of the Millennium Stadium, a city in the rain.

"I misread everything," she said. "If only I'd seen it was about me, and not about her."

"She wasn't to know how things would turn out. She would never have meant for me to go to prison," he said. "I see that now, although at the time, I thought she was punishing me. I thought I deserved to be punished, for what I'd almost done to her. But I can see now that she wanted a way out, for us all."

"I failed her," Viv said, the tears coming at last. "Completely and utterly failed her. I let Deian go off to Preston, I turned everyone away."

"You didn't fail her," Iestyn said. "You made her a saint. She's the most talked about saint this island's ever had. It's become a legend. Everyone knows about her. It's become a myth. In centuries it will be like that story about Elgar, no one will really know the ins and outs of it, they will just know that her name's important, that is speaks out, that it stands for something."

Viv stared out of the window. It was beginning to rain, the droplets flooding down her window, shrouding the island in blue mist. It was the first rainfall they'd had this summer.

"I want you to leave," Iestyn said. "I want you to go back and see what's changed. That's all Delyth ever wanted you to do. That's why she did it. She knew how much in love with this place you were, you both were. But the mainland isn't like it used to be. Wales isn't like it used to be. We're strong now. Stronger than ever. The language is strong, too. People don't have to live on the margins anymore."

She looked up at him. Those battered, worn eyes. She wondered whether he would look any different now, had he stayed. People who lived on the island their whole life were healthier, smoother round the edges. And yet perhaps those rougher edges were important, too.

"No," she said, firmly, thinking of the residents of the island of St Kilda that Sister Mary Catherine had told her about. They had been forced to leave and it had forced the life out of them. Most of them had been dead by the end of their first year. "This is my home now. Some of us *like* living on the margins."

"I'm not asking you to leave forever. Just go and see it," he said. "See what they've done. What it's actually like. Go to Cardiff, Mam. Wipe away those memories of my court case: just go and see what's there."

She stared at him, again, finding it difficult to recognise herself as she was now, like this, talking to her son, with ease, at the kitchen table. The son she'd pushed away so readily. The son that had become a victim of her stubbornness; her refusal to stay and fight. She realised that she owed Iestyn everything now, but still couldn't bear the thought of it somehow, walking to the Cavern knowing she was going further than Aberdaron – knowing that she was travelling inwards towards Wales, inwards towards herself, towards what she had always wanted, always anticipated. She would not go. She wanted to please her son but she couldn't put herself through this. She was too old.

Then, suddenly, Elfyn nudged her, his brown eyes wise and warm.

32

As he walked towards the lighthouse that evening, he had the feeling of walking along a plank, not knowing whether he would have the confidence to jump off himself, or whether he would have to be pushed. Tomorrow, he would be leaving the island. It was time to go. After hearing everything Iestyn had to say that morning, he knew that the summer was over. He clung on to the headscarf in his pocket, knowing that he had the one thing that could never be taken away from him. And he knew that she'd done it for him, in some strange, perverse way. His mother had disappeared in order for him to become apparent. It should have marked him out from everyone else, made him more determined than ever to use the language, to live in Wales, to use that anger, that tension in him to wonderful effect. Become a politician, become a writer. Use the language as a force. But he hadn't. He'd been sitting in a flat in Preston watching the seasons go by, using somebody else's language, the island like a dream, somehow, the map of Wales a mere doodle on his bedroom wall.

Tomorrow, most of the others would be leaving, too. He'd heard that Mererid and Elin had already packed up. Greta was ready to go, even if Leri wasn't. The dig was finally at an end. That morning Howard had come up with the JCB to pour the soil back into the field. Deian had finished his report for the board, a beautifully fabricated document, comprising mainly of indecipherable riddles of pure jargon. He would be taking it over tomorrow to Gwyn, who would merely flick across the black and white patterns before ordering some volunteers to start work on the cemetery. And after Leri's half-conscious confession in his arms yesterday, he had taken the bones back to the hermitage, returning them to St Deiniol's display, thankful that he had never mentioned them to anyone but Fran. He felt as though everything was back where it belonged, neatly in its place. All they needed now was for a few pets to die. Elfyn had his sights on the right hand corner, although Deian suspected that one of the twin goats would be the first to tumble in.

He knew Mererid would be in her room, the computer battery dying, her screen blank. Calling to say goodbye felt like the most natural thing in the world for him to do. He suggested that they went for a walk across the south end. They hopped over the white-washed walls and began walking out towards the sea, the island's final, green finger reaching out to sea, becoming thinner and thinner. This was it, this was the plank, he thought. A bird swept down close to them and Mererid's face lifted up to look at it. She was standing so close to him now, he could see each freckle as though it were an island unto itself. With the sky darkening, the wind churning around them, he reached out, and trembling, geared a tentative lip out towards hers.

They kissed for a while, awkwardly at first, his tongue sliding a little too eagerly into her mouth, taking up all the space. But soon, they were able to establish some kind of rhythm, something softer, sweeter, her tongue fleshily locked with his. She pulled him into the comfort of the bird hide. He lifted up her small frame so that she was sitting on him, tiny legs wrapped around his thick-set waist, her slim fingers uprooting his white T-shirt from his digging trousers. He wondered whether she could smell the soil on him, but remembered that the body was allowed to have its own perfume on this island. Once he felt those small breasts dancing against him, he wanted to unwrap her, and had the nerve to push his hand up through the small opening of her shirt to locate a small, hardened nipple protruding through her bra. For some reason he thought suddenly of his mother, what she would think of him now – here, in this bird hide, with this woman. With this Welsh-speaking woman. This poet. She would be so proud, he imagined Iestyn saying, and tried to stifle a laugh. A groan escaped him as Mererid's hand formed a slender circle around his penis.

They said nothing to one another after that; the intensity of their eyes was dialogue enough. There was none of the awkwardness he usually felt in situations like this. Their clothes peeled away like layers of silk; their bodies, despite their having no room to move, seemed free and limitless, adjusting to one another's rhythms; fitting together. Before he knew it, he was inside her. He looked up at her face, saw that her eyes were closed, her mouth slightly parted. She was still wearing her black mackintosh, which neatly disguised them – should anyone peer through the gap – as a couple embracing, but very suddenly he didn't care who saw them, and began hoisting it above her body, over her head. The small shirt underneath he wrenched open, showering a cluster of small buttons onto the floor. The black bra stood there like the final barrier between them, and she unhooked it for him, her breasts a thrill to his fingers; her raw taste tingling across his tongue.

They hovered on the peak of pleasure; keeping completely still at times, and at others giving in to their bodies so that the bird hide felt like it would burst open about them in neat segments, announcing their desire, their naked bodies to the whole island. He didn't want it to be over, Deian thought, feeling his climax coming ever nearer, seeing her whole body arc back, away from him, a perfect, white landscape, the eyes of freckles winking at him. This scene was too much for him, her hair swaying behind her, her breath gasping, her palms banging the wooden ceiling, and he came; a burst of bright light behind his eyelids, the warm body around him urging him on, grasping him harder. It took a few more shifts of those pale hips to satisfy her, and then they were both perfectly still.

She looked at him. He still didn't want to say anything, any single word would seem somehow ridiculous. So he pulled her towards him and kissed her again, their faces mingling in a steady stream of sweat. Her hair, her face, they were all new to him; exhilarating in his hands. He realised that this was the first time in six years he'd had sex with anyone except Fran. And it had been wonderful, he wanted to tell her, like nothing else. He no longer felt lost, the way he had always felt after sex with Fran, these past few years. As if whatever Fran was looking for in the very act of having sex wasn't there at all. He thought of all the times she had insisted that they do it there and then, that it was *time,* only to end up crying in the bathroom because it was *her* time; another disappointment in bright, red streaks. And then, even worse, she would run off to her own home; keep her pain resolute behind her own doors, despite his repeated requests for them to move in together, to share the pain they both felt.

This was different. This was sex because they wanted one another, loved one another, even, in the passing, sporadic way only islanders could. They had so much more than he and Fran had, in so many ways. They had the island, they had this summer, and no one else would ever understand what it had been like. He'd wanted this for much longer than he'd realised. There was beauty in having Mererid in his arms right then, and to have given her what she wanted; which was merely himself, rather than the duplication of himself that Fran wanted so badly.

Mererid kissed him again, before eventually climbing off him. She reached for her knickers. They were a metallic green, which surprised him, although he didn't know why. Maybe he had some strange preconception about what a poet's underwear would look like. She lifted her trousers back up as he reached for his belt.

They sat back down, side by side. After a few minutes, Mererid reached for his hand. He hadn't realised until he felt her hand on his how much he'd longed for it, more than anything else, all these weeks. Once it was within his grasp he squeezed it hard, as drops of sweat fell away from his forehead and onto the wooden floor; a stain the only sign of what had just happened between them. He stared down at the shape it made on the floor, and saw it form a kind of long stripe like the outline of the south end of the island, wriggling its way toward the sea.

Things seemed much easier for him on this side of the island, much simpler, he thought, they always had. He seemed freer here, he thought, caressing Mererid's fingers, one by one.

Once they returned to the lighthouse cottage, they crossed a strange border back into their own lives. Elin was on the doorstep, sullenly pulling on the dregs of a cigarette, hitting her heel against the concrete. She looked at them both accusingly – for a moment Deian thought she must have seen them – and got up to greet them, both arms crossed. She seemed to him more distant than usual. Her folded arms implied she wanted to lock Mererid in; to keep him out.

"It's our last night," she said, resentfully, in Welsh. "I made dinner."

"Where's Ben?" Mererid asked.

"He's gone," she said, sukily. "He left this afternoon. Didn't say a word. I didn't even get to... you know... he wasn't even that into me..."

Elin turned on her heel, back into the cottage. Mererid turned to look at Deian, saying resentfully, in English, "It's our last night."

He didn't know whether she meant hers and Elin's, or hers and his. And he realised he should have asked, made sure, before shrugging his shoulders and walking off into the purple-tint of an evening. He found himself wondering that very thing all the way back to the bird loft that evening, replaying that sentence in his head, carefully scanning it for intonation, detonation. *It's our last night.* But he realised that it didn't particularly matter. It was the last night for them all.

And for the sake of taking leave, for the sake of nothing and everything, he should have stayed at the lighthouse that evening. He found himself approaching the top of the island, with the lighthouse cottage looking just as far away, just as inaccessible as it had three hours ago, when he was plummeting down to meet it.

But with one colossal difference. Something in him had been released. The very stuff he'd been told by an apologetic doctor all those months ago would never amount to anything, that would never be able to get Fran pregnant, would never secure him a future.

And the release at last gave him purpose, somehow, a direction. It made him feel alive again. Alive, and hopeful, as he caressed that headscarf in his pocket, that there were other ways of living on.

33

When gentle persuading would not do, they resorted to dragging her out. Leri felt the scrape of her back against the rumpled bed of stones, and looked for something to hold on to. But there was nothing. The cold walls pushed her fingers away. She felt like a corpse being slid out of its tray at a morgue, and soon enough, curious, upside-down faces appeared above. "Is she alright?" she heard one say to the other. "Well, she's not dead, is she?" said another, harder voice. "Why is she looking at me like that?" the voice added, trying to shoo away Leri's gaze in a flap of hands. Leri now recognised her as Greta, the blue-black hair covering her mouth.

She knew they would come, sooner or later. Leri had already played out the scenario in her mind, and knew what she had to do. She had run from them on the mountain, she could run from them again. She could outwit them; it was what a clever documentary-maker did, Clive said. A whiff of potent liquid caught her by surprise, blurring her vision. She tried to block out the pain as Mwynwen pressed a cloth to her cheek and wove her way around the wound, her fingers tearing at the skin.

"You might need stitches," she said. Leri thought of the cross-stitch on her BAFTA dress, the amber and gold patterning down the front. "Hopefully it won't scar. But then, even if it does, it won't go deep. Does it hurt?" Mwynwen asked. "I don't feel anything" is what Leri thought she said in reply, until she saw Mwynwen looking up at Greta with questioning eyes. "Why won't she say anything? Why does she just keep staring? Do you think she's concussed?"

"I think she's playing up," Greta replied.

Voices were strange to her now, ugly almost. She remembered

how she had first pined for Greta's voice, lying on her back in that cave, wanting her to come and silence the haunting sounds that crept into her consciousness. The whisper of creatures all around her was deafening. They slid onto her hands, writhed around in the grass outside, while something came all-a-patter about her ears. But soon enough, the island's natural sounds had become part of the rhythm of her silence. She saw it as a wonderful thing; to be here when the dusk fell, to hear the sounds gushing from the earth; the birds calling to one another, the grasshoppers pulsating in the grass, the beetles battling it out in the dust. She wondered how she had ever lived with the mundane noise of her own world, those lorries that shuddered past her flat in Canton as though they were charging through her living room. The howling of the next-door neighbours who hurled things through windows, banged on the locked doors. The boy racer at the bottom of the street announcing his music tastes to the world, his exhaust scraping across tarmac.

Mwynwen hooked one of Leri's arms about her neck, and slid the other around Greta's shoulders. Leri had no idea what time it was, or how many days she'd been in the cave. It was early morning by the looks of it, the dew still dribbling towards the root. The mist swam in front of them in grey swathes, obscuring the island from view. It was like they had planned it, she thought, so that Leri could see no further than the step in front of her, her feet smoothing out the carpet of grass as she went. Each step took her further away from a closed off world that no one could permeate, where her own failure could not break through stone and cackle in her face.

When Mwynwen let go of her briefly by the mountain wall, she saw her chance, and tried to run back up the path. The mountain came smacking her in the face, a green punch which winded her, leaving her powerless by Greta's feet. "Well that was a silly thing to do, wasn't it?" she heard Greta say.

Elgar never had this problem, she thought bitterly. The whole world had let him be, while he sat up there munching on grass and listening to the sounds of the earth. Certainly nobody had forcibly removed him like this, or treated him so shabbily. She wanted to tell them so, only the words would not come. No words at all could allow themselves to leave the small, dry opening of her mouth, as though they were now shut in her body's cave instead, shunning the daylight.

She sauntered on towards the main path, her fingers taking hold of Greta and Mwynen's hands. The mist was rising, the sky bringing down its soft curtain over the scene, each and every detail falling into place. Behind and in front, there were small clusters of people all walking in the same direction. Leri listened to the chorus of feet trudging onwards. No one spoke, as if they were all too busy clinging to their own thoughts. They knew, like she knew, that this was to be their last journey towards the Cavern. Far away, the rickety wheels of a trailer squealed. The lighthouse released one final foghorn. Rounding the corner by the boathouse she saw the white boat docking silently by the jetty. From the direction of the lighthouse, Mererid and Elin were being towed into view by Howard's tractor. They leaned on either side of the trailer facing away from one another, their faces sullen as they rocked back and forth amongst their belongings, like some sombre carnival float.

Seeing Iestyn and Deian arriving with their bags was the final straw. Leri felt as though they were all staring at her now, disgusted by the blood patterns on her face, smelling the stench of her cave-musty skin. She wondered if it was a conspiracy; some kind of plan to get rid of her. Perhaps they intended to give her a surprise sea burial, to throw her to the mercy of the tide-race, chanting together as she sunk from view. She wanted so much to be clean again. Clean and unwounded. She felt herself falling limply into Greta's arms.

"Leri, don't do this to me now, please. A few more steps, and we'll be on that boat."

"My stuff," Leri croaked, the words sharp in the back of her mouth.

"It's all packed," Greta said, without looking at her.

"The camera," she whispered.

"I've labelled all the tapes we've got left. The camera's a write-off, Ler. It really doesn't matter. We've got some good stuff. Look, try not to speak, OK? We'll be back in Cardiff before you know it. Then, everything can get back to normal."

Nothing would ever be normal, she wanted to tell her. Not in

Cardiff anyhow. Cardiff was as abnormal as you could get. All those nights at the Cameo Club sucking up to various directors. Chapter Arts and its ersatz bohemia, those one-stone blonde darlings in scarves, fanning themselves with their scripts. The lunch meetings at Ha-Ha's that never amounted to anything apart from a woozy afternoon; hours wasted, giggling over a photocopier. It was all wrong for her. She hated it all. She could never go back. Never.

She was the first to be deposited onto the boat. The cargo chain of islanders stood back to make way for her and her entourage, bowing their heads as she passed. It was almost as if she were royalty, she thought, wanting to laugh out loud in their faces. She was handed over into Brian's sandpaper hands, and slotted into place on a damp, white seat. Brian did not, it would seem, know what to do with her. For a while, there was no one on board but the two of them, sat in uneasy silence, the boat swaying their stares from side to side.

"Get a move on, the lot of you," he shouted to the others.

Over on the jetty, she saw Greta saying goodbye, a flurry of kisses and whispers. She saw Iestyn hug Greta with warmth he had never shown her, before yielding himself to a chain of other embraces along the jetty. Last in line was Elin, who he kissed on the mouth – a long, hard, and forgiving kiss, which she received greedily. Leri found herself wondering whether she would be kissed like that ever again, by anyone. Her mouth felt as though it now hosted half the creatures of the night, wriggling on the pink walls. They had formed a barrage on her tongue, so that when Iestyn came over to talk to her, she only stared at his shadow.

"I hope things work out for you," he said. "I'm sorry if things didn't turn out like we planned, but these things hardly ever do."

She kept her eyes on the pacing silhouette on the boat's deck.

"I'm staying on for a bit. Taking over Mam's duties. Won't be becoming a monk or anything. No offence, Father," she heard Iestyn say, as a nebulous shadow appeared beside him. "I belong here. I've never really been at home anywhere else. Not that I've been given much of a chance, but still, there was never any point in getting even. It wasn't the island's fault, nor my mother's either. It was just something that happened. And now I've got a chance to undo some of it."

Leri looked up into his eyes. Don't talk to me about undoing, she thought. He spilt those ribbons of tape across the wind. She wondered where that ribbon had ended up, whether it had taken its revenge out on some poor seal down by the seal cave, wrapping itself tightly against its neck, dangling it from the ledge as a warning to other seals. Her story was now among the seaweed, tangled up around the anemones and the purple starfish. She should have gone down with it, she thought. Captains went down with their ships, it was only right that she drowned along with her story.

She clung on to this thought. It wasn't too late. This might truly be her only chance. If she couldn't go back to Cardiff, then where could she go? The sea was there in front of her. In the peculiar light of a September sunrise it looked inviting. Purifying, like a shining medicinal liquid. She felt so dirty by now, a speck of dirt in every pore, each of her fingernails a black frown. This was her chance to wash away the stench of the last few days, to throw healing salt water on her wound. She imagined the water embracing her, letting her body go loose. Its blubber engulfing her, dragging her away from the world and its clamour, towards a slick, floating silence. The moment before you drowned was supposed to be the most wonderful calm one would ever experience, she remembered someone saying.

While Brian was busy helping others onto the boat, she wriggled her way out of her life jacket. This was it, she thought. This was how it was all going to end. She heard a shuffle of voices somewhere in the distance, and, just as she was nearing the edge of the boat, felt the familiar grip of Greta's hands.

"Leri, what on earth are you doing? Sit back down will you? This is embarrassing enough as it is."

There was no compassion in Greta's eyes, only coldness. Exactly the kind of coldness she wanted to drown in.

"Leave me," she tried to say. "This is what I want." Her voice had been reduced to a mere squeak.

Greta looked over her shoulder now, catching Deian's eye. He came towards them and grabbed Leri's hands. They were warm. But it didn't make any difference. She had the warmth of Deian's hands and the coldness of Greta's eyes, and she still wanted to die.

"I want to… it's not… and I definitely don't ever…" she managed, forcing the words out into the air.

She was turning into Elin, she thought. Or she had swapped places with her, at least, for Elin herself was far, far away, churning out finite sentences with grace and ease on another side of the boat, unaware of the commotion. Suddenly everything was a distant blur, grace and ease falling to the margins of her consciousness, (although now they had become Grace and Ease, her two new attendants, which sat on either side of her, scowling). She felt Brian's hands on her once more, pulling her down into her seat, tying the edges of her life jacket to the life jackets of Deian and Greta. Binding them together like children.

As the boat moved away from the island, Leri found it impossible to distinguish one thought from the other.

I want to.

It's not.

And I definitely don't ever.

She thought.

34

Mererid cannot bear Leri's sobs. Thick with mucus, they seem to go on forever, in tiny aching waves, hurting them all. She doesn't know her well enough to reach out, to gently squeeze her arm and say it will be alright, or even to shake her, to tell her to pull herself together. Before she started crying, the boat had a kind of neutrality. They had sat side by side, in their orange puffs, not looking at one another, each making a solitary journey. Now, however, they are forced to look at one another again. It has become Leri's journey, and they are merely passengers.

Mererid hasn't thought much about what it will actually feel like, this moment, the island moving away from her and her moving away from the island, but she feels that even now, it isn't what she expects. She's imagined a tearing sensation, a feeling that the island is being wrenched from her. But it's gentler, somehow, as though she's only leaving for a while, knowing she'll be back. She wishes she could cry. It would seem like the most logical way of letting it out, but she knows it would seem silly. She's only been here six weeks. Most of the others have been here for months. Most of them can't imagine the island carrying on without them. But Mererid knows she saw something like relief in Mwynwen's eyes that morning. The islanders turned their backs on the visitors a fraction of a second sooner than they had all expected, their waving arms falling back at their sides.

The island becomes smaller and smaller. The jetty disappears, then the lighthouse, then the mountain. They curve around a bulk of mainland, and the whole island is gone, just like that, with nothing to indicate their departure but the rippling of the boat's path across the water. Mererid watches as this too, fades away, the tide's crinkled surface being stretched taut, the waters around them becoming stiller.

She watches Deian on the other side of the boat, smoothing his palms with his fingers. She thinks of those fingers yesterday, making their journey into her hair, across her breasts, between her legs. She thinks of the clasp around her waist, and shudders, slightly, as the pleasure tingles through her again. The boat speeds up, nearing the end of its journey. The sea salt in her nostrils, the warmth all over her body, the pain she feels in knowing that soon Deian will be gone, is all mixing up inside her, deliciously complex; an erotic poem, a villanelle perhaps, haunting in its repetition. If only, Mark, you could find this in me, she thinks. If only you knew I really was capable of all this.

Porthmeudwy is dotted with faces. This isn't her stop. She's going on to Pwllheli; there's no one here for her at Porthmeudwy. Brian and his helpers dock the ship in shallow water and prepare the smaller boats. She sees Deian untie himself from Leri, only to get caught up in the chain of embraces as he walks towards her, being swept away from Mererid in a tide of arms and elbows. She keeps an eye on him, like a card in a pack, afraid she'll lose detection and he'll be gone. Then, there it is, a sudden break in the web, a path from him to her. He kisses her, quickly, but deeply, on the mouth. She gasps when he pulls away, wanting more. She looks around to greet what she assumes will be the faces of wonder. But no one has witnessed the kiss; no one but an apathetic seagull and perhaps Brian, in one corner of a bitter eye.

As they sink away from her in a dinghy, Mererid sees that Leri is still crying. Viv now has her arm around her. Maybe as much for herself as for Leri, so she doesn't have to look up, acknowledge the world around her. Mererid remembers the fear in Viv's eyes when she had to step off the jetty.

Mererid can no longer hold back. She looks straight into Deian's eyes as he drifts away from her. It is now that she feels the real tearing, an exquisite pain that floods her entire body.

It's only her and Elin left on the boat. Brian says nothing. He just gears them on, skimming the water, towards the sun, until a shining Pwllheli comes into view. Mererid isn't prepared for this. Even from this distance she can see people milling about, blue and white shirts rippling in the breeze, holiday hats swaying, dogs barking. They glide in among a host of other, bigger boats, dwarfed by the magnitude of yachts with names like Northern Star and Arabella, flashing in bright turqouise and magenta. They drag their cases behind them, the wheels rollicking loudly against the wood of a massive jetty. Everywhere, it seems, people are shouting and laughing. A man with a brown wrinkled face is cackling at something his wife has said, his wife is chortling, bits of her prawn sandwich falling out of her mouth in pink clumps.

A few minutes later, Mererid is sitting among their cases outside the main reception building, waiting for Elin to bring her car round to meet her. She sinks into the hot tarmac and watches a young man and woman fighting over a packet of chips. The polystyrene tray squeaks from the woman's hand, the chips are splayed in a yellow shower on the pavement. She tries to squirt tomato sauce over him, it squishes from the packet and misses. He breaks his resolve and laughs. They kiss, wetly, sucking one another's lips, before going to buy another packet. Next come two teenage boys in a car, opening the doors and letting the heavy music flood out, along with their chemical, Malboro Red smoke. The cigarette butt is thrown out, and fizzes in a patch of red sauce. They boom off, the wrong way down a one way street, beeping their horn all the while.

She knows she has to ring Mark, because despite everything, she still has to go home. She has to get her car. It's the only thing she's got left that is really hers. It rings four, five, times and is curtly answered by Margot. Margot says Mark is still asleep. Mark's voice comes from somewhere, apologetic and low, softer than it was that night they last spoke.

"Sorry, Mer," he says, "don't know why she answered."

Hearing his voice ignites something in her, and she has to be careful, she thinks. It isn't that she doesn't love Mark, it's just that she doesn't love him enough. A little bit of love can still draw you back in.

"I need to come by, I suppose," she starts.

"It makes sense, Mer. All your stuff is here. You need to pick up the keys to the flat."

"The flat?"

He pauses, trying, she imagines, to get away from Margot's ears, her hair, her awful smell.

"I got you a flat. It's a nice one. Down by the pier, thought you might like it, after coming back from the island and everything. One bedroom." She doesn't say anything. She hasn't expected him to sort anything out for her. She's expected spending tonight ringing up old friends, maybe even driving home to Swansea to her mum's flat, crying all the way down the A470. "I'm sorry that I did that; I was just, you know, I didn't want you not to have anything. It might give you the space you need."

Her heart soars. Her own little flat. She can't think of anything better tonight. She'll buy a few beers and sit in an empty room with candles around her, looking out at the pier. She can create her own little island.

"No, Mark, it's fine. It'll be perfect. I just didn't expect…"

"I can't have you sleeping on the street, Mer."

But you can, Mark, she thinks, you can.

"Do you want me to come and get you?"

The sincerity of his voice. He wants to come and get her. She knows him. She knows that a week of sleeping with Margot has been intolerable for him.

"No, it's OK, I've got someone who can bring me."

It joys her to say this. She's got someone, Elin, this person who she feels now will always be in her life, who is now gliding towards her in a huge silver car. The sight of Elin at the wheel is such an unfamiliar thing, she laughs. Elin comes out and she is laughing too. She sits in the car – a Vauxhall Meriva, Elin tells her, her mum's – and puts the safety belt on. It feels alien and rubbery, and loud, gliding from its hook like a black tongue.

They drive on in silence until they reach Felinheli. They both look at one another when they turn off towards the restaurant. They've talked about it so many times around that small table in the kitchen. They've already ordered from the imaginary menu many times and have virtually tasted everything that's on it. The red and gold carpet is sticky under their feet, the plastic menu lifeless against their eager fingers. They can't decide what to have – everything seems novel and precious and just so easy – that they opt for some kind of combo, a little bit of everything to share. They sip their orange drinks and listen to the thundering jukebox. The meal arrives and after a few bites, they feel full. They've forgotten the density of grease, on their fingers, in their stomachs. It's too much. Mererid stares at a pulverised chicken wing and decides that it's something she can live without. She craves those things that they could make last on Bardsey – a jar of olives, a piece of goat's cheese. She would even gladly eat Elin's toffee, that rubbery substance that left them both feeling a little bit sick. She realises that she'll have to rely on these things to bring Bardsey back, now, for in every sip of this too-rich orange drink, she's being sterilised once more to mainland life, in all its ordinariness.

She's not sure why she doesn't want Elin to meet Mark. She makes her park a few streets away, to say her goodbyes. Elin is hers, she thinks, and Mark belongs to another Mererid that Elin doesn't really know. She watches the last silver glint of the Meriva around the corner.

She's back on College Road. Facing Mark's red door – their red door – is strange. A door with a lock seems like an oddity. It glints boldly, its surface smooth, so unlike the chipped, sun-peeled paint of their cottage door. Her black car is still parked outside. The same kids still make faces at her as she crosses the road, and the sound of laughing students fills the air; so loud, somehow. He must have seen her through the window, for here he is now, standing at the door, a tall shadow waiting to greet her, a strange, awkward look on his face. She walks in and he chatters, endlessly. She sees her stuff in neat little bundles all around the place. He's tried to pack her up. She catches sight of a stray, blonde hair on their dark blue sofa, and can imagine Margot's voluptuous fall from grace, hair by hair, garment by garment. She can imagine Mark, sweating, his T-shirt still on.

She wonders what he sees, now, looking at her, whether or not he can see what she's left behind, whether he's having to fish in the strange new tide of her eyes, catching nothing.

"About the flat, I didn't mean to…"

"It's fine, Mark. It's for the best. It was thoughtful of you."

"I over-reacted, I mean, we could still work this out, couldn't we?"

Mark is crying. His large hands about his large face in their small kitchen, and she wishes she could cry, too, to show him she cares. He throws the keys at her, silvery and new in the air. Gives her the address of the flat. As she drives off, she sees Margot rushing down the street towards the house. She tries not to think of Margot touching a stray, beautiful strand of Mark's hair.

The flat is white and pure. Even the carpet is a neutral colour, half way between beige and white. There is an empty fridge that hums quietly, a lounge with no television, a bedroom without a light. Perfect, she thinks. She goes out to buy candles, some rice cakes, olives, and some white beers. She smells the musty odour of stale hops on the streets of Upper Bangor. She tells the man in the off-licence that she's just come back from an island. He looks at her strangely as he places the bottle opener in her plastic bag. She feels unsafe as she manoeuvres her way down Love Lane in her car, towards the pier.

Half an hour later, she is surrounded by candles, drinking her beer, the window slightly ajar so she can listen to the clinking of boats in Dickie's Boatyard across the road. They collide gently in the water, establishing a kind of gentle harmony as they clunk against one another. There are no waves here, she thinks: the rippling water is boxed in, going nowhere. And yet, seeing the sea in the far distance, she knows she is still on some kind of island, an island of her own making.

The poems will not come. She wants to capture the essence of Deian, but the lines are weak and wilting. Then she realises why. Deian is not a poem. Deian is more than that, a narrative unto himself, a complex web of stories. Deian cannot be separated into stanzas like Mark, segmented in four lines or tested in triplets; he needs to stand complete, unbroken. To stick him in a poem would be like insulting him somehow. He deserves better.

And with this in mind, she decides to write nothing; for the time being.

35

A wave of fatigue hit Viv as she sat down in the back of Greta's car. As soon as they had travelled their first mile, she was lost in something which vaguely resembled sleep, the moving dark throwing her from side to side, the imprint of a seat belt across her chest a reminder that she was protected; for now, at least. The dark gave way to occasional bursts of colour. She saw Iestyn on the jetty, waving at her, a lopsided smile on his face. She saw the path at Porthmeudwy, rising in front of her, its golden dust strange and enticing. She saw that first shock of road, navy and shining, as Greta steered the car around the corner. Throughout her dreams, she was aware of the engine chugging beneath her bottom, a vigorous purr so different to the tractor she had once driven.

When she opened her eyes again, she saw that they were on a dual carriageway. The white stripes were being swallowed by the car, whoosh, whoosh, whoosh, in great gulps of tarmac. Greta was listening to Radio Cymru. The news bulletin announced that the bodies of two girls had been found in a woodland area, and that the police had arrested a man and a woman. Leri looked out of the window, tapping her fingers against the window pane, in a series of staccatos.

It was starting to get dark, now. Tall, dark trees seemed to loom at them from every direction. They drove a further eight miles into the night. Soon enough, things started to change. On either side, bold road-signs sprang out of the earth, and Viv recognised them as the signs she and Delyth had spent so many years of their life painting over, taking down. She saw the Welsh above the English: Caerdydd, Cardiff. A small, yet colossal feat that she'd long forgotten. While all these years, she had let Sister Mary Catherine get away with writing Bardsey Island on her envelopes, rather than Ynys Enlli.

In the distance, she could now see the orange promise of a city, staining the air. Soon enough, the green on either side had morphed into grey pavements, large buildings, suburbs. The north end of the island had become North Road, where everything had an angle, a jagged edge, buildings you could cut yourself on. They careered over a red flyover, sliding, it would seem, into the city, flowing into the bright stream of traffic. Viv admired Greta's composure as she manoeuvred them all safely around those circles and stripes, further on into the lit-up city. No one beeped at her, like Viv remembered people had done at her and Mwynwen all those years ago, when they had tried, in vain, to get to Cardiff Crown Court on time.

She couldn't help but think about Iestyn. What would he be doing now? He'd be sat at that window, probably, staring out to sea. The moon would be out, she thought, seeing its half-smile above her. Even Cardiff couldn't swallow a moon. If only she had been allowed to bring Elfyn with her, she thought, missing his furry warmth at her feet. But not having him with her liberated her a little. The noises here would be too much for his soft ears. And he didn't speak English. He was probably the only monoglot left in Wales.

Their first stop was a place called Beda Road, where Leri lived, Greta explained, turning into the street a little too sharply. Viv didn't get out to say goodbye; it didn't seem appropriate somehow to have her feet touch this unfamiliar street before anything else. In the rear view mirror she watched the exchange between the two women. They embraced awkwardly, a mess of limbs, before Leri lifted Greta's face to hers. Greta pulled away, and Leri collapsed in a sea of bags in the middle of the road. Greta made a phone-call. Five minutes later, an overweight man with a beard arrived. Greta placed Leri in his arms, and he shouted after her. She began running back towards the car, got in, and revved away.

Greta didn't mention any of this to Viv, as though the whole scenario had never happened. Viv wondered whether it was because she was a nun. Maybe people didn't like dragging nuns into this kind of fiasco. Especially a hermit nun, she thought, who'd been living on an island for twenty odd years. Maybe she thought that a nun wouldn't understand what had caused the hurt in Greta's eyes that evening as she walked away; or what had roused Leri to cry out as the boat had moved away from the island. But Viv understood both sentiments perfectly well. Too well, she thought, feeling the sharpness in her stomach.

But she wasn't a nun anymore. She had to remember that. Nuns didn't escape in cars down the A470. They didn't ignore God's voice, who was booming at her from above, telling her to stay put on the island. They certainly didn't get talked into making documentary programmes about their experience, as she'd now agreed to once again. Greta had promised her there would be none of the gimmicks that Leri had proposed. All she wanted was to present Viv's emotional journey, explore the reasons why she had run away from Wales, from her campaign, in the first place, and what it would take to make her go back. She would look after her, Greta said, and Iestyn could stay on to look after Elfyn.

Viv opened a window as Greta drove them back into the city. They flew over yet another bridge, and she saw the jutting, white peaks piercing the night sky, light shining up from its core.

"That's the Millennium Stadium," Greta said. Viv couldn't help but let out a laugh, thinking about Sister Mary Catherine and the others, wondering what they would make of this new boldness of hers.

The name St Mary Street sprung out at her, making her think of the saints of the island, long dead in the cold earth. She opened the window. There was nothing saintly about St Mary Street. On either side, young girls – glittering like fish – teetered on the edges of their stiletto heels, while young men in shirts bucked one another with tucked-shirt bravado. She could smell the aftershave from here. She stared on at their wild-haired abandon, as they eased their way into Friday night in tiny clusters, a swaying path of laughter down the street. It seemed strange, yet thrilling, that two realities could co-exist like this within the same country; the long-forgotten saints of Enlli, and the more unorthodox saints of St Mary Street, arm in arm, without knowing it.

The moon slid from view, presenting her with a deep, starless sky. It was somehow invigorating to be without the stars for once, to have this dark canvas enveloping her. They were always showered with stars on Enlli, so much so that being without them felt exotic, like a sin. She stuck her head out, and laughed again. Greta laughed too, squeezing her hand, tight.

"Nearly there, Viv," she said, as they passed by a sign that said Cardiff Bay.

The next bridge unfolded another view. On the balcony of a towering yellow-brick building Viv could see a couple kissing. It was strange somehow, to view a kiss so high up in the air. Directly beneath them a woman leaned over her balcony, breathing smoke into her phone, punching the air with erratic gestures. Facing them all was the black water that seemed to hold the building in place. Viv turned her head to peer into the depths and saw hundreds of balconies, all identical, shining white at her in the water.

They parked the car. In front of them was an enormous building, a slumped, golden creature on its haunches, with light bursting forth from its body. *In these stones horizons sing*, it said, *gwir fel gwydr o ffwrnais awen*. It dwarfed her; made her feel minute, like she could slip through the cracks at any moment. But there were no cracks, not any more. Tiger Bay and its grey dust was now a sparkling new forecourt with light and fountains. It made her realise that she had spent the past twenty years feeling very enormous on her little patch of land, when she wasn't that big at all.

Greta slipped her arm through hers. Viv wondered if they looked like mother and daughter, strolling along like this. She could be anything she wanted to be; no one would know. Looking up again at those shimmering words pouring out of the building she realised for the first time in her life that she was anonymous. Bathed in this white, synthetic light, she was no different to anyone else who walked by and gawped at the spectacle in front of her. She wasn't Sister Vivian, she wasn't Viv. She wasn't anyone, because this city asked nothing of her.

Rounding the corner, her breath fell out of her. There it was, right in front of her. Above the water, its glass panels gleamed at her. It was as wholly transparent as they had all said, the light inside inviting and warm. Here was the building that she never thought would be possible, the building that had only ever existed in her mind. Even her imagination could never have conjured anything so beautiful, so dazzling. It stood there, squat and angular, a gleaming ship of promise, guiding her on, urging her to step on board. She slowed down, wanting to savour each and every inch she travelled towards it. Greta's warm arm told her that she understood. Up they climbed towards it, over the smooth slate, step by step, until Viv's face was almost touching the glass, looking right in.

"They close in half an hour," Greta said. "Do you want to go in?"

She looked in at the people hovering about, the visitors trickling down the slate steps; stopping to peer down into the chamber below. The security guards upturning bags and beeping visitors through the gate.

"No," she replied. "Not today."

She was afraid of doing everything at once. She didn't want to wake tomorrow and feel that it had all been a strange vision in her sleep; that it hadn't been real at all. She needed to see it in the daylight. To check it was really there. To see what an ordinary day in the life of the Assembly really looked like. She heard the purr of a camera beside her but didn't mind, for once, that she was being filmed. There were no words, no glib sentence that would ever capture what she was feeling. But she knew it was there somewhere, reflected on her face along with the light.

She turned her back on the building and looked out across the water. How peculiar, she thought, that what she was stood on now was also a kind of island, a piece of land completely segmented from the rest of the city. The water surrounded them, holding these huge buildings afloat, it seemed, with nothing to be seen in the distance but the dotting of tiny lights, which were minuscule in comparison to the huge streaming light which now poured through this building and through Viv, throwing their shadow onto the water as one. And they truly *were* on an island now, she thought, all of them: the building behind her confirmed it. All the time she had been away, Wales had been prising itself away from the mainland at its border. She wondered what they would say if they could see her now; Iestyn, Mwynwen, Howard. If they could see that she was not on the margins anymore, but at the very centre of something; something that was fast becoming as much of an island as Enlli could ever hope to be, an island that really spoke out to the rest of the world; the waters around it still and calm, the boats never ceasing to come and go.

And there was only one way to ensure that they would see it, she thought, starting to speak as her eyes challenged the camera's stare.

36

His car wouldn't start. It was no wonder really, Deian thought; it had been there for months by now, sitting abandoned in the car park at Porthmeudwy. It had probably given up on him, just like Fran had. Deian tried to recall the last time he'd been sitting in this car, all those months ago. Fran had been at his side, chattering excitedly, or at least, that's how it had seemed at the time. He'd thought they were embarking on a new phase in their relationship. She was coming with him to the island, it had meant everything. Looking back, he could see it was her nervousness that had made her whitter away like that; hands butterflying, eyebrows twitching. She must have known that only minutes later she'd be jumping from that dinghy and into the water. She knew, even as she was squeezing his hand, offering her support, that he would end up travelling to the island alone. And now he'd come back alone, too, to a car that smelt of dying perfume and sun-curled stray hairs, where Fran's lighter had exploded into a thousand fragments, all over his dashboard.

There was no one around to help him. He'd foolishly waited until everyone else had gone, before starting the engine, so he could be alone, so he could say his own silent goodbyes to the summer. But now it was the summer saying goodbye to him, the sky no longer that dense blue but a greying white, a blank stare of a morning. He tried the ignition one more time. It coughed hopefully, before exhaling its last, pathetic splutter. He crossed his arms and sighed. It was so tempting, he thought, to do nothing but sit here, and let the morphing shapes of the day pass over the sunroof of his car. He could let his thoughts fall away into the afternoon, night, another day, even. It was only then that he would have the option of going back. He imagined how Brian's face would contort when he saw him coming down the path.

But he wouldn't do it. He couldn't go back. Not now. Perhaps he would never go back. The survey had been completed; his mother's plaque was in place. He didn't need the island to unearth his memories for him, or his mother, either. He felt closer to her now, sitting here in the deserted car park, hand on her headscarf, than he had in years. Iestyn was the only thing really left for him on the island now, and even he had wanted him to leave, had needed him to. "I'll be fine," he'd said to him, refusing to use English this time. "It's about time I got acquainted with this place again, made it accept me on my own terms. I can't have you holding my hand for me anymore, Deian. You should really find other people to hold hands with," he'd said, cracking open a brown-toothed smile.

"I know," he'd said, addressing his friend in the language of their childhood, "I think it's about time I did that, too."

He thought about ringing Mererid. She and Elin would be just about getting into Pwllheli by now; it wouldn't be too late to ask them to turn back. But then he couldn't do that, either. He couldn't make Mererid, who had already travelled inland, onwards towards that house she shared with that *fiancé*, to start her winding journey back down towards Aberdaron, towards him, towards the end of the earth, as if she were going back in time. *We can't keep going back in time,* he remembered his mother once shouting at Viv, *because it's like saying that everything's over, that there's nowhere more to go from here.*

He couldn't drag Mererid back here to stand above the bonnet, push his car; as though he had never been inside her, as though those tiny hips around his had meant nothing. The boat had taken her away from him, and it had seemed the right thing at the time, a decorous ending. She had not jumped into the water to get away from him, after all, and the white boat sailing gracefully away from him had seemed, if nothing else, like some kind of progress.

And with that in mind, there was only one other option. He phoned to get the island's manager to come and help him, and had to endure a forty-minute discussion about the finer details of the fabricated archaeological survey, while Gwyn sweated above the engine, the cleft of his buttocks creeping above his belt, smirking back at him. But at least at the end of it, his car was purring with satisfaction, and he was soon revving his way towards the car park entrance. In the rear view mirror he saw that Gwyn's mouth was still moving. He was more than likely quibbling to himself about bones, animals, or some other island minutiae. Maybe he was wondering whether he'd been right to employ a writer who'd done no writing; or trust a documentary-maker whose documentary was now dust. Either that or he was trying to make sense of any number of the lies Deian had just told him about the dig and its findings.

Deian beeped his horn and waved at him, pulsating through the dust, away from Porthmeudwy for good.

An hour into the A55, driving had ceased to feel alien; and his tractor-speed had soon accelerated to ninety-five. He took his time getting back to Preston, however, and acclimatised himself again to the strange realities of the world by staring at unhappy couples in service stations, irate lorry drivers in fast-food outlets. He'd stopped at a pub in St Asaph for lunch, watching children diving in and out of a bright ball pool in the kids' corner. He felt the island drifting away, detail by detail. He built up the world for himself again, swallowing it along with the too-greasy fish and chips, washing it down with a long-craved for pint of stout.

For large parts of the journey he muttered to himself in Welsh, enjoying the new slick feel of those words on his lips; shouting out the passing place names to himself: Pen y Clip, Penmaenmawr, Abergele, Rhuddlan. He listened to Radio Cymru while he still could, singing along to pop songs he didn't know, talking to DJs he'd never heard of, laughing along with the unseen audience of some comedy programme. The more the language filled his mind, the more he thought about Mererid's lips pressed to his, her hand cupping his face in earnest, pressing her whole body onto him. He had daydreams of them both strolling along the pier in Bangor, holding hands, walking their dog.

Radio Lancashire came squealing across the frequency, with a rendition of an American eighties classic.

The dog ran away; jumping off the pier.

Fran was outside his house when he got back, shivering on the doorstep. From the look of her she'd been there a while. He wasn't sure why she was standing outside like this; as far as he knew she still had her own key, to come and go as she pleased. His headlights lit her up, and she was smiling, despite the cold chattering along her teeth. Was he supposed to feel guilty about Mererid? Fran probably wouldn't even believe him if he told her. And he hadn't done anything wrong. There was no clearer way of telling someone that it was over between you than swimming away from them. There was no greater indignity than a back-turned breast stroke in shallow water. He had been rejected; rejected men were free to do what they wanted, and act in all manner of inappropriate ways.

"How was it?" she asked, quietly.

"More or less the same old island," Deian lied.

"Except for the findings," Fran beamed. "What did you do about those bones?"

"Dem bones," he laughed, "were really nothing. Well, they were something if you're into saints. Which, as we all know, I'm not. You were right, as usual. What are you doing out here? You're cold. Let's go inside."

"I've got a surprise for you," Fran said.

"OK," he said, hesitantly, as they walked into a dark house. Deian felt Fran's arms around him. He hugged her back, without conviction. He hadn't anticipated having to share his first night back with anyone, and it slightly annoyed him. He reached for the light switch.

"Don't," Fran said, "leave it off for a bit."

Hugging Fran's cold body, he couldn't help but think of Mererid and him in that dark kitchen. He should have kissed her then, he thought. Maybe then he'd have so many more memories, so many more hours to treasure; he wouldn't have to hoard them all in a swaying bird hide.

"I'm so sorry about what I did," Fran said. "I wasn't thinking. I should have realised it would be hard for you to go to the island alone. It was just one of those spur of the moment decisions. Nothing made sense to me just then. I mean, all this talk of a baby when I wouldn't even move in with you, it was mad. Totally crazy. I had no right putting that pressure on you. To push you like that. The doctors, and everything. We weren't even ready for it. I needed time to sort my head out."

"Fran, it's OK," he said. Deian hated that pleading, tinny voice of hers in the dark. It was too noisy.

"No, it's not OK. I should have come with you to the island. Everything would've turned out differently then."

You're telling me, he thought. Thinking now of the past few weeks, it was impossible to envisage her beside him; checking the dig with her usual precision, marking the soil, pushing back her auburn hair. Placing her in those scenes made the others fade from view. His hands on Mererid's thighs would have been nothing but a mere mirage.

Fran moved to a corner of the room. She turned on a light, though not the light he was used to. It was a dimmer lamp that he didn't recognise as his own, and it gently lit the room for him, each corner slowly pigmented in a peachy hue, before coming into clear, bright-white focus. He saw what Fran had been trying to hide from him. All around his house there were new objects, artefacts, items of clothing; a new sofa in the corner. It seemed that the very opposite of a burglary had taken place.

"What do you think?" she said, looking up at him, eyes widening with hope.

"I think it's a funny way to break up with someone," he said.

"I didn't want us to break up, Deian. It was just too much for me, what with all the disappointments. It doesn't matter anymore," she said. "When you rang me about those bones, I was thinking, about all the pain you went through. Sometimes children don't really fit with what adults want. I mean, your mother had you to worry about and she still…"

"She did what was right for her," he said, resenting her tone. "It's not her fault I wasn't really listening to what she was telling me. I understand now what she wanted me to do, how she wanted me to turn out."

"You've turned out beautifully," Fran said, touching his face. "She'd be proud of you. I'm proud of you. Which is why I want it to work this time. I want us to live together. No more pressure, I promise."

"You don't want children, then," he said.

"I don't have to have my own children," she answered, trying to coax his hand into hers. He held it firmly behind his back. His hands had last touched Mererid. They weren't yet ready to touch anyone else.

She turned to admire the room. "Well? What do you think? Aren't you pleased I moved in?"

He looked around at his once sparse house now covered with floral scatter cushions; strange pieces of Chinese art were now decorating the white walls, and a funny sculpture of some sort had replaced his egg plant. It was uneasy on his minimalist eye, positively insulting his frugal tastes. And yet, he saw that it made a bizarre kind of sense. It was what this room needed. Fran was a mainland person, she understood what it was to really live somewhere, with these comforts, to fill up your life with comforting peripherals that somehow defined you, that fought against the emptiness on your behalf.

She knew what it was like to have a dimmer switch, to bring things into gradual, artificial focus.

"Say something," she pleaded with him. "Tell me you're pleased, at least."

"I am pleased," he said, grabbing her shoulders firmly between both hands. "I think it's great you want to live here. I mean, I was going to need a tenant, anyhow. This makes things much easier for me."

"Tenant?" she stared at him. "Deian I thought we…"

"We don't have to discuss the finer details now. Stay as long as you want. I'll let you know when I've sorted something."

He retreated back towards his car. He had a sense of urgency now, quickening his pace, hearing Fran breathlessly trailing after him.

"Deian! Where are you going?"

"Home," he said, fastening his seatbelt. It was one of those decisions that was never going to make sense until he'd actually made it. It felt right and real and the only logical thing for him to do. He didn't quite know where that was exactly, or how he was supposed to get there. He couldn't go to Mererid, as much as he wanted to, not yet, at least. That dog on the pier wasn't theirs to keep. He couldn't go to the island either, Iestyn had told him as much. But he couldn't stay here. Not in this cul-de-sac so far from the sea, this red-bricked house without a garden; with this woman and her dimmer switch.

Fran's face was pressed to the car window. Her nose was all squished up, her breath bursting in tiny clouds on the glass. When she stepped back, he saw that her breath had left a smudge, right there in the centre of the window pane. It resembled the very jagged shape that he'd doodled on his bedroom wall all those years ago, the crouched mass that his mother and Viv had tried so hard to kick in the ribs, though it had never bent double, as they had wanted. Two welcoming arms penned in the grinning, uneven, coastline, as it floated separate and alone on his window.

And all around it was a new, clean, sea of glass, which reflected only himself.

Acknowledgements

I gratefully acknowledge Academi and the Bardsey Island Trust for awarding me a writer's residency on Bardsey Island which enabled me to write this novel. I am also greatly indebted to the islanders for their kindness and openness in sharing with me the histories and mysteries of Enlli, past and present, although I should emphasize that the characters in this novel are fiction. Thanks also go to Peter Florence, Director of the Guardian Hay Festival for his much-valued support.

I would also like to thank the following for their unfailing encouragement, advice and friendship – Kate Woodward, Lowri Hughes, Elin Royles, Dafydd Llewelyn, Owen Sheers, Stevie Davies and Gayathri Prabhu – and also my wonderfully meticulous aunt, Siân Elfyn Jones, who has been my most valued reader over many years. Thanks also to Gareth Pierce for being the funniest, most reassuring and warm-heated confidant a girl could wish for.

I would also like to thank my parents, Wynfford and Menna, and my brother, Meilyr, for all they have given, alongside my surrogate sisters, Mari and Nerys.

Colossal thanks to Gwen Davies for believing in this book, and for being an inspiring editor who provided me with a sharp critical eye when it was most needed.

And most imporatantly, *diolch o galon* to Iwan – for his love.

Praise for Fflur Dafydd

"The most compelling novel I've read in years; a love story, a thriller, and a profound meditation on language and identity."

— **Peter Florence**

"Wry, engaging and perceptive, *Twenty Thousand Saints* is a beautifully-rendered story of multiple forms of enquiry and excavation – spiritual, linguistic, filmic and sexual. Dafydd's laid-back narrative voice seems perfectly tuned to her cast of characters and the changes that befall them when they encounter this novel's most dominant personality, the isolated island of Bardsey herself, and all the secrets and history she holds."

— **Owen Sheers**

"The author rips to shreds that myth of the island of twenty thousand saints. Her imagination and originality are remarkable. The Bardsey of this novel is an island of mischief and insanity."

— **Glyn Jones**, bbc.co.uk, on *Atyniad*

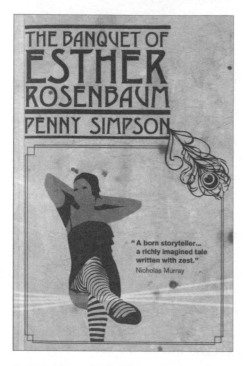

THE BANQUET OF ESTHER ROSENBAUM
PENNY SIMPSON

" A born storyteller...
a richly imagined tale
written with zest."
Nicholas Murray

It is Berlin, 1929. The inflation-hungry city is edging towards disaster, but seven-foot Jewish orphan Esther Rosenbaum is serving up a banquet for friends.

"An extravaganza where the real and the imagined take turn and turn about... sumptuously detailed and fantastical... at once full of disturbing delicacy and at the same time [forceful]... marked by its humour, verve and hallucinatory strangeness."

— **Clare Morgan,** *Times Literary Supplement*

"Casts an intoxicating spell, blending tragedy, satire and magic realism to create a sensuous exploration of food, revolution and the resurrection of community."

— *New Welsh Review*

£9.99
ISBN: 978-0-9555272-3-4

'Offbeat, subtle, haunting, fresh.'
Kate Long

SALVAGE

Gee Williams

ALCEMI

A sophisticated thriller ranging between Wales, north-west England and Goa, which explores possession, betrayal and how much we can afford to lose.

James Tait Black Memorial Prize for Fiction Nominee

"Turns the whodunnit into the whodonewhat ... a compulsive page-turner."

— Prof. Colin Nicholson, Chair of the Judges

£9.99
ISBN: 978-0-9555272-0-3

ALCEMI

www.alcemi.eu

TALYBONT CEREDIGION CYMRU SY24 5AP
e-mail gwen@ylolfa.com
phone (01970) 832 304
fax 832 782